A WALLFLOWER TO LOVE

Love's Addiction
Book One

Marie Higgins

Dragonblade Publishing, Inc. is an imprint of Kathryn Le Veque Novels, Inc.
P.O. Box 23
Moreno Valley, CA 92556
ceo@dragonbladepublishing.com

Produced in the United States of America

First Edition November 2022
Trade Paperback Edition

ARE YOU SIGNED UP FOR DRAGONBLADE'S BLOG?

You'll get the latest news and information on exclusive giveaways, exclusive excerpts, coming releases, sales, free books, cover reveals and more.

Check out our complete list of authors, too!

No spam, no junk. That's a promise!

Sign Up Here

www.dragonbladepublishing.com

Dearest Reader;

Thank you for your support of a small press. At Dragonblade Publishing, we strive to bring you the highest quality Historical Romance from some of the best authors in the business. Without your support, there is no 'us', so we sincerely hope you adore these stories and find some new favorite authors along the way.

Happy Reading!

CEO, Dragonblade Publishing

Julian Stratford has a plan. He will steal the duchess and make her confess that her husband killed for a title. Once that is accomplished, Julian can take back his rightful title of Duke of Linden. Everything goes smoothly until he steals the wrong sister. Now it's time for a new strategy. Alexandria Templeton is a hopeless wallflower, but with his guidance, she will be a great asset while trying to find evidence against his cousin for killing Julian's father and brother.

Disaster endangers his well-thought-out plan but also threatens to destroy his heart.

PROLOGUE

North Devon, England, 1857

"MEN, KEEP A sharp eye out. Private Bywater is here. I know it."

Major Julian Stratford tied his horse to a post as he scanned the area. Searching through buildings for Private Bywater would slow his men down a bit, but it must be done. Although the missing soldier wasn't dangerous, the man needed to return to duty. It was Julian's responsibility to make certain that happened.

It irritated him that the private would go missing on Julian's watch. Bywater was distraught because the woman he loved ended their engagement three months ago, but Julian wouldn't tolerate such mutiny. He needed to bring the private back to show the other men that this type of disobedience was unacceptable.

Today's weather seemed more pleasant than of late. A light breeze blew through the trees and teased the hair on Julian's nape. His regiment had been searching for Private Bywater for three days, and his irritation level grew each evening when they returned to camp empty-handed. He had received reports that the missing soldier had visited the tavern and consorted with *ladies of pleasure*. However, if the private knew Julian was looking for him, he would hide elsewhere.

Julian removed his hat and pushed his fingers through his hair as he studied the buildings across the street. The tavern, The Drinking Hole, was already full of patrons for only being two o'clock in the afternoon. As much as Julian wanted a drink, he would wait to celebrate when he captured Private Bywater.

From the corner of his eye, Julian noticed a man leaving the leather shop. He held his breath. *Father?* But then realization struck him, and his throat tightened. His father and brother were dead—a message he had received only two weeks prior. The news still disrupted Julian's life because he couldn't mourn the way he'd wanted. His wish was to return to the family's estate as soon as Private Bywater was found. There were too many unanswered questions about his father and Forbes' death, and not knowing was eating through Julian's soul and needed to be stopped.

He had been told in a letter that his father and older brother died of the plague. Yet he had heard nothing about the servants on the estate suffering the same fate. If it were the plague, others would have been affected too.

Julian Stratford was now the Duke of Linden. He would be expected to step into his new role soon. His last act as Major Stratford would be to catch Private Bywater.

Releasing a deep breath, he turned toward his men. "Four of you search the north end, and the next four will search the west end." He pointed to the soldiers nearest to him. "And you will go with me."

As the men went their separate ways, Julian moved toward the tavern. If the missing soldier were inside The Drinking Hole, the man would undoubtedly see the regiment through the windows, since already most of the people walking the street had stopped to gawk at Julian's men. In that case, Bywater would want to escape out the back way.

Instead of going straight to the tavern, Julian hurried in a different direction. As they passed the bank, Julian peeked in the window. As he'd suspected, several people watched him as his men sneaked around the building, but the private wasn't amongst them.

Bywater was a hard man to ignore. His straggly orange-red hair and bushy beard were noticed, even in night's shadows. He was also taller than most men. And when he laughed, his voice belted strongly through the air.

An eerie feeling came over Julian, and the hairs on the back of his neck rose. He halted, which also stopped his men. Julian scanned the perimeter for anything out of the ordinary. As a soldier, he trusted his instincts, and currently, they were sending him a warning.

None of the people along the street seemed dangerous, which made him wonder if someone watched him from inside a building. Yet he couldn't worry about that unless it was the private.

Julian dismissed the suspicion and continued on his way. The sun was high in the sky, and the brightness made him squint. As he brought his hand up to block the glare, something from a distance caught his notice. Up on the hillside, three people stood by a shiny object. Because of the way the sun hit the large piece of metal, Julian couldn't tell what it was, and the people were too far away to recognize.

He ignored them and moved around the building. Once again, the eerie feeling gnawed at his conscience, telling him to turn back.

Irritated by this unknown emotion, he stopped again and looked at his small team. "You three go around the building. The rest of you come with me."

"Sir?" Private Winkle tapped Julian on the shoulder. "Is something amiss?"

Julian met his man's stare briefly before watching ahead. He was hesitant to tell his men about the sensations rushing over his body in warning. "No, Winkle. I feel that we need to go this way."

How could he explain to his men something he didn't know

himself? Yet following his instincts was something he did.

Suddenly, a boom ripped through the air. The ground shook. The scent of gunpowder filled him.

His heart sank. He knew exactly what would happen next.

As the cannonball hit the ground, Julian flew through the air. He hit the ground and rolled. Searing pain ripped through his right leg, and he cried out, clutching his bloody limb.

Dizziness assailed him, but he struggled to remain alert. All around him, he heard the cries of the injured and screams from the bystanders. Although he wanted to help, his injuries kept him immobile.

As the air cleared, he looked toward the hillside. The shiny object had been a cannon. If only he had seen it sooner.

He gritted his teeth against the pain and struggled to stand as he drew his pistol, determined to stop those responsible for this terrible disaster. The three men he had spotted earlier were running.

Julian lifted his shaky arm, pointed the pistol, and shot. One man fell to the ground. But within seconds, the man jumped up again, clutching his left arm.

Before he could reload and shoot, the spinning in his head finally gained control. Julian fell to the ground again and closed his eyes, giving in to the consuming darkness.

CHAPTER ONE

The warped floorboards in the hallway creaked. She held her breath as the terrifying sound sliced through her. She glanced at her white fingers, clutching the dagger's handle so tightly she feared numbness would soon take over her limbs. It didn't matter that her heartbeat pounded so fast she could scarcely breathe; she was determined not to let them take her.

Mr. Blackwood—the handsome man she had briefly met—was to blame for the turmoil growing inside her. That man had been entirely too charming, too sweet, and swept her off her feet with his words and impassioned glances. Although she wasn't a stranger to flirtation, this man seemed too experienced for her. For some reason, he could read her thoughts and know her feelings without her having to express them to him.

Now she surmised his purpose. He had wanted to get close to her for her money. Why else would he make such bold advances in a short amount of time?

She should have seen this trickery through his sugarcoated words. She felt like a fool for trusting a man so easily and allowing him to sweep her mind into oblivion. Sadly, it was too late to stop him from charming her. Now she feared for her own safety.

The wind outside whipped around the small cottage where she had lived since she was a child, but tonight, the sound did not comfort her. Every member of her family was dead by the

murderous hand of the man who'd captivated her so completely.
For certain, she was next.

Alexandria Templeton stared at the passage she had written while nibbling on her bottom lip, a habit she'd had since she was a child. She had always told herself that doing this helped her think better.

She thought about the plot—or what she had plotted so far—and this passage didn't make much sense. *Why* had the woman's family died? And more importantly, *why* was this man, Mr. Blackwood, trying to kill her heroine?

Placing the quill on the desk, Alexandria released a frustrated breath. Once again, she had started a story before she had time to really think about what would happen to her characters and *why*. In the four years she had been writing stories, she should have learned not to write before the plot's conflict was outlined.

Then again, she knew why she hadn't learned the lesson yet. Writing was her retreat from reality. Every day she anticipated the moment when she entered her own little world and created her characters, making them do as she wished without their talking back or putting up a fight. Controlling her characters was what she enjoyed and loved more than anything.

Writing was her escape from a world where she had no choice but to let people control her.

Perhaps it was time to write a letter to her cousin, Maxey Langley. Alexandria's cousin also dabbled in storytelling, and with Maxey's help, writing a mystery became easy.

Closing her eyes, she stretched her neck and rolled her head from side to side, releasing the tension building in her muscles. As she fluttered her eyelids open, she peered out the nearest window. The sky was a baby blue, and from the closest tree that stood so still, it was obvious there was no summer wind today. This would be the perfect weather to ride her horse, Buttercup.

Alexandria scooted her chair away from the desk and stood. She placed the lid on her inkwell and the quill back in its cup as excitement built inside her. Galloping around the estate on days like this really cleared her head and made her think better, especially while working on her next mystery novel. One day someone would notice her writings and want to publish them, but until then, she would keep reaching for her dream.

She donned her riding habit with the short-waist lavender jacket, black skirt, and matching hat. Fitting her hands into the purple gloves, she walked out of her room. As she moved down the corridor, the door to her sister's room opened, and out stepped Alexandria's brother-in-law, Martin Hinsdale, newly appointed Duke of Linden. A frown creased his forehead as he dug his slender fingers in his bushy blond hair and scratched his head.

Tightness squeezed her chest. Her sister must still be quite ill. Her brother-in-law had worn that expression for the last five days. Alexandria prayed nothing life-threatening was wrong with Charlotte.

Frustration mixed with Alexandria's concern. Martin refused to keep her as informed as she wished to be, nor would he allow her to visit Charlotte. Alexandria wished she knew why her sister's cough wasn't getting any better.

Martin lifted his head, and his gaze locked with Alexandria's. She held her breath, fearful of what he might say, since he had never been very polite. His glare pierced right through her as he proceeded up the corridor. She had never seen him smile except when he looked at her sister. It was too bad he didn't do more of that, because he looked much better when happy.

She really wished he would at least let her know about Charlotte's welfare. It irritated her that he was so secretive about her sister's condition. Bunching her hands into fists, she grumbled under her breath. This time, she wouldn't let him stop her from seeing her sister, even if she had to go behind his back to do it.

As long as he didn't catch her, anyway.

Taking slow steps, she waited for him to disappear into his study and close the door. Quickly, she turned and hurried to her sister's bedchamber. Slowly, she opened the door, hoping the hinges wouldn't squeak. Thankfully, no sound came.

Holding her breath, she stepped into the room, waiting for the floorboards to groan. Once again, she was relieved when silence greeted her.

No candles lit the room, but a pale shaft of light escaped the drawn bedroom curtains, bringing a small measure of brightness to the otherwise gloomy chamber. Charlotte lay in her bed, her arms resting outside the many blankets covering her. She wore a pink gown with a ruffled neckline, fluffy sleeves, and pink ribbons around the wrists. Charlotte's blonde hair—a shade darker than Alexandria's—was braided and hung over her left shoulder as wisps of hair sprang free. Her pale face contrasted greatly with her gown.

Alexandria looked from the bed to the other furnishings: the armoires, two tables, two sofas, and three Persian rugs. In her opinion, the only good thing about Martin was that he provided lavish comforts for his wife. Although Alexandria and Charlotte had never suffered poverty as children, they were not used to seeing such expensive furnishings. Martin made certain his wife was happy and that she was made to look like a queen. Too bad Charlotte didn't look like one now. In fact, she resembled someone who was on her deathbed.

Frowning, Alexandria felt her heart tighten with sadness. Taking soft steps so as not to awaken her sister, she crept to the bed and stopped beside it. Carefully, she placed her hand over Charlotte's. Her sister jerked and her eyes flew open, her attention landing on Alexandria. Within seconds, a tired smile touched her lips.

"Xandria, you have finally come."

"Oh dear." Alexandria panicked but kept her voice low for fear her brother-in-law would hear. "I didn't mean to wake you."

"Nonsense." Charlotte slowly shook her head. "I have wanted to see you."

"Indeed?" Confusion filled Alexandria. "Then why was your

husband keeping me away?"

"He was? Are you certain?"

"Of course I'm certain. He specifically instructed me not to come into your bedchamber and disturb you."

"When did he say that?" Charlotte's brow creased.

"On the first day you became ill."

Charlotte chuckled lightly, but Alexandria could tell her sister struggled to do so.

"Oh, Xandria, he probably meant that you shouldn't disturb me on that particular day. I'm getting better, I assure you. If you had only said something to him, I believe he would have allowed your visit."

"Don't be too certain about that," Alexandria grumbled. Although her sister had only been married a little over six months, Alexandria knew her brother-in-law's mood swings and how uncommunicative he was.

Charlotte lifted her hand, placed it over Alexandria's, and gently squeezed. "You should not be so shy around him, my dear. He is your brother-in-law, not a stranger off the street." She took a ragged breath and cleared her throat. "I realize you are reluctant to talk to men, but Martin is different. Truly, I wish you would think of him as family."

Alexandria would rather not. Besides, if she had to think of him as family, why didn't he think of her the same way? Not once had he gone out of his way to talk to her or get to know her.

"I shall try," she answered in a soft voice.

"Oh, Xandria, please don't fret. If only you would talk to men like the characters in your stories, you wouldn't be considered a wallflower. For once, you need to put yourself in your characters' shoes and talk to a man." Her grin lifted one side of her mouth higher than the other. "I think you would be surprised how easy it is."

Alexandria shrugged. "Perhaps that is the reason I enjoy writing so much. It's because I can be a different person in my stories."

"Just pretend you are one of your heroines. I'm certain you would be able to relate better that way."

"Perhaps." Alexandria took a deep breath and slowly released it. "So, tell me, are you truly feeling better? You are not just saying that to calm my nerves?"

Charlotte nodded. "I'm gradually feeling better. The physician assures me I shall be out of bed by next week. In fact, I rarely cough."

"I pray you are recovering now. I do miss our talks."

Charlotte skimmed her gaze over Alexandria's attire and arched an eyebrow. "Are you going out riding?"

Alexandria patted her high neck collar. "Yes. I was on my way when I saw your husband leave the room. That's when I decided to sneak in and see you."

"Are you, by chance, having problems with your story? Usually you only ride when this happens."

Alexandria chuckled. "You know me so well."

"Indeed, I do." Charlotte's eyelids drooped, and she yawned. "Go and ride now so I can rest. Return to me tonight. I'll be stronger then."

Alexandria bent and kissed her sister on her forehead. Although her heart still twisted with pain to see her sister in such a weakened condition, Alexandria was relieved to have a chance to speak with Charlotte.

The moment Alexandria stepped out of the house, the sun hit her face, and she squinted from the brightness. She blinked before proceeding to the stable. Martin had been given some fine horses to go with his new title. Four Arabians took up residency in the stable, as well as four Shetlands, two Clydesdales, and her favorite—the only Highland pony—Buttercup. Never before had she seen a horse so beautiful. The beige coloring of the animal's coat blended well with the darker brown of her mane.

As she waited for the stable boy to saddle Buttercup, Alexandria glanced across the estate. Martin was a very fortunate man, indeed, to have inherited such a grand piece of property. The circumstance in which he had acquired his title wasn't very fortunate, though, since Martin's uncle, the third Duke of Linden, and two cousins—Forbes and Julian Stratford—had all died within a few months. The duke and his eldest son, Forbes, died of what was assumed to be the plague, even though it hadn't struck anyone else on the estate. Julian Stratford, however, died in battle. Alexandria had heard that he had been promoted to a major only three months before he was killed while his troops were training in the field.

Martin had married Charlotte two months before he inherited the duke title. Thankfully, he'd also allowed Alexandria to live with them, since her parents had died two years hence, and she had no other place to call home.

Heavy footfalls crunched on the gravel outside the stable, shaking her from her thoughts. Martin marched toward her, pinning her with a stern expression.

"There you are," he snapped. "May I have a word, please?"

Gulping, she nodded and stepped away from the horse. Charlotte wanted Alexandria to act like one of the heroines from her stories, but right now, she felt like a coward as she forced herself to face her angry brother-in-law. Perhaps if he didn't always look so menacing…

"Yes?" she asked in a squeaky voice.

"I've been thinking a lot lately, and I've decided to find you a husband. You are well past the marrying age, and if we wait any longer, men will not find you a worthy mate. So, starting tomorrow, I will contact several acquaintances to see who would be willing to take you off my hands."

She inhaled sharply, clasped her fingers together, and held them against her bosom. *Take me off your hands?* His rude words stung just as much as a slap across the face. How dare he! Could he truly do something so despicable? Yet he was her guardian. Therefore, he could.

Panic rushed through her, tightening her chest. She could scarcely breathe. How could she write herself out of this mess?

CHAPTER TWO

TEARS BURNED BEHIND Alexandria's eyelids, and she blinked to keep them from showing. She didn't dare show her frustration in front of her brother-in-law. Then again, if she did, it would be the first time in history she acted like that in front of a man.

"I—I understand," she whispered.

"Splendid." Martin nodded. "That is all I wanted to say. You can go about your ride now." He flipped his hand through the air, turned, and marched back toward the house.

Her eyes filled with tears, so she hurried back to the horse. The stable boy assisted her on top of Buttercup, and as soon as she grasped the reins, she kicked her heels into the animal's sides and urged the horse into a run. As she guided Buttercup away from the house, she allowed the tears to fall freely until they blurred her vision.

Her heart broke into pieces. She knew there wasn't anything her sister could do about this particular problem. If Martin wanted Alexandria out of his house and married to one of his acquaintances, it *would* happen. After all, he was the duke, and people would bow to his command.

None of this was fair. She was called a wallflower for a reason. How could she marry a man if she couldn't even look him in the eye? She would never make a good wife. Not only that, but she also wouldn't be able to get to know the man before he married her. Therefore, how would she know if she was getting a decent husband?

When it became too hard to see, she stopped her horse just inside a group of trees. Leaning her face against Buttercup's mane, she sobbed harder. What could she do to prevent this from happening? What could she possibly say to Martin to make him change his mind? There had to be a reason he didn't want her living in his large manor. She had done all he had asked so he wouldn't think she was a burden. Her efforts had been all for naught.

Martin's words buzzed through her head viciously, making her stomach churn. *I will contact several acquaintances to see who would be willing to take you off my hands.*

Take you off my hands… Off my hands…

Her tears fell harder and faster, and she didn't have the strength to stop them.

From deep inside the cluster of trees came the snort of another horse. Sucking in a breath, she whipped her head toward the sound. She tried searching for the horse, but her tear-filled eyes kept her blinded. She wiped away the tears and searched again. The bushes moved, and within seconds, a man rushed toward her.

She blinked, doubting what she saw. Before she had time to react, the man's large hands gripped her waist.

"What do you think you're—" she demanded, but her breath was ripped from her lungs as he yanked her off Buttercup.

Thankfully, he didn't let her drop to the ground. Instead, arms of steel circled her so tightly that it was impossible to wiggle free. She slammed the back of her head against his chest repeatedly, hoping that would make him release her, but it didn't. Pain shot through her skull with each blow, so she stopped.

"Let me go," she cried out, struggling harder.

"I'm sorry, *duchess*, but I cannot do that."

How odd that he had called her duchess, yet his tone sounded sarcastic, so perhaps he was saying it to be mean and disrespectful.

He pulled her farther into the wooded area. She screamed louder. The sound startled Buttercup, making the horse jump and run off. Panic tightened her throat. What in heaven's name was this man trying to accomplish? She screamed again, but this time her voice sounded hollow and scratchy.

His chest shook with laughter. "You can scream all you want, *duchess*, but nobody will hear you. You're too far away."

"What—what do you want with me?" she asked in a hoarse voice.

"You shall soon understand my method of madness. But for now, I need to get you out of here."

Out of here? What did he mean by that?

The man finally stopped dragging her, but it was only to wrap a large woolen horse blanket around her, covering her head and arms, and then he wound a rope around her to secure the covering. She tilted a few times, thinking she would plummet to the ground, but he held her and kept her upright.

Suddenly, he lifted her in his arms and flung her over a horse. As her stomach hit the animal, her breath whooshed from her lungs, but she kept still. She breathed deeply, trying not to panic. It was too late. Her head throbbed with fear. Wiggling wouldn't do her any good because she would probably fall off the horse. She also needed to save her strength for later when she attempted to escape his clutches.

And she would indeed escape.

He mounted behind her and lifted her effortlessly, adjusting her body to sit on his lap. The man's thighs were muscular and felt strangely comfortable underneath her buttocks. For a moment, she imagined what he must look like, and her cheeks burned from the picture in her head. She quickly pushed the embarrassment aside and concentrated on breathing normally, even if terror spun through her body and caused her to tremble.

Another thought interrupted. Although she knew what was

happening to her was real, this would certainly make a great scene in one of her stories. Then the realization hit her full force. Finally, she was able to experience something she could write about. That had never happened before.

Rolling her eyes, she quickly ushered the idea from her head. Why was she thinking about her writing? Obviously, she had been kidnapped and needed to focus on that. Yet how could she prepare for something she had never experienced before? And what would happen when the man took her back to his hideout? Shy little Alexandria Templeton would *never* be able to handle this. Her characters could, but *not* her! If the man had friends helping him, how would she be able to communicate with them? Hopefully, there was a woman in his gang of criminals, because at least that would give her someone to talk to.

For a little while, she concentrated on the sounds of the rhythm of the horse as they rode, surprised about how they lulled and calmed her. She had no idea where they were headed, but she figured they had already been riding a good hour.

Remarkably enough, his arms were strong, and as she leaned against his chest, an odd fluttering stirred in her bosom. Never had she been this close to a man, and although this was a bad situation to go through for her first physical contact, she couldn't stop analyzing the feelings inside her. The cocoon of his thighs, chest, and strong arms caused her to relax. Her eyelids grew heavy, and she had to fight the urge to sleep. She needed to be alert to whatever was happening and how far they were riding.

After what seemed forever, the horse slowed. "Whoa, boy," the man said, his tone deeper than it had been earlier.

Snapping to awareness, she stiffened and prepared for the worst. Hopefully, he wouldn't hurt her. In all the stories, when the villains kidnapped the heroines…they were not after a nice social visit. The villains wanted something and would stop at nothing to obtain it. This man who had taken her was probably no different.

He dismounted and kept one hand on her, saving her from

tipping over. He lifted her from the animal as if she was a sack of feathers. Gently, he set her on her feet, and within seconds, the ropes around her loosened and came off. Next, the blanket was removed.

She blinked against the sudden brightness. As her vision adjusted, she noticed they were at a small, run-down cottage in the middle of nowhere. For a moment, she wondered if anyone lived here, but then she noticed the smoke rising from the broken chimney. The fresh aroma of bread baking from within the cottage wafted through the air. Her stomach grumbled. How long had it been since she last ate? It couldn't have been more than two hours, yet the terror she had been through made her weak and hungry in the worst way.

"*Duchess*, may I present your new castle for the next few days." He swept his hand toward the cottage and bowed slightly as if he were a humble servant.

She was finally able to get a good look at him. He wore the clothes of one of the grooms, but he was in *no way* a boy. She doubted he was a servant, as well. His dark brown hair was tousled, and he sported a day's growth of stubble on his face, making his upper lip and around his mouth and chin a charcoal color against his tanned skin. As she had surmised from being held by him, he was all muscle, from his strong arms to his strong legs.

When she caught herself gawking, she blushed profoundly and turned away. For certain, her flushed cheeks would show him her further embarrassment. Good heavens! This man—her kidnapper, no less—was so very handsome. Devilishly so! But she had never seen him before in her life. Although he resembled the men she wrote about in her stories.

"You're probably wondering who I am," he said.

She sneaked a peak at him over her shoulder. Her cheeks continued to burn as she nodded.

"For now, you may call me Grey."

She arched an eyebrow. "Gray, as in the color?"

He rolled his eyes. "No, Grey with an *e*—as in the man's name."

Embarrassment washed over her again. She hated feeling stupid. "Fine," she mumbled.

He grasped her upper arm, led her to the front door, opened it, and shoved her inside. She stumbled but, thankfully, didn't fall. That, too, would have been humiliating. He followed her in and shut the door behind him.

The furnishings in this front room were few and extremely worn. The only couch was red and gold, but the colors were faded terribly, and the edges were frayed. Even the cushions were so badly worn that the stuffing was spilling out. There was another cushioned chair against the other wall. She had no idea what color it used to be, but it had turned brown over the years. Spots of yellow were littered over it, and she wasn't certain if those splotches were supposed to be there or not. Two rickety wooden chairs sat near the fireplace, but she didn't dare sit on either.

So many questions ran through her head, yet she couldn't ask them. It wasn't her nature to question authority, or question a man about anything, really. Unfortunately, the man named Grey wasn't supplying her with answers, and curiosity would drive her insane.

Charlotte's words echoed through Alexandria's head. *For once, you need to put yourself in your characters' shoes and talk to a man. I think you would be surprised how easy it is.*

Alexandria's heartbeat quickened and moisture formed on her palms. Could she really do that? Could she indeed talk to a strange man like her characters did and have the self-confidence needed to find out why this man took her?

She switched her attention to Grey. He had moved to the fireplace and was breaking apart the burning logs with a poker. He was powerfully handsome, indeed. She could *never* talk to a man who looked so incredibly attractive. If she were to talk to him, she wouldn't be able to look directly at him. If she met his stare, she would become tongue-tied for sure.

There was no other way out of this dilemma, though. She *must* become one of her characters. The sooner, the better.

CHAPTER THREE

J ULIAN GREY STRATFORD watched the Duchess of Linden and inwardly seethed. He had actually expected more from this woman. Why hadn't she screamed louder? He'd expected her to kick or bite, but once he placed her on his horse, she ceased her fight. Their ride to the cottage was less than an hour, but he wanted to make the duchess think they had traveled farther, so he'd kept riding around the vicinity.

It hadn't taken long for her body to relax against him, which was when havoc invaded all his senses. Not only did she smell like fresh-cut spring flowers, but her soft body pressed against him so intimately that his lonely mind couldn't stop imagining what could possibly happen between them. Naturally, she was vulnerable, but he wouldn't take advantage of that. It didn't matter that he hadn't held a woman this way for a very long time. He would never force a woman into submission.

Kidnapping her was entirely different. He wouldn't hurt her, though. But he wanted revenge and needed answers.

At the cottage, as he untied her, he had expected her to spout words no respectable lady would say, or at least threaten him in some way, but again, the woman surprised him by doing none of that.

Her beauty also caught him off guard. His cousin, Martin, would have certainly found a lovely lady to claim as his wife, but

Julian never figured her to be *this* beautiful.

The Duchess of Linden wore a light purple riding habit, and the outfit hugged her slender form quite nicely. Her hat had fallen off when he first grabbed her at the estate. Locks of blonde hair escaped a once well-coiffed bun to give her a disheveled appearance.

A few moments earlier, when she had studied him as if though he was nothing but sweetmeats she wanted to devour, he'd had to bite the side of his cheek to keep from grinning. Perhaps *devour* wasn't quite the word, since she had looked stunned by her indecent thoughts only seconds afterward.

Her gaze stayed on the floor for several awkward moments. Gradually, the rhythm of her chest deeply rising and falling took on a faster motion. Clearing her throat, she lifted her attention to him and squared her shoulders.

"Do—do you intend to starve me, sir?"

He arched an eyebrow. What an odd thing to ask. "No."

"Then would it be permissible to…eat something now?" Her voice squeaked.

He couldn't understand why she wanted to eat when only two hours ago, he'd seen her through the dining room window eating breakfast. "You are hungry?"

She narrowed her eyes. "But of course! Would I have asked otherwise?"

The sudden snip in her tone startled him at first, only because she had been so shy thus far. Yet she was now beginning to resemble the duchess he had been told about.

Julian folded his arms over his chest and lifted his chin. "Well, *Your Grace*, if you will come with me into the kitchen—"

"Why can I not stay here by the fire?"

"I fear you will try to escape. Although I'm certain you won't get very far before I catch you, I'm really not in the mood to run after you."

She huffed and threw him a scowl. "I assure you, I'm very hungry."

"Then please"—he swept his arm toward the kitchen—"let's adjourn into the other room so I can prepare you something to eat."

Her mouth tightened, and she stomped past him into the next room. Grinning, he followed. Soon, she would learn who was in command here, and it wasn't the high and mighty Duchess of Linden, that was for certain.

She came to an abrupt stop. He sidestepped her quickly to keep from bumping into her. The hurried movement brought a twinge of pain to his right leg. He gritted his teeth and tried to rub the ache from his knee. His injury was still rather new, and he needed to remember to give the wound time to heal. Unfortunately, all he had planned to accomplish now wouldn't allow him time to be patient. He would have to endure the agony from time to time and get used to it.

He studied her disgusted expression as her focus swept the room, and he tried to see this room as she was seeing it for the first time. So perhaps he should have cleaned a little better, but considering this cottage was on his friend's estate, and it hadn't been used for several years, it was no wonder the place was filthy.

Dented old pans hung on the walls, and the copper had faded many years ago. The shelves needed dusting, along with the canisters and bowls filling them, and the floor looked as if it hadn't seen a broom or mop in months or even years. At least the two fireplaces worked properly. One held a large black kettle of boiling water, and the other the baking bread that smelled as if it might be done. The table near the only window in the room was as rickety as the three chairs surrounding it.

Julian moved to the fireplace to check on the baking bread. Earlier this morning, he had prepared the bread, hoping it would be ready by now, since he, too, was hungry. He used a cloth to lift the lid on the cast-iron pan slowly. The heavenly aroma filled the air, and he closed his eyes, breathing in the scent deeply. It smelled exactly the way he had made it while in the military.

In his early years, his regiment had praised him countless

times for his excellent cooking. As he had climbed the ranks, there was little time to cook, and he had to rely on his men. Strange to think that none were as good as Major Stratford. Some couldn't even boil water.

He glanced around the small space and toward the shelves, searching for some plates, but he was yet to see any.

"Is there something I can do to help?" she asked in a small voice.

He looked at her and crinkled his forehead. A duchess offering to help in a kitchen? How odd. "If you can find some plates for our bread and some cups for our tea, that would be most helpful."

She moved past him, and the skirt of her riding habit brushed across his legs. Her sweet fragrance filled his head again. Now he recognized the flower. *Lilacs.* As much as he enjoyed a woman's scent, he tried not to enjoy this particular woman's smell. He didn't want to like her. She was the enemy's wife, and he only wanted one thing from her.

A confession.

Julian was convinced Martin was the reason the original Duke of Linden, Julian's father, and his brother, Forbes, had died so quickly. The physicians had written to Julian and explained that his family's sickness was a form of the plague. What confused Julian was why this illness took Father and Forbes' lives, and yet it hadn't made anyone else on the estate sick.

Very curious—as was the suspicious accident that nearly took his own life shortly after his hearing of his father and brother's deaths. Julian and a few of his men had been in town trying to locate a missing soldier. Julian hadn't planned on being in this town for very long. Out of nowhere, a cannon hit near the tavern where Julian and his men had been, killing several of his soldiers. The blast had injured Julian along with many civilians.

He rubbed his right leg, grateful that the surgeon hadn't removed the limb. By the grace of God, his leg had been saved as well as his own life. Of course, the flesh wounds were still very sore, and he had to take care not to get an infection. By this point, Julian realized none of these mishaps were accidental, especially since they only targeted the Stratford men.

"I can't find any dishes," the duchess said irritably. "It's hard to believe you would plan a kidnapping and not have the supplies to take care of your prisoner."

Julian studied the woman, not quite sure how to take her. Although her words were what he had expected from such a high and mighty woman, her tone still lacked confidence. And she kept her focus lowered, rarely looking at him.

"Forgive me, *Your Majesty*, but this cottage was supposed to have been stocked. I assure you, I'll take care of the matter after I feed you."

He turned back to the bread, took the pot from the fire, and slowly carried it to the cooking table. He used a knife to cut out chunks of the bread, careful not to burn his fingers.

He couldn't help but wonder what had happened to his friend, Vincent Wallace, Earl of Trenton. The earl was supposed to have stocked the small cottage in preparation for the kidnapping. Where was he now? If it weren't for Vincent, Julian would not have suspected Martin of killing his family—at least for a few months. The earl had watched Martin since he took over as duke, and Vincent had become suspicious of the new duke's actions. Julian didn't know what he would do without his friend and the assistance he had offered in catching the murderous cousin.

"We'll make do without dishes," he grumbled, keeping his attention on the bread. "Sit at the table, and I'll serve you."

Silence filled the room. He couldn't even hear the duchess breathing. Panic gripped his chest, and he swung around, looking for her. She was gone!

How long had it been since he last spoke to her? Good heavens, he couldn't remember. But he shouldn't fear because she wouldn't have gotten very far.

He dropped the knife on the table and rushed out of the room. The pain in his leg returned, and he gritted his teeth. Yet he couldn't worry about his injury now.

He listened for any sounds that would tell him where she had gone. The front door was open, letting him know where she had exited.

He quickly limped outside, stopped, and scoped his surroundings. His knee throbbed, and he rubbed it, praying the pain would disappear soon. *Where's my horse?* There was no way the duchess would have had time to mount by herself in just a few minutes; if she had, he would still be able to see her.

He whistled for his horse. By now, the animal knew when to come to his master. Immediately, he heard the animal's neigh and swung his head toward the sound. The horse was grazing in a nearby pasture without the duchess. Would she have been so foolish to try to escape on foot?

The fine animal raised his head and trotted toward Julian. He stroked the horse's mane as he glanced around the area. Where could she have gone?

"Duchess, you may as well come out now. It's impossible for you to get very far. If you haven't noticed, we are quite a distance from town."

Slowly, he walked away from the horse. Julian looked behind each bush he passed. Irritation grew inside him as the minutes ticked by. She really couldn't have gone far.

"If you insist on making me search for you," he said louder, "my anger will only worsen, and I can assure you, that's not something you will enjoy."

He stopped and waited. Within seconds, twigs snapped behind him, and suddenly, a sharp point jabbed the middle of his back. He stiffened.

"I haven't gone anywhere yet," she said roughly. Her voice was almost foreign. "But I have a knife, and I know how to use it. I suggest you take me back to the estate immediately."

Inwardly, he groaned. This could not be happening.

CHAPTER FOUR

Julian was still trying to wrap his mind around why the woman kept stammering while talking to him. Even though her voice became stronger with each word, she still didn't resemble the woman he'd been told about. Although she was frightened at the prospect of being kidnapped, he'd heard rumors about Duchess Linden that made politicians quake in their boots.

This wasn't the first time someone had held a knife to his back, and it probably wouldn't be the last. Releasing a heavy sigh, he raised his hands in surrender. "It appears you're in control now, duchess. I suppose I have no choice but to comply with your demands."

He gave her only three seconds to experience the powerful feeling she thought she held. Because he had been in this situation before, he knew her arm would relax, lowering the knife from his back. Just as he figured, the pressure from the tip of the knife lessened.

Taking advantage of the moment, he swung around and grasped her wrist. She screamed, and the knife dropped. He yanked her against him. As the front part of her body touched his, she gasped. His injury throbbed with pain, but he tried his best to ignore the discomfort.

Her wide, frightened eyes stared at him. He shouldn't have scared her, yet he had to let her know who was in control, and it wasn't the high and mighty duchess. The lesson he hoped to teach was one she would probably never forget. By her expression, he highly doubted she would pull this stunt on him again.

For a split second, guilt streaked through him. Perhaps he shouldn't have treated her as one of the men from his military experience. She was a naïve woman who had been protected all of her life. He needed to keep that in mind in case of future incidents. She was as delicate as a flower and smelled just as delectable. For some odd reason, she fit remarkably well in his arms. So soft—even though she was trembling.

Silently, he cursed. He could *not* have these feelings for his cousin's wife. He had kidnapped her for only one purpose, and lusting after her just would not do.

"Now, my little duchess," he said in a softer voice, sweeping a finger across her pale cheek as he pushed back a stray lock of hair, "shall we return to the kitchen and feed you?"

Her body quaked, and she nodded.

He kept her in his arms as he led her inside the house and into the kitchen. She stumbled a couple of times, but he suspected she wouldn't gain her full strength for a few more minutes.

"Let's sit you down right here before you end up on the floor." He helped her to the table, continuing to hold both of her wrists in his large hand. "Now, if I let you go, will you be a good duchess and stay seated?"

She nodded quickly.

"Very well, then."

He released her and stepped back to the baker's counter. He picked up the knife, turned back to the bread, and cut a chunk out. Using the kettle's lid as a plate, he brought the meal to the table and set it down.

He pointed to the bread. "Eat."

Julian turned from her again and moved to the kettle. At least there was a tea kettle and cup—but only one. It didn't matter. He wasn't thirsty anyway. He swiftly prepared the tea and placed the cup in front of her, noticing she had already eaten half of the bread slice.

Standing back, he folded his arms and scowled. Hopefully, it wouldn't take long before she confessed what her husband was up to. Julian didn't really blame her for wanting to be Duchess of Linden. Most women coveted that title and had tried to seduce his older brother just to get it. But this woman would soon discover she had married the wrong man. Martin would not make a good duke, and as long as Julian was alive, he had to make certain his cousin would never kill another person.

It would be difficult to convince the duchess that she needed to tell Julian the truth. He suspected she didn't know her husband was a murderer, but she would be able to tell Julian where Martin had been during the days of his brother and father's deaths—and of Julian's accident—and what men Martin had met with and paid off for assisting with these so-called accidents. The duchess had married Martin before he stepped into his new title, so she ought to know something about her husband's crooked lifestyle.

Julian prayed she would give him the answers he needed soon. He had never lowered himself to kidnap anyone before, and he could tell already that this particular woman would sorely try his patience.

It took several minutes, but soon she had eaten her chunk of bread and finished her tea. Slowly, she stood and squared her shoulders, but her eyes were downcast as she clasped her hands to her middle.

"I thank you for the food," she said.

Julian arched an eyebrow. Why had she thanked him? What game was she trying to play this time?

She took a deep breath and brought her gaze up to meet his. "Now, would you please tell me why you have kidnapped me?"

"No, not yet. I need time to think, and you need time to worry about what I'm going to do with you." He motioned toward the door leading into the other room. "Shall I show you to your room now?"

Her face paled, and she nodded. He escorted her up the stairs and to the room that would serve as her bedchamber as long as he held her prisoner.

As they walked inside, she held a grim expression, just as she had done when they first entered the kitchen. Julian realized this room wouldn't compare to her bedchamber at Linden Hall, but at least he had provided her with a bed, a decent mattress, and a few blankets. There was one small end table to hold a lamp.

After he adjusted the lamp and brightened the room, he pointed to the bed. "Forgive me, *duchess*, for not having more accommodations for you, but this will just have to suffice."

She nodded and quickly wiped away a tear sliding down her face. Another wave of guilt swept over him, and he pushed back the feeling, reminding himself that he was not at fault for any of this. She was, as well as her murderous husband.

Julian left the room and closed and locked the door before returning downstairs.

The cottage had been abandoned for several years, but Vincent had promised Julian it would be in tiptop shape. He didn't have a problem living in squalor, only because there were times while he was with his regiment that they were forced to hunt for their own food and camp out under the stars with only a thin blanket. Being in the military had given him skills—which he needed for this very occasion.

Though his leg pained him, he should sit and try to relax. But that wouldn't happen anytime soon. His thoughts were in turmoil, his body restless. He moved around the small living room and kitchen, straightening things and getting them as clean as possible.

He was thankful for his friend Vincent. Lord Trenton had been a godsend of late. As young lads, they weren't very close, but they'd seemed to frequent the same gaming tables before Julian went off to join the military. Right after his father and brother died, Julian received a letter from Vincent informing him of his family's deaths and about the peculiar activities that Martin had been up to before assuming the role of duke.

If not for Vincent, Julian wouldn't be desperately trying to find proof against his cousin. It had been Vincent's idea to hide out on the estate and keep watch over Martin and his wife. Julian knew that eventually Martin or his wife would slip up and give him the evidence needed to prove his family was murdered. Of course, when he waited and watched for the duchess to venture out of the house, he grew impatient. When he saw her today, he knew he had to take the chance and grab her.

Julian finished cleaning and stood back to study the two rooms again. They looked much better, but he still needed to find dishes for the kitchen. He had no idea how long they would stay here. It all depended upon the duchess and how much information she would give him.

Julian moved to the stairs and glanced up, listening for any sounds. The longer he stood concentrating, the more he heard the woman's soft sobs. Just as before, guilt clenched his chest. Perhaps it was time he brought her back down and grilled her about her husband.

He hurried up the stairs and opened the door. She was gone.

The open window indicated what had happened in his absence. He bunched his hands into fists. That woman could not be trusted. He shouldn't have left her alone.

Growling, he swung around and hurried down the stairs as fast as his painful leg would allow. How long had it been since she escaped? He couldn't recall how much time it had taken him to clean up the place. Had she taken his horse without his knowledge?

Julian yanked the front door open and marched outside. He stepped toward the spot he had left the animal, but it was empty. He scanned the perimeter for his horse as his heartbeat quickened in panic.

For being a trained soldier, he could have done things differently with her. However, he hadn't expected the woman to attempt to flee *twice*. Why hadn't she learned the first time?

Irritation stimulated his footsteps around the cottage as he searched for any signs of where she could have headed. The neigh from a horse stopped him. He swung around and peered toward the field. His horse grazed peacefully as if nothing was wrong in the world. Julian wished for that kind of solitude.

Once he had mounted his horse, he took off riding. He scanned around him, hoping the color of her dress would be what caught his eye. Now, if he could remember what she wore…

Finally, his mind opened. She wore a lovely riding habit trimmed in silver. The color he hoped to see was lavender.

After a few minutes of circling the area and not finding her, he gnashed his teeth. She couldn't have gotten that far. Unless…

Julian pulled the reins, bringing the horse to a stop. What if she had just opened the window to make it appear she escaped, and had been in the shack hiding, waiting for him to leave before she made her getaway? Could the duchess be that clever?

Then again, she had taken the kitchen knife and used it as her weapon earlier. So, why not do something intelligent now?

He jerked the reins, maneuvering the animal back toward the shack. One way or another, he would find her.

He neared the shack and searched in the distance. The sun's rays highlighted the purple material of a woman's dress moments before her shapely figure came into view. She ran toward the northeast side of the shack, where more trees could hide her. As soon as his anger calmed, he would have to commend her for her quick wit.

She must have heard him coming, because she glanced over her shoulder. Her eyes widened, and she ran faster. He was by her side within moments, blocking her with his horse.

"Leave me alone," she yelled.

"Not yet, *duchess*." He leaned over and grabbed her arm. As he lifted her to his lap, she squirmed. He gripped her tightly and placed her in front of him.

Her glare was wicked, but it didn't bother him.

"I don't know why you have kidnapped me." Tears filled her eyes. "I've done nothing wrong."

"Perhaps, but I'm ready to talk, and I need your company. Talking to myself won't get me any answers."

She folded her arms and pursed her mouth, trying her best to look away from him. The little duchess was feisty, but he would get her to talk one way or another.

The return ride to the shack didn't take long, but in the few minutes, unexpected sensations he didn't want to feel shot through his body. Although this feeling wasn't foreign to him, it had been too long since he experienced the rush of desire taking over his thoughts.

He could not… No, he *would* not have this. The woman on his lap was not only married, but had been foolish enough to marry his cousin.

They reached the shack, and he stopped the horse before dismounting. She continued to sit with her arms folded and her chin lifted stubbornly. He held his hands out to assist her.

"I don't need your help," she snapped without meeting his eyes.

"Please, *duchess*, don't take my gesture for one of help. I only wish to make certain you don't try to run from me again."

Finally, she looked at him. Her arched eyebrow warned him of her spirited attitude. He couldn't blame her. After all, she had just been kidnapped.

"Fine." She slid her hands into his.

As he helped her down, her body bumped against his. Once more, that feeling returned, growing hotter this time.

Silently, he groaned. *This is not the time!*

"I'm ready to talk," he said in a tight voice. "Come inside with me, and I'll tell you why I've kidnapped you."

CHAPTER FIVE

THE DUCHESS MARCHED into the shack, wiping at her eyes, and Julian followed closely behind her. She didn't stop until entering the front room. She came to a halt in front of the fireplace. Her shoulders were pulled back and her body appeared stiff.

The duchess peeked over her shoulder at him for a moment before returning her attention toward the embers slowly burning in the hearth.

Irritation ran through him again. Why didn't she want to look at him? How could he carry on a conversation with her if she wouldn't meet his eyes? It would be nearly impossible to study her reactions otherwise.

"There are only a few answers that I need from you," he began, limping closer to the hearth. The warmth would help the pain in his leg immensely. "If I'm satisfied with what you tell me, I'll return you to your home. It's as simple as that."

Immediately, she swung and faced him with wide eyes. He had to admit, having her look at him this way made him catch his breath.

"That's all I have to do?" she asked.

"Indeed, that is all."

"Then pray, please ask these questions so we can be on our way home soon."

He almost chuckled from her response. She seemed to think it would be that easy. She was definitely in for a rude awakening.

"Fine." He took another step toward the fireplace, since she made no move to sit on the couch. "I want to know..." He paused, carefully placing his words together in his thoughts. "Where was your husband this past March, on the thirteenth day?"

Her head tilted slightly. "My *husband?*"

"Yes. Martin Hinsdale."

A smirk grew on her mouth, and surprisingly, her sapphire eyes sparkled with humor. "I'm afraid you are mistaken, Mr. Grey. Martin Hinsdale is not *my* husband. He is married to my sister."

He waved his hand. "I'm not *Mister* Grey, just Grey." Then it struck him what she had said after that. "And don't try lying to me, Your Grace. I know Martin married Miss Templeton."

"Indeed he did. He married Charlotte Templeton. I'm Alexandria, her younger sister."

As he studied the woman, panic grew inside him. No! He couldn't have taken the wrong sister. She was exactly how Vincent had described her. Blonde hair, slender, lovely, but with the tongue of a viper. Although the lady he had taken had most of these, he still questioned the sharp tongue, since he had only noticed this a few minutes ago.

"I don't believe you." He shook his head. "If you are the younger sister, why are you living at the estate with your sister and her new husband?"

She shrugged, holding up her hands. "I came with the marriage deal. Charlotte didn't want to leave me behind because our parents have since passed, and she is my only sister. Miss Maxey Langley is my close cousin, but she lives near Manchester. Charlotte wanted me to stay close to her instead of moving to Manchester."

Julian shook his head. "Martin would have never agreed to something like that."

Her expression changed suddenly. He liked it better when there was a hint of a smile on her face instead of a frown and misty eyes.

"That would probably explain why earlier this morning, he had told me he was going to find me a husband who would *take me off his hands*." Her throat jumped in a hard swallow. "When you found me in the group of trees, I had been crying, correct?"

"Uh, yes, I believe I did hear you crying."

"Because Martin had just given me the startling blow."

"Impossible." Frustrated, Julian ran his fingers through his hair and paced the floor. He wouldn't accept this possibility. If he had stolen the wrong sister, then he wouldn't get any answers at all. He couldn't have done all of this for naught.

He stopped his pacing and looked at her. "Why are you lying to me? You are the woman my friend described to me. You *are* Martin's wife."

"I suppose I resemble Charlotte in some ways, but if it is Charlotte you're after, she has been in her room for the past five days. She has been extremely ill and hasn't moved from her bed."

"Five days, you say?" His hopes dropped even lower. He had only been spying on the estate, trying to figure out a way to kidnap the duchess, for the last three days. Perhaps this was why he had only seen this woman moving around inside the manor.

"Yes. Five days exactly, Mr. G—um, I mean Grey."

Groaning, he scrubbed his hands over his face. If only he had waited for Vincent to join him, but no—Julian had been too impatient and needed to kidnap the woman *immediately*. He certainly had a mess on his hands now. For once in his life, he didn't know how to fix this mistake.

ALEXANDRIA WRUNG HER hands as she watched Grey closely. Her captor was on the edge of admitting defeat, she could feel it. Now she knew why he kept referring to her as *duchess* and *Your Grace*. Now that the truth was out, she prayed he would return her to the estate. Hopefully, she would find the right words to encourage him to do so. Although returning would only mean Martin's threat would come to pass, her sister needed her, and Alexandria definitely needed Charlotte.

"Grey? What is it you need my sister for? To ask her questions as well?"

He dropped his hands as his stare locked on hers. "Yes. I need answers from your sister, unless, of course, you can answer them."

Her mind jumped back to the question he had asked her about March thirteenth. Could she possibly remember where Martin had been on that day? "I shall try to recall where Martin was on March thirteenth."

"Yes, please try. It's very important that I know this."

Slowly, he nodded. His eyes grew wide and stayed on her. It was uncomfortable to have the scrutiny of such a handsome man, but if helping him was the only way to get back home, she would do it.

She turned her head and stared into the fireplace again. She could think better without looking into his mesmerizing green eyes.

"Martin would have probably been gone a sennight," he said.

Sometime in the middle of March was when Martin would have been gone. Her sister married him in the last part of January. Martin had stayed at their small country estate until the end of March, when he took over as duke.

Instantly, Alexandria's mind opened. She inhaled quickly and swung her head toward Grey. Excitement bubbled in her chest. "Martin was indeed gone a sennight. Charlotte had told me he was trying to locate them a place to live. That would have been in the middle of March."

"Are you certain?"

She nodded. "I'm very certain. I recall thinking that this was the last time my sister and I would spend quality time together without the presence of her new husband."

A whoosh of air escaped Grey's mouth, and a smile stretched across his mouth. "Splendid."

"Is that all you need?" she asked.

"No, but it's a good start."

She wondered why this man was so interested in her brother-in-law. Obviously, her captor didn't like Martin very much, but her curious mind wanted to know every detail of why he was so desperate for answers. Another thing she couldn't understand was whether she should fear Mr. Grey. Obviously, his issue was with Martin and not her.

"Sir? May I ask what crime Martin has committed against you?"

Grey was silent for a few awkward moments, and although he said nothing, his expression spoke volumes. Malice colored his narrowed eyes, and his handsome face was marred with lines of anger. Indeed, her brother-in-law had definitely done something dreadful when he upset Grey.

"What if I told you," he began slowly, "that I believe Martin to be involved with the deaths of two men, and he was the reason a third man nearly died as well?"

She gasped. "Martin is a murderer?"

"Two men for certain, and he injured a third with intent to kill."

"Surely you jest?"

He shook his head. "I do not jest. I stake my life on it, in fact. All I need is proof now."

"Oh my."

She placed her hand against her bosom, feeling the erratic rhythm of her heartbeat. She thought back in time to right after Charlotte married Martin. Although Alexandria hadn't wanted to converse with the man because of her shyness, there were many times she heard him barking at the servants for doing something wrong. One particular time he had a visitor, and as she sat in the small library, she could hear him and this other man arguing loudly. Parts of the threat he had thrown at the visitor made her blush. She couldn't help but feel sorry for the other man.

Then there were times she overheard her sister and Martin arguing. Apparently, he was most disagreeable with several people. With a temper like Martin's, it was possible that he had a mean streak…one that could harm others.

Worry whirled through her of all the possible things he could do to her as well as Charlotte, but then her mind switched and took a different path. Hope bubbled inside of her. If her brother-in-law were put in the gaol for his crimes, he wouldn't be able to marry her off to a man she didn't love. She and her sister would return to their country home instead of living in such a large house. She and Charlotte could resume their simple life in the family cottage before Martin entered their lives.

"What do you think will happen to Martin if he is caught?" she asked.

"I'm quite certain he'll hang for his crimes."

Dare she believe? Dare she hope Martin was the man Grey thought him to be, so that her brother-in-law wouldn't be able to control her life any longer? But therein lay the problem. Could she trust her captor enough that he would obtain his goal and get Martin out of her life?

CHAPTER SIX

JULIAN STUDIED HIS prisoner still standing near the hearth. Was she the duchess, or was she really the younger sister? He scratched his chin. The duchess would be a few years older—or at least look like she was a few years older. This particular woman appeared young, perhaps midway in her twentieth year. Martin's wife would be in her late twenties.

Although this woman was stunning, she wasn't the flashy beauty he had heard about from Vincent. The earl talked about Martin's wife as if she were a woman most men stumbled over their feet just to look at. Vincent had told Julian that most men went out of their way to give her trinkets just to hear one kind word from her. Julian studied the woman he'd kidnapped. She didn't quite measure up to Vincent's description. However, this sister was indeed lovely, but naturally so.

Now, in her hesitation, there was a certain gleam in her eyes, as if excitement built inside her. Confusion filled his head. Would the true duchess show as much excitement at the prospect of her husband's hanging? Probably not. But this woman appeared as if she did—and that she couldn't wait.

"So, tell me," Julian said in a rush before she could get another word out. "If you are indeed the younger sister, why have you not married? If your sister is the duchess, I'm quite sure many suitors have sought your hand in marriage."

Her face flamed a brilliant red, and again, she dropped her focus back to the floor. "I…I haven't married because…"

She paused, seeming unwilling to reveal her reasons. Finally, she took a deep breath, squared her shoulders, and lifted her eyes to his.

"Grey, I'm what men like yourself consider a wallflower. I am shy around men, and I have difficulty conversing. My sister has always been the center of attention, not I." She cleared her throat. "If it were up to me, I wouldn't marry at all, but unfortunately, my brother-in-law thinks I need assistance in this matter."

Julian cocked his head. This was the second time she had mentioned her brother-in-law in this respect, with irritation coating her voice. Was Martin truly trying to marry off the younger sister? Then again, if Julian had a sister-in-law living with him and his new bride, he would also want to get her married.

"Is there anything else you wish to know so I can convince you that I'm not the duchess?" she asked timidly.

He tapped his finger on his chin. Should he believe her? Part of him felt he shouldn't, yet he really didn't think Martin's wife would behave this way. This particular woman was definitely not acting the part. "So, you are Miss Alexandria Templeton?"

She exhaled a loud sigh. "I am, yes."

"Miss Templeton, do you think you know your brother-in-law well enough to help me?"

One of her slender shoulders rose in a shrug. "I can try, but whatever you do, promise me you will not kidnap my sister and bother her about this matter. As I mentioned, she is very ill, and I don't want you to make it worse for her. If you don't believe me, return me to the estate, I'll try to sneak you inside her bedchamber, and you can see for yourself."

Brave woman. Would she really risk having her brother-in-law catch her? Of course, Julian would find another way, because *he* couldn't risk being noticed at the estate just yet. It was too soon to let Martin know the real Duke of Linden was still alive.

"Perhaps later," Julian said with a nod. He moved to the

couch to sit but stopped instead. Hopefully, she would join him. "So, Miss Templeton, what can you tell me about Martin that I might not like?"

Her sapphire eyes widened, and she blinked. The corner of her mouth lifted slightly. "That *you* might not like? How would I know that, sir?"

"Point taken." He blew out a breath. "Instead, why don't you tell me what things you don't like about him?"

Her attention moved to the couch. Uncertainty flitted across her eyes as she switched focus from Julian to the far side of the furniture. He motioned with his hand for her to sit. She fidgeted a few moments more before moving to the end and perching on the edge of the cushion. The couch might be dusty and worn, but it wasn't going to bite her, for goodness' sake! However, now he could sit.

She folded her hands in her lap and her attention jumped around the room but only landed on him a few times before continuing to wander. He wondered why she didn't like looking at him for very long. Strange woman.

"To be honest, I don't know His Grace that well at all," she began.

"Actually," Julian said, "will you refer to him as Martin? In my opinion, he doesn't deserve the title of duke."

She nodded. "As I was saying, Martin courted my sister a month before asking for her hand in marriage. During that courtship, I only met him three times, when he came to our house for supper. Like all men, he only had eyes for Charlotte, so I couldn't engage him in conversation for any length of time." She shrugged. "Which is good, because I am not talented that way."

Julian crossed one leg over the other. "What about after your sister married him and you moved into the estate?"

"One thing I noticed during those first few weeks was that he rarely stayed home. I found it odd that he didn't want to spend more time with my sister, especially since they were newly wed."

"Did he have an excuse for being away so much?" Julian

studied her reactions and the way she answered his questions. So far, she appeared sincere in trying to help him.

"All Charlotte said was that he had to get his affairs in order because of his newly appointed status as duke. Charlotte assured me their life would return to normal soon."

Julian rolled his eyes. He would bet that some of Martin's affairs had to do with women and his gambling debts instead of business. "Can you remember if anyone visited him after he took the title of duke? And if so, did he appear as if he was embarrassed about their being there?"

She frowned and shook her head. "I'm not certain what you mean."

He licked his dry lips. "I'm thinking about ruffians or similar. Men who were lower class whom Martin might have been embarrassed talking to in public."

"No, not really. Most of the people who came to visit were associates of Martin, and he didn't appear to be embarrassed by them at all. He introduced his wife to them without hesitation."

"But not you?"

She shook her head. "I stayed in other rooms and only observed from a distance. While he was with his friends, I was either in my room writing or riding my horse, Buttercup."

"Hmm, I see." He scrubbed a hand over the lower half of his face, realizing he needed a good shave soon. "Perhaps Martin met with those particular people in secret so as not to draw attention to his misdeeds."

"Perhaps."

Her attention shifted to the wall as her expression changed. Strange, but he could actually tell the wheels in her mind were turning, and she was on the verge of remembering something.

"You know, I do recall a time when I had gone to the stable to ride Buttercup, and I saw Martin with two men behind the barn. The way they stood huddled with their voices low and their eyes constantly shifting gave me the impression they were discussing or planning something that they did not wish others to discover. I recall thinking at the time how different these two men were compared to Martin's other associates. He gave them money, as well. I had assumed they were new servants, but then I never saw those men again."

Excitement shot through Julian. This could be something important. He dropped his leg to the floor and scooted closer to her on the couch. "Do you think you would recognize these men if you saw them again?"

Her eyes widened as her gaze slid over his face and rested on his chest. Her cheeks flushed with a deep red. She placed the back of her hand against her cheek and glanced up at him again.

"Most definitely. You see, although I had just noticed them that one time, I used their descriptions in the story I was writing at the time."

Surprise washed over him, and he arched an eyebrow. "You were writing a story?"

"Yes," she muttered, and looked down at her folded hands.

He wished she would stop looking away. Reaching over, he touched her chin, and immediately, she studied his face. "Miss Templeton, there is no reason to be embarrassed. Writing stories is a wonderful talent to have."

Her mouth stretched into a shaky smile. "Thank you."

"Have you had any of your work published?"

She shook her head. "Of course not. Nobody would take a woman seriously, anyway."

"Maybe…maybe not. You would have to know someone with connections." He grinned. "Anyway, back to these men. What did they look like?"

"They appeared to be in their early thirties and slender. They wore the clothes of the lower class. The taller man of the two had bright auburn hair—almost like a burnt orange. He had a scar on his cheek that was an inch long. It didn't appear to be fresh, though." She paused for just a moment. "And the second man was very blond, as if the sun had colored his hair. He walked with a limp—worse than yours."

Julian held his breath. *She noticed my limp?* Immediately, his hand moved to his aching leg. He had tried his hardest not to limp and show the pain he was still experiencing. He hadn't realized how astute she was until now. She was also descriptive, and he could picture these men from just her words.

"This information is very helpful." Julian knew he and Vincent would find the evidence needed to catch these buggers now.

"I hope you will be able to locate them," she said sweetly. "As I mentioned earlier, I only saw them that one day."

"I'm confident I'll find them. When I'm determined to do something, there is nothing that will stop me."

"Splendid."

Miss Templeton smiled, but it still wasn't the full smile he wanted to see on her face. Then he remembered he was her captor. Because he had made the mistake of stealing the wrong sister—and then threatening her when she held a knife to him— he needed to figure out a way to make her feel that he was no longer a threat. In fact, from this point forward, he would think of her as his partner in the search for justice. He would have to charm her. That was the only way to soften her heart so she would assist him.

"Tell me, Miss Templeton, has Martin ever threatened you or treated you unkindly?"

She frowned. "How do you mean?"

"Has he ever struck you or acted as if he was about to?"

"Oh, heavens no! He has never lifted a hand to my sister or me."

"Does he talk unkindly to you?"

Her stare wandered away again as she scratched her cheek. Slowly, sadness etched into her expression, and surprisingly, his gut twisted. Anger shot through him. He knew his cousin's words had been what cut this woman deeply. Immediately, Julian felt the need to punch Martin in the face for being so unkind.

When it finally struck him how protective he was feeling toward Miss Templeton, he mentally shook off the feeling. He had no right to experience this with her at all.

"Actually, yes," she said softly. "We don't converse much, but he is not polite when he talks to me. He makes me feel like an imbecile and that I don't have a brain...or at least that I don't know how to use it. I realize now that I'm just a thorn in his foot, but I have never understood why he cannot be nice toward me." She released a deep sigh. "Perhaps he is correct in assuming I'm worthless because I'm a wallflower, and I don't enjoy mingling."

Just as before, anger pierced Julian, hotter than he had expected. If Martin were standing in front of him now, he would throttle the imp within an inch of his life. Then Martin would know what *worthless* felt like.

"Miss Templeton, you cannot be more wrong." He scooted closer until his leg brushed against her gown. Gently, he took hold of one of her hands. Her eyes widened, and her body stiffened, but that didn't make him pull away. He needed to get his point across, and sitting this close was the only way he knew how to do it. "You are a lovely and intelligent woman. From what I've noticed, you are extremely levelheaded as well. I have never known anyone like you."

She shook her head. "No, I'm nothing like you have described."

"You don't see yourself the way I see you, my blossom. Here you are, a woman who has been wrongly kidnapped, and yet so far, you have pointed out my mistakes, dared to threaten me with a knife, and then you have softened your heart and offered to help me with my goal. How many women do you know who would have been so brave?"

"Brave, sir?"

He grinned. "Very brave, Miss Templeton." He squeezed her hands gently. "On top of that, you write stories. Martin would kill to have a gift like yours, considering the fool doesn't have a creative bone in his body."

Immediately, her face lit up and she laughed. Her sapphire eyes twinkled like stars in a night sky. He hadn't realized how utterly amazing and mesmerizingly lovely she was until now. His heart leapt at his knowing he had made her feel such happiness.

"You are too kind," she said with a slightly stronger voice.

He shook his head and tried to stop his heart from beating fast and his smile from widening further. But it was impossible not to feel giddy. Her cheerful expression made his heart light, and he wanted to keep her smiling all the time.

"Anyhow…" He cleared his throat. "I wanted to know how Martin treated you because I'm wondering how he'll react when I take you back home."

The enthusiasm in her expression quickly disappeared. "Well, when you return me, he will certainly follow through with his threat and find me a husband." She shook her head. "As much as I love my sister, I cannot allow him to marry me off to the highest bidder."

Inwardly, Julian groaned. "He would do that, to be sure. However, I just thought of a way that will bring justice to both of us."

"What way is that?"

"I need you to spy for me. Come to think of it, you could snoop through his study and bedchamber when he is not there."

Panic filled her eyes as the color faded from her face. "I couldn't possibly do that."

Still holding her hand, he brought it to his chest and pressed her palm against his heart. Her attention moved to his chest, and her expression softened, but the rhythm of her breathing quickened. Surprisingly, his heartbeat sped a notch just from her touch. This wasn't good at all. How could he think straight if her touch affected him in such a way?

Charming her was working, and he would have to keep it up if he wanted her full cooperation.

"Miss Templeton, if you help me with this, I promise you here and now that I will not let Martin marry you to someone you don't know or love."

After a few seconds, she lifted her eyes to his face. "I…I,

um…believe you."

Hope grew inside of him. She was slowly beginning to trust him. He needed her help desperately, and if he had to seduce her to get it, he would.

CHAPTER SEVEN

ALTHOUGH ALEXANDRIA SAID she believed him, part of her wanted to fear him because he had kidnapped her. But the more time she spent with Grey, the more she couldn't stop herself from enjoying his company. It was hard to believe, but it became much easier to talk to him, and she rarely blushed anymore. So far, she had been doing as her sister had encouraged her to do—become the women in her novels. At first it was difficult, but the more she conversed with Grey, the more confidence she gained. Perhaps she could do this after all.

Another thing she noticed was his attitude toward her now that he realized he had taken the wrong sister. She no longer felt he would hurt her, but she still didn't know if she could fully trust him. He definitely wanted to see Martin put behind bars, but could she help Grey as he wanted? Men who were out for revenge were not in their right minds—or so she had been told and, of course, written about.

She dared not get her hopes up too soon.

Nevertheless, she found herself gazing into his green eyes more often now, feeling her heart melt and loving the way her chest fluttered. His intense stare didn't make her as uncomfortable as it had before.

She reined in her feelings quickly. She couldn't feel this way about him. He hadn't yet proven to her that she could trust him.

Of course, she couldn't let him know. Perhaps if she *acted* like she trusted him, that would be the way to convince him to take her back home.

They talked for two hours, and it became easier. Grey continued to persuade her to help him spy on Martin, and it amazed her how much courage she gained by just listening to Grey's kind words. But could she actually spy on her brother-in-law? The mere thought started a churning pain in the pit of her stomach, slowly at first, but it heightened the longer Grey begged for her help. Could a meek woman such as herself accomplish what Grey had instructed?

"But you don't understand," she said, standing and walking to the hearth to stare at the fire that was nearly out. "Martin is used to me hiding from him. He will certainly notice when I watch him more, especially if I'm not in my room most of the day."

Grey moved to stand near her. He took the poker and knelt to break up the logs. He was starting to douse the fire—did this mean he would take her home? Her hopes rose and then quickly fell. She was utterly confused. Although she was still considered *kidnapped* and with her abductor, she didn't want to return home to face Martin's threat.

"I fear Martin will question me about my actions." She rubbed her arm. "And what if he tries to harm me?"

"Miss Templeton." Grey placed the poker back against the stone wall, stood, and faced her. "I will not let you out of my sight as long as Martin is around."

"I don't understand." She shook her head.

"For the past few days, I've been outside the estate spying on Martin. That is why I thought you were the duchess. I could see you in the sitting room reading a book. I saw both of you at the dining table when you partook of your meals. I saw him in his study, and I saw you whenever you went riding."

Heat climbed up her neck to attack her face once more. He had been watching her, and the mere idea made her shiver. She swallowed hard. Could he possibly have seen her while she was in her bedchamber? She seriously hoped not.

"You watched us *all* the time?"

Grey shrugged. "Well, perhaps not every moment of the day. Of course I didn't watch you sleep."

She hoped that meant he couldn't see inside her room. "How were you able to spy on us while outside?"

He grinned, and her heart flipped. That blasted smile of his gave her this reaction every time.

"There are a few places on the estate where I can hide. I have a spyglass, and that's how I have been able to watch the two of you so closely."

She tilted her head, keeping her attention on him, even though it was hard. "Sir, I don't know whether to think that's a good or bad thing."

He chuckled and folded his arms over his wide chest. "I'm not insane, if that is what you're referring to."

"You certainly couldn't prove it in front of a magistrate."

His eyes widened for a moment before he threw his head back and laughed. She couldn't help but smile as his rich baritone filled the silence of the room. This was the first time she had conversed with a man and he found her humorous. She quite liked the warm feeling spreading through her chest.

When he finally met her stare again, he shook his head. "The point is you don't have anything to worry about. I'll be watching you, and if Martin tries to harm you, I will stop it. Just make sure you're by a window, and I'll see it."

As much as she wanted to believe him, it was hard. The truth of the matter was, she really didn't know Grey well enough to put her fate in his hands.

"I thank you. That makes me feel slightly better." She glanced at the dying embers in the hearth. "Why did you put out the fire?"

"Because, as promised, I will take you home. Does that ease your mind some?"

She hesitated before nodding, but his narrowed eyes told her he wasn't convinced.

"Miss Templeton? What are you worried about?"

"The same thing I was worried about five minutes ago."

He touched her shoulder and squeezed softly. "Will you trust me?"

"I shall try." And she really meant it as it left her mouth.

A half-hour later, they started back to the estate, riding on his horse. Although she wasn't wrapped in a horse blanket this time, she still sat on his lap. The position was so improper and yet so incredibly cozy. His arms and legs bracketed her body intimately.

Warmth spread over her like a comforting blanket. There wasn't any other place she would rather be at this moment. She never felt this rush of emotions, and since she was tired of questioning them, she decided she would just enjoy them for now. Besides, he couldn't see her face, so he wouldn't know how much she enjoyed this moment.

"Remember," he said after a while of traveling in silence, "make certain to be in rooms that have windows so I'll be able to keep an eye on you the best way I can. If Martin tries to corner you in the hallway, casually lead him into the nearest room with a window."

She swallowed hard, praying she would be able to accomplish this. She *needed* to do this. How else could she become the women she wrote about in her stories? But it was more than that. Grey had spoken to her as if he believed in her. Never had she allowed a man to get this close to her until she felt like a confident woman. She couldn't let him down.

"Where exactly will you be, Grey?"

"Mostly, I'll be hiding in the group of trees on the east side of the stable. There is also a small hillside directly opposite the west wing with trees and tall bushes that will keep me hidden."

She looked over her shoulder and into his eyes, and her heart skipped a beat. She quite enjoyed his smoldering gaze and could look at him like this for hours without getting bored.

He was entirely too close. She cursed her insane emotions, but she did like the newfound feeling. "Grey, I get the impression that you know the estate quite well. Did you used to visit there as a lad, or do you live nearby?"

He blinked and moved his focus back to the road, and his jaw tightened. She received the distinct impression that he was hiding something. Of course, he wouldn't be completely honest with her yet. Perhaps he was waiting for her to prove he could trust her. Funny, since that was the game she played with him.

He nodded. "I have spent a lot of time at the estate. That's why I know where everything is located."

She dared not push him to tell her more. She must believe he would in due time. Yet she had shared information about her life, and it seemed almost unfair that she didn't know much about him.

"Is Grey your real name?" she asked hesitantly.

His stare locked with hers again. "Why do you ask?"

"I just want to get to know you a little better." She shrugged. "Is it wrong to want to know the man I'm helping—the same man who assured me he wouldn't allow Martin to marry me to the highest bidder?"

His face relaxed, and he smiled. Her breath caught in her throat again. This had been happening too much already. Yet, when he looked so incredibly handsome, how could she not react? Nevertheless, she must find a way to stop herself from feeling this way.

"No, I suppose it is not wrong."

"So, is Grey your real name?"

"It's my middle name."

"Do your friends call you that?"

"Actually, no. I hold a title, and they call me by my title."

He stroked her arm, making her belly flutter. Silently, she sighed and relaxed. It was then she realized just how muscular he really was. His wide chest made her body buzz with awareness.

She hitched a quick breath and sat up straighter. The knowledge of what he'd just said to her finally stuck in her mind. She must have heard him wrong. If he held a title, that meant he was a nobleman, and noblemen didn't go around kidnapping innocent women…or doing all they could to see someone hanged. "You are a noble?"

"Indeed."

"What is your title?"

Chuckling, he shook his head. "I don't want you to worry about it right now, my blossom. I give you permission to call me Grey."

Oh! His secrets were going to drive her insane, she just knew it. She didn't know why he kept referring to her as *my blossom*, but it made strange things happen to her stomach. "Do you plan on ever telling me your title and given name?"

He took a glance at her before returning his attention to the road. "Yes, I shall tell you when the time is right."

She faced the road once more. Gradually, she relaxed against his chest. It was hard to keep from touching him in some way…another first for her. Even though he was incredibly muscular, resting against him like this was actually comfortable. Really, she shouldn't enjoy this closeness. Obviously, Grey wasn't a respectable nobleman, especially if he went around kidnapping people. He must have strayed from his upbringing, which meant he would not be a gentleman to her at all. If that were the case, it was utterly ridiculous of her even to conjure up such fantasies about the kind of man she wished him to be. Being a wallflower all of her life, she was used to daydreaming about men giving her some attention as they did to her sister. Moreover, just as all of the daydreams she had had before, this one would eventually end.

The steady rhythm of the horse lulled and relaxed her until she couldn't keep her eyes open any longer. She closed them but tried to remain alert. The only things she could hear were the horse's hooves, Grey's breathing, and, of course, his occasional sigh. She found herself sighing along with him.

Gradually, one of his arms moved around her, holding her against him tighter. She smiled and, in her sleepy state, cuddled closer. If only she could stay in her dreams and be like this forever. If only he were a true gentleman—a real knight who came to her rescue and saved her from the horrid brother-in-law who didn't care a whit about her welfare. If only…her dreams would come true.

Her eyes hadn't been closed for very long before the horse came to a sudden stop. As she blinked herself awake, the heaviness consuming her body let her know she had been asleep much longer than she had realized. "Where are we?"

"Home," he whispered near her ear.

Her chest tightened as she glanced down the grove at the estate—Linden Hall was how Martin referred to it. It had only been a few hours since Grey took her away from here, and she knew the place would be the same when she returned, yet studying the grand house made her realize how lonely she had been since the first day she and her sister settled in. Strange to think she had enjoyed herself with Grey even when she was frightened to death and couldn't trust him—more than she had since moving in with her sister.

Would he make good on his promise by keeping her safe? Only time would tell.

CHAPTER EIGHT

F EAR FILLED ALEXANDRIA quickly. She didn't want to come back to this place, not as long as Martin still resided at Linden Hall. Although she didn't fully trust Grey, he was her only hope of freedom right now, so she must help him.

Grey maneuvered the animal into a cluster of trees and stopped. He dismounted, carefully hooked his hands around her waist, and lifted her down. She held on to his shoulders, keeping her eyes on his as he lowered her. Alexandria brushed against him, but he didn't seem to mind…and remarkably, she didn't mind either. Silently, she cursed the fact that she had been a wallflower all of her life and had never enjoyed such privileges.

His throat jumped, and he licked his lips. "I'll let you go from this point. We don't need Martin or the servants to see us together," he said softly.

"No, we don't."

"Remember, you shall be fine. I won't take my eyes off you."

He said the last part so very tenderly, and his eyes darkened slightly. It was hard not to trust him with her full heart at this moment, but she couldn't get rid of the nagging thought in the back of her mind, reminding her that he hadn't proven to her that he could be trusted.

She realized he still held on to her, and she held on to him. Suddenly, her throat turned dry, and she didn't want to move away. "I'll remember."

"I think we should meet later tonight," he said.

Hope sprang in her chest. Perhaps she had interested him in some way. Dare she believe? "You do?"

"Yes. I want to know everything that has happened with Martin and what has not. Then we can plan for tomorrow's day."

She nodded as her hopes slowly deflated. He didn't show any signs of being repulsed by her company, which was slightly encouraging. But at least she would see this handsome man again.

"Yes, Grey. That is an excellent idea."

"Where should we meet?"

Her mind froze, and for the life of her, she couldn't think of anywhere on the estate that would be private. Of course, it didn't help her un-functioning mind because she was in his arms and couldn't stop gazing into his irresistible eyes.

As he watched her, his mouth slowly stretched into a grin. "There is a grove of trees by the pond. I'm sure you've ridden by that place many times since you've been here."

"Uh…yes, I have."

"In the evening, the grove of trees is very private. Not even the moonlight will disturb us. I think we should meet there."

"All right." She licked her dry lips. "What time?"

"What time do you have supper?"

"Eight o'clock."

"Then meet me there after supper."

"Should I bring you something to eat?"

His smile stretched more, if that were possible, and his green eyes glimmered with happiness.

"I thank you for thinking of me. And yes, it would be wonderful if you could bring me something to eat."

"Then I shall be delighted to do so."

She didn't know how long she stood standing in his embrace, but he acted as if he didn't want to move. Finally, he cleared his throat and slowly dropped his arms. She quickly folded her arms to keep them occupied because they suddenly felt empty. A strange, hollow feeling encased her.

"I shall see you later this evening." His voice came out low.

"Yes."

He didn't move, but his attention dropped to her mouth. Urgency swept through her, and she wanted him to yank her back in his arms and bestow upon her the first kiss ever...the kind of kiss she had dreamed about since she discovered boys were not as disgusting as she first thought.

She scolded herself for thinking this way. He was *not* the kind of man she should share her first kiss with, but since he had realized she was the wrong sister, he had been so gentle. He had listened and believed in her, which was something men had never done to her before.

He swayed toward her, and she held her breath. But he took a step back. She released the pent-up air in a rush between her lips.

"Don't forget, I'll be watching you." He winked, turned, and mounted his horse. He glanced at her one last time before riding toward his hiding spot.

Disappointment washed over her. She had been rejected many times in her twenty-three years, but never had she felt this lonesome before.

Alexandria made it to the stable before anyone on the estate noticed her. Nobody would know she had been missing for a few hours, only because she wasn't important around here anyway. The setting sun brushed the sky with reds, yellows, and oranges. One of the stable boys gave her a nod before returning to moving hay around the animal's stalls. Immediately, she noticed Buttercup had returned. She was grateful her horse knew the way back, but it hurt that it hadn't alarmed anyone when she didn't return with it.

Sighing heavily, she pushed weary fingers through her hair. She had styled her waves into a bun this morning, but they had all come out over the course of her adventure. She could only imagine what she looked like—a horrid mess. And to think this was what Grey saw the whole time he held her captive. *How humiliating!*

Well, tonight, she would certainly show him what a proper lady looked like. With any luck, she would be able to help him become the respectable nobleman she knew he could be. Excitement gave a bounce to her step. She was absolutely giddy, like a schoolgirl again. She wanted to laugh as she skipped to the manor. It took all her willpower not to throw her arms out and twirl around in pure glee. Perhaps she would when she entered her bedchamber, where no one would see her.

"There you are."

The grating voice of her brother-in-law brought her thoughts to a stop. The happiness inside her disappeared quickly. She ceased moving any farther, locking her feet together in a military stance. She stiffened and waited for him to come into view. There was no way she would make the first move to look at him. At least they were outside for Grey to watch, and she didn't have to worry about trying to find a window to stand by.

When Martin finally walked beside her, he skimmed his gaze over her in disgust, from the top of her messy hair to the bottom of her mud-encrusted riding habit. His lip curled, and he glared at her with beady, hateful eyes.

"So, the wanderer returns."

"Wanderer?" she asked, keeping her voice steady, refusing to look directly at him.

"I suspected you would run off after I informed you about my intentions. When your horse returned without you, I thought you had run far away from here."

"No, Your Grace. I was just…just…walking. I needed time to think."

He cocked his head. "And pray tell, what were you thinking about all those hours?"

Wouldn't you like to know? "Several things, actually."

He shrugged. "I see you've come home for something to eat, as usual."

She held in a gasp. What had he meant by that remark? Did he think she was fat? *Augh!* Never before had she wanted to clobber a man so much. "No, not really. I shall be fine."

"Tell me, have you come to terms with what I told you earlier?"

This time, she couldn't stop looking at his face. He slowly circled her, hooking his hands behind his back as he glared her way.

She arched an eyebrow. "About finding me a husband?"

"Yes."

"No, I have not come to terms with it yet. Perhaps in a couple more days."

The distaste in his expression deepened. He stepped closer and grasped her wrist. Pain shot through her arm, and she grimaced, holding her tongue to keep from crying out. Anger pumped through her, overriding the pain.

"I suggest you accept this notion faster than a *couple more days*. I want you out of Linden Hall within the week. You had better not get any ideas of how you can discourage these men, either. I swear I shall give you to one of them regardless of your thoughts. Do I make myself clear?"

She wiggled her hand, trying to get out of his grip, but he was stronger. Whimpering, she glanced around the yard and searched for someone to help her. Unfortunately, nobody would come to her rescue. After all, this was his home, not hers.

In the corner of her eye, movement near a cluster of trees caught her attention. *Grey!* As if the mere thought of his name made him materialize, Grey marched toward them with a noticeable limp, his sword halfway drawn. Malice laced his expression as he focused on Martin. Thankfully, Grey was behind her brother-in-law, or he would be able to see the man coming to her rescue.

Her heart leapt nearly out of her chest. Grey would risk being caught just to save her. She didn't understand why he would want to show himself to Martin, because she knew Grey must stay hidden until they found the proof needed to put Martin away for good.

Panic rushed through her. No matter what, Grey could not make his presence known yet.

Finding strength she didn't know she possessed, she yanked her hand out of Martin's grip. "No!" she shouted, holding up her hand to stop Grey, but looking at her brother-in-law.

"No?" Martin asked, irritated.

"Um, I mean, *yes*, your warning is very clear indeed." She lifted her chin and squared her shoulders then glanced at Grey. Thankfully, he had stopped, but he hadn't retreated into the trees. "I understand you completely, and I shall comply with your wishes the best I know how."

"You had better, or you shall not like the consequences." The insipid man flipped his hand in a dismissive wave. "Now go and get yourself cleaned up. You look hideous. I cannot have my sister-in-law looking so dowdy when I try to find her a husband."

"That's exactly what I had planned to do, Your Grace." Before turning toward the house, she noticed Grey had darted back into the trees.

Sighing with relief, she continued into the house and directly to her room to change for the evening. Shock was a mild word for what she was experiencing right now. She still couldn't believe Grey would risk getting caught like that. His actions just a few moments ago meant only one thing: she could trust him. He was really going to keep watch over her and protect her.

She closed the door to her bedchamber and leaned against the hard frame. Placing her hand over her erratic heartbeat, she smiled. Had she been wrong about Grey this whole time? Perhaps he was indeed a nobleman, and if he was, could he possibly be the man of her daydreams?

A chuckle escaped her, and she moved away from the door. As she plucked the buttons on the jacket of her riding habit apart, she reminded herself that she couldn't let her dreams take away her logical mind. She couldn't jump to conclusions, either.

Although Grey had proven himself to her, that still didn't mean he would stay around and want to court her after all this was over. It was foolish for her to believe such a thing.

He was a nobleman, and they only wanted to marry noble-women with large dowries, which she did not have.

As she pulled the jacket off, her wrist burned with the sting from Martin's strong grip. She seethed, hating the way he had always treated her. Why hadn't Charlotte noticed? Charlotte had landed herself a duke for a husband, so did she really care about Alexandria anymore?

Sadness crept over her as tears swam in her eyes. It had seemed that ever since Charlotte met Martin, she hadn't cared about her younger sister's welfare. Perhaps Martin was wise to find Alexandria a husband after all.

Pausing, she stared at the pitiful woman in the full-length mirror. A shiver ran through her, twisting her stomach. No, Martin wasn't trying to find her a husband. All he wanted to do was find her another person who would be responsible for her care.

If only her parents hadn't died. If only her extended family lived closer. Her grandparents had lived across the ocean, and her aunts and uncles, in America, were too far away to be of any aid. There was no one for her to turn to.

She rubbed the moisture from her eyes and continued clean-ing herself up. Determination drove her now. She would help Grey all she could or die trying. Her choice was made. She could only believe that they would find evidence to put Martin away, because the opposite was too unbearable to think about.

Taking deep breaths, she tried to regulate her heartbeat. She shouldn't fear Martin any longer. Grey had promised to protect her from the wretched Martin Hinsdale. Although she struggled to believe the stranger's words, seeing him running out to protect her earlier made her want to trust him.

She changed into one of her day dresses. This one was blue with white trim around the short sleeves and the hem, and had a fashionable sash to tie around her waist.

It took her a while to brush out her hair, but she didn't restyle it fancy, only because a maid would assist her with that before tonight's dinner. Satisfied with the coil on the back of her head, she left the room and headed for the library.

All the books she loved to read repeatedly were in one spot. Thankfully, Martin didn't spend time in the library, and so he didn't rearrange her books. She found the right book and moved to the cushioned chair she usually sat in, but her thoughts stopped her.

Sit by the window.

She glanced at the brown leather chair near the window and frowned. Martin had used that chair the very few times he came in. Dare she sit there now? It wasn't as if the chair had his name on it, so why couldn't she sit in it?

On shaky legs, she stepped toward the chair. She listened intently for the creaking floor that would announce Martin's entrance into the room. So far, she heard only her own rapid breaths.

She stopped at the window and looked out. Was Grey watching her now? That man had no idea about her shyness. Being up front with Martin would nearly kill her. But she must. Her sister didn't deserve to be married to a murderer.

Alexandria stepped closer to the chair and cautiously lowered herself to the seat. She sat back against the cushions and opened her book. How was she expected to read at a time like this? But she must stay in her daily routine, even if her routine was to sit on the sofa instead.

It took a while, but finally she was able to concentrate on the words in the book. Soon, her mind focused on the story, and her body relaxed as she climbed into the book to experience everything the characters were feeling. Reading was the next best thing to writing. The fiction world took her to a time and place where she could experience true happiness.

The loud noise of a man clearing his throat jerked her out of the story. Immediately, she met her brother-in-law's harsh glare. Her stomach twisted in dread, and she nearly threw up.

"Oh, dear." She quickly stood, and her book dropped to the floor.

"May I inquire as to why you felt it necessary to sit in *my* chair when you have one in that corner of the library?" He motioned toward the sofa.

Her throat grew dry, and she could scarcely breathe. "Um…" She swallowed hard, hoping the moisture would soothe her throat. "I…wanted to be closer to the window."

He arched an eyebrow. "And why is today more special than the other days?"

Panic filled her. Whatever words exited her mouth couldn't be about Grey watching them.

"Forgive me, Your Grace, but…" She licked her parched lips, grasping at words floating around in her mind. She was a writer. She could think of something to say.

"But?" he asked.

Taking a deep breath, she squared her shoulders. "I was cold, Your Grace, and sitting by the window gives me heat from the sun."

He shrugged. "Well, I'm here now, so you can leave."

She held her breath. That was all? Then again, that was enough. She didn't want to be in his company any longer.

"Yes, Your Grace." She scooped up the book and hurried out of the library.

It felt odd, but she was almost proud of herself for not crumbling under pressure. Perhaps helping Grey would be a positive turning point in her life. She looked forward to her next challenge and prayed that she could stay strong.

CHAPTER NINE

JULIAN PEERED THROUGH his handheld spyglass—the one he had used quite a bit during his military life. This handy gadget helped him tremendously.

He scanned the perimeter of the house slowly, looking for anything unusual. So far, everything had been going smoothly. Alexandria must have pulled off a splendid performance, because Martin was strutting around the house as if nothing was amiss.

Gnashing his teeth, Julian steamed with anger when he recalled the brutal way Martin had grasped Alexandria's wrist. Fury and hatred had pushed Julian at that moment. He could imagine wrapping his fingers around his cousin's throat and squeezing. Indeed, he would have done that very thing if she hadn't stopped him. She had no clue why he wanted Martin out of the house, but she handled the situation with her brother-in-law quite well. Just thinking about her thoughtfulness made Julian's heart swell. Until now, he hadn't been certain he could trust her.

As the evening progressed, he watched her wander from room to room, staying by the windows. Occasionally, she glanced out toward his hiding spot. Of course, she couldn't see him, but it lightened his heart knowing she was watching for him, nonetheless.

Alexandria and Martin were in the dining room now. She was at one end of the table and Martin at the other. Julian's cousin spoke a few words to her, but thankfully, nothing more than that. Julian's little blossoming flower kept her head down and ate her meal the whole time Martin talked. Julian's gut twisted. He knew that she had to tolerate his cousin's company, and he prayed she wouldn't have to do that too much longer.

Suddenly, Martin threw his linen napkin on his empty plate, pushed away from the table, and stormed out of the room in a terrible fit. Julian switched his spyglass back to Alexandria, and a grin stretched across her pretty face as she looked toward the window. Julian's heart leapt. Now he wanted to know what was so humorous about Martin leaving the room that way.

Within minutes, she had moved away from the table and left the room. Exhilaration shot through Julian. She would be coming to their secret spot any minute now.

A movement by the front of the house drew Julian's attention there. Martin dashed out of the manor and stomped his way toward the stable. His voice was raised in anger as he shouted commands to the servants to prepare his horse. Soon, the obtuse man was on the animal, riding away from the estate. This would make Julian and Alexandria's meeting more relaxed indeed.

Chuckling, Julian shook his head as he hurried toward the place they had planned to meet. He couldn't believe how much he'd enjoyed watching her this evening. She was certainly different from when he kidnapped her earlier today. Then again, when he kidnapped her, he thought of her as someone else. Strange how things had worked out for the better. Fate certainly had more interesting plans for him.

This evening, she wore a lovely baby-blue gown with yellow floral designs. Her sleeves ended at her elbows, and the round neck of the gown looked to be decorated with white ribbon. Seeing her dressed this way made him want to change into his own evening attire and step into his rightful role as Duke of Linden.

While she was in the sitting room earlier this evening reading a book, he'd noticed her blonde hair was up in a presentable bun, and wisps of her locks were left unattended as they curled around her forehead and ears. Alexandria was breathtaking, and he couldn't stop staring at her. The more he watched her, the more he missed talking to her. Even his arms reminded him how it had felt to hold her those brief times earlier today. An ache of longing filled him. He wanted another moment to hold her again. Would she allow it? He wasn't certain he liked these feelings, since he hadn't felt this way in quite a while.

Visions of when he returned her to the house floated through his memory. He had continued to hold her after lifting her down from his horse, and she had allowed the intimate moment. She had stared at him with her beautiful, wondrous sapphire eyes and even watched his mouth a time or two. During those moments, he had felt the distinct desire to kiss her passionately. It was a struggle not to follow his instincts, and thankfully, he was able to pull away and leave without giving in to temptation.

But now, because he had watched her for these past few hours, he wanted her back in his arms. He wanted to know what it would feel like to kiss and caress her and have her return those same affections.

However, it was still too soon. They barely knew each other. She certainly didn't know him that well, and he wasn't ready to tell her the truth about his identity. Although he knew more about her, he still thought she would be safer if she didn't know his real name. He would tell her, just not now.

He blew out an exasperated breath. It would certainly be difficult to control his urges while seeing her tonight and dressed so pretty as they hid in the shadows together. Good heavens, he was a man with needs. It would be near impossible to keep from pulling her against him and kissing her senseless, but he must.

Eventually, he would find a woman to have a serious relationship with, but now was not the time. After he took over his role as the Duke of Linden, he had so much to finish before he could even think about looking for a woman who would be his wife.

He made it to the grove of trees before Alexandria arrived. He paced from tree to tree until he saw her coming his way. She wore a black, hooded cloak, probably to keep herself from being noticed. He hurried to the edge of the trees until she saw him. Reaching his hand out, he took hold of hers and pulled her inside the shadows.

"Do you think anyone saw me?" she asked, lowering the hood.

"No, I think you are safe. Martin left the estate on his horse. I'm sure he won't be back for a few more hours."

"I hope you are correct. That will give me time to visit my sister and hopefully look through his study."

"No." He touched her shoulder. "Don't search through his room tonight. Because we cannot presume how long he'll be gone, I don't want to risk the chance of you getting caught."

"Yes, you are right, of course." She smiled.

Even though they were cloaked in shadows, the outline of her delicate face was visible. He couldn't quite see the color of her eyes, though. He had no trouble drawing her lovely face from memory to fill in the missing details in the shadows. He suddenly wanted to pull her out of the trees and into the moonlight so that he could see her and stare at her loveliness.

"Tell me what Martin said to you as you were entering the house after we arrived," he said.

"When you tried to rescue me?"

"Yes."

She frowned. "He told me how disgusting I looked, and he threatened me once again that he was going to find someone to marry me. He had mentioned that if I didn't go along with his plans, I wouldn't be happy about the consequences."

"He's the devil," Julian grumbled. "I actually wanted to strangle him at that moment. I didn't approve of the way he was grasping your wrist. I wanted to break every finger on his hand—"

"And I'm glad you didn't." She gently touched his arm.

He nodded. "Thank you for stopping me."

"I knew the timing was not right."

"You were correct."

Shaking her head, she pulled her hand away. "I had wanted you to strangle him as well. But I couldn't let him see you."

He smiled, but he didn't think she could see his face well. "I shall never forget your thoughtfulness."

"And I shall never forget yours."

Her voice was so soft, so sweet. It took all of his willpower not to pull her into his arms right now. "I'm sorry he hurt you." He rubbed her shoulder, not wanting to take his hands off her, even though he should.

"Don't be," she replied. "His words and actions made me want to find the evidence to have him arrested. Believe me, Grey, I *will* find some proof that he was responsible for those murders. After all, that's the only way to stop him from marrying me to one of his friends."

Julian loved how she had blossomed in just the small amount of time he had known her. From what she had mentioned before, she didn't enjoy talking with men because she didn't know how. She was doing such a fine job of it at this moment, and he couldn't help but feel proud.

"What about at the dinner table? I could see him saying something to you, but then he stormed out of the dining room, angrier than an irritated bee."

Alexandria parted her cloak. "Oh, speaking of dinner, here is your food." She untied the rope that held the bulky burlap sack to her waist.

He took it from her and fastened the rope around his waist. "Thank you. It smells divine."

"There is roasted duck, a few apples and grapes, and some bread and cheeses."

"It sounds heavenly."

"Indeed, it tasted heavenly as well."

"All right now, tell me what happened with Martin during the meal."

She laughed. "Oh, that. Yes, it was very humorous, and I struggled not to laugh at the time, but it was very difficult."

"What happened?"

"He kept throwing insults at me, and I refused to acknowledge him in any way." She flipped her hand in the air. "I realized tonight he absolutely hates it when I ignore him—just as much as he gets irritated when he can see his words don't affect me."

Julian threw back his head and laughed. "Oh, my little blossom. I can't believe you did that. Martin deserves a dose of his own medicine from time to time. That man needs to realize he cannot push people around."

Her voice softened. "I wouldn't have been able to do it without your help, you know."

"My help? What did I do?"

"You encouraged me. You made me feel that helping you was of great importance. I wanted to feel important to someone."

His heart clenched. The poor, sweet woman. How could she have gone all these years without feeling important? "You *are* helping me, and you'll never know how much I appreciate it." He took her hands in his and squeezed lightly. "And you are very important to me. I don't want you to ever forget it."

"I thank you for your kind words, Grey."

It was on the tip of his tongue to tell her his real name. He wanted to hear her say *Julian* so badly, but it was too soon.

"I will continue to bestow my kind words upon you as long as you continue to bless me with your sweet presence, my blossom."

He was sinking into temptation fast, and the urge to take her in his arms grew stronger by the second. Perhaps he needed to get them into some light just so this moment wouldn't seem so private and intimate. Yet, at this point, he didn't think it would help. He was just a normal man, after all. How could he resist her innocent charm?

"Grey, you say the kindest things to me. I fear if you don't stop now, I will be lost forever," she said breathlessly.

"It is I who feels lost, my blossom. I fear I cannot think of anything but your sweetness." He slid his arms around her shoulders, pulling her closer. She slipped her arms around his waist.

He cupped her head, sweeping his thumbs across her lips. Her lilac fragrance enveloped him and nearly drove him mad with wanting. He envisioned dropping his face to the softness of her neck and partaking of her creamy skin with his mouth. Blast it all, the dream was getting harder to fight by the second.

Slowly, her eyes closed, and her lips parted as if she were offering a silent invitation. How could he turn her down? But he must. If only he had the courage to stop himself.

Julian lowered his head and brushed his cheek against hers. That wasn't good enough. He needed more. He moved his mouth closer, hovering his lips above hers. A tangy-sweet scent breezed from her mouth. Grapes. She had been eating some for dinner.

She held her breath, which made him want to do the same. She trembled in his arms, but he suspected it wasn't from fear. How could she be frightened of him at this moment when she was practically melting in his arms? Instead, he was certain she held a different kind of fear. Would he be the first man to kiss her? The mere thought made his heart hammer faster in anticipation.

The excitement building inside him was just too much to control. He had to kiss, taste, and devour her with his inflamed affection. He would think about the consequences later. Right now, however, he *must* follow his desires in haste.

He swept his lips across hers so very gently. Curses, she was so delicate. He felt if he took the kiss fast and as wild as he wanted, he would surely break her. But the longer he held himself back, the more his body shook from the exertion. He needed to end this torture before something dreadful happened.

As he settled his lips over hers, a tree branch broke from behind through the stillness of the night. At first, he wasn't certain that was the exact noise he had heard because of the pleasurable sigh escaping her throat, but then came another branch snapping. And another... The sound grew closer by the second.

He sucked in a breath and broke the brief kiss. Ending their close contact, he clutched her arms until she regained her footing, and then he whipped around, keeping her behind him.

"What's wrong?" she asked.

"Shh. Someone's here," he whispered.

Shadows played all around him. It was too dark to see who was coming toward them, but he was ready. Quickly, he reached for his sword.

Drat! He had left it on his horse. He was without a weapon, which generally didn't happen to him. It didn't matter. He had his strength and would knock down their intruder in a single blow of his fist. If that was what it took to get rid of the person who dared disturb his and Alexandria's privacy, then so be it.

CHAPTER TEN

A LEXANDRIA'S MIND WAS in a dreamlike cloud full of happi-ness. Why on earth would someone disturb it? And who could have possibly seen them in this cluster of trees, especially when there wasn't enough light? Nobody could be just taking a leisurely stroll, especially in this section of the estate.

There could only be one explanation. Her heart dropped. It had to be Martin.

As the sound of the footsteps neared, a tiny light followed. Whoever it was carried a low-lit lantern. She clutched Grey's coat and pressed herself up against his back. She had no qualms about his protecting her.

The lantern was a ghostly light bobbing in the dark as it drew closer. When the lantern bearer was nearly upon them, the lantern rose, shining a soft patch of light on her and Grey.

"Greystone, is that you?"

The tenseness in Grey's frame relaxed, and he exhaled a heavy breath. "Indeed it is, my friend. You scared the wits out of me, Trenton."

The other man chuckled. "Can you imagine my fright when I saw a shadow too large to be one man? Pray, who do you have with you?" He came closer, holding the lantern higher.

Grey pulled Alexandria around to his side. "Miss Templeton, may I present my good friend, Vincent Wallace, the Earl of

Trenton."

Being introduced to someone she couldn't see very well was a little awkward. Nonetheless, she felt shy once again, just as she had always done when introduced to a man.

She curtsied. "It's…nice to meet a friend of Grey's."

"Trenton," Grey continued, "this is Miss Alexandria Templeton."

Although it was hard to see him, she could tell when Lord Trenton bowed. "It's a pleasure to meet you, as well." He stepped closer. "Tell me, Greystone, what has been going on so far since we last talked? Do you still have *her* in my woodsman cottage?"

Confusion filled Alexandria. *Greystone?* Why did Lord Trenton refer to Grey that way? And was *she* the woman Lord Trenton referred to at the woodsman cottage?

Grey shook with a quiet laugh. "Actually, no." He slipped an arm around Alexandria, maneuvering her closer to Lord Trenton. "This is the woman I kidnapped earlier today, believing she was the duchess. As remarkable as it sounds, I took the sister."

"Not good, Greystone," Lord Trenton replied with humor in his voice. "And I suppose you are now returning her?"

Laughter escaped Grey. "I'll explain things to you later. Right now, Miss Templeton and I are ready to discuss the plans for tomorrow."

There's that name again! She really wished she had the courage to ask Grey about the strange name Lord Trenton kept using, but she didn't dare voice her thoughts. She had to wait until she and Grey were alone again.

"Do you want me to meet you back at the cottage, then?" Lord Trenton asked.

"If you don't mind. I won't be long, I assure you."

"As you wish. I shall bid you a good evening." Lord Trenton bowed. "And Miss Templeton, it was a pleasure meeting you. I hope to see you again soon."

"As…do I." Her voice squeaked out, so she quickly cleared her throat.

Grey stayed quiet as Lord Trenton retraced his footsteps back out of the trees. Finally, Grey chuckled and turned toward her. "I'm actually surprised he found me here."

"Did he know you were hiding?"

"Yes—we are in the shadows, yet the bloodhound still tracked me down."

She laughed lightly. "Indeed he did." She cleared her throat again. "Tell me, why did he keep referring to you as Greystone?"

He released a heavy sigh and rubbed his forehead. "Do you recall me telling you I have a title?"

"Yes."

"Greystone is my title."

"You used your middle name as your title?"

"No. It was just a coincidence that the title I inherited held my middle name. Associates of mine usually don't call me Grey. They either call me Greystone or my first name."

Confusion grew inside of her. Why wouldn't he tell her his name? She didn't want to push, but she felt as if he didn't trust her enough to know that bit of information about him. Her heart twisted. She realized he was in danger because of Martin, but she wished Grey would be more open with her. After all, she was risking her neck and becoming someone she had never been before, just for him. She felt like she was becoming the person she had always hoped to be, but she never thought she had the courage to do so.

"Oh, I see," she said softly.

"My blossom." Keeping his voice low, he stepped closer to her and cupped her chin. "Please do not worry about my name. I gave you permission to call me Grey."

"You would rather me call you that than Greystone?"

"Actually, yes." He stroked her skin. "Only because if Martin would find out you are helping someone, I don't want him to know who I am."

"But I would never tell."

"You don't know that. If Martin has killed before—which is

what I truly believe—I'm certain he would torture you until you released the identity of the man helping you."

"Martin doesn't know your title?"

"No, because I was only recently given this title. However, Martin would be able to ask around and find out I am Lord Greystone."

Inwardly, she groaned. Grey did have a point there, and she shouldn't argue. There was still something she needed to know. Strange how she had blindly trusted him without knowing all the answers.

"Grey? Would you tell me why you don't want Martin to know about you? Would you at least ease my mind on that matter?"

Silence stretched between them, and she would give anything to know what he was thinking. She wrung her hands against her middle, patiently waiting for his answer and praying he would give her one. Already she knew how elusive this man could be. He certainly held secrets.

After a few minutes, he blew out a breath and ran his fingers through his hair. "I don't want Martin knowing about me because..." He released a sigh. "I don't want him to know one of the men he thought he had killed is still alive."

Shock vibrated through her. Martin tried to kill Grey? Why on earth would anyone want to kill Grey? Then again, perhaps he was speaking of someone else, since he didn't directly say it was him Martin tried to kill. Yet the hint was there. If only Grey would trust her enough to tell her everything.

"And this is why you are so adamant about finding the proof against him?" she asked.

"Exactly. I don't want him to know I'm alive." He took her hands in his. "This is why I so desperately need your help."

Her heart beat with renewed life, especially when she recalled earlier this evening when Grey had nearly come out of hiding to save her from Martin's violent actions. She wanted to sigh but refrained. Why she had doubted Grey a minute ago, she didn't know, but from now on, she would trust him with all her heart.

She squeezed his hands. "And you shall have my help, as much as I can possibly give."

"That's all I ask."

Dare she hope he would kiss her again? Yet it was so improper. She shouldn't have allowed his heavenly lips on hers to begin with, but ah…the kiss was so very wonderful. He wouldn't have kissed her unless he had some kind of feelings for her, would he? Yet they had only known each other for a few hours. She had never believed in love at first sight, and she highly doubted she was now falling in love with him. No, this was definitely infatuation. Nothing more. So how could she convince her quickening heart of that notion?

PERHAPS JULIAN SHOULDN'T have given her that bit of information, but he figured she needed to know his motivation. He didn't want her to think he was a madman, although there had been a few times since they first met where his actions proved otherwise.

He was grateful he hadn't mentioned what men Martin had murdered, or Alexandria would have known his identity within seconds. She was a bright woman and had a quick wit about her—once she opened up to him, of course. Indeed, she was shy around men, and there was a remarkable difference in the way she was with him and how she responded to Lord Trenton.

It didn't matter that he couldn't see her face right now—his mind knew what her expression would be because her voice was so soft and caring. If he could see her clearly, he supposed she was gazing up at him with her sparkling, wondrous eyes.

He swallowed hard, his throat suddenly becoming dry. They were alone again, and he wanted more than anything to continue the kiss from moments ago. He really should end these feelings now. There was no way he could get emotionally involved with

Alexandria Templeton. She was the kind of woman who was after marriage and a family. While Julian wanted those things someday, he wasn't ready yet.

Thankfully, he needed to return to the cottage to update Vincent about what had happened. Having her return to the manor was the key to stopping these insane notions flowing through his head whenever she was around.

Julian felt Alexandria would be safe tonight, since Martin was out. Julian would be back at this spot bright and early in the morning to continue to watch over *his* estate.

He lifted her hands to his mouth and brushed his lips across her fingers. "My blossom, it's getting late, and I think you should retire. I thank you again for the food. You are a gem indeed."

"Yes, I suppose I should get back inside."

"Go directly to your room and lock the door. I feel you shall be safe. I'll be back here tomorrow."

"As you wish." Her tone had changed to one of disappointment as she slowly pulled her hands away. "When should I search through Martin's rooms?"

"Wait until he leaves the estate tomorrow."

"What if he doesn't?" she asked quietly.

"He will. I've been observing him closely the past few days, and he leaves to ride into town at least twice a day."

"I wonder why I haven't noticed."

He chuckled. "Because you are either in the library or riding your horse during those times."

"Oh," she said with a laugh. "I suppose you have been watching us."

"Indeed I have." He leaned over and kissed her forehead. "Now hurry inside. We shall talk tomorrow."

Julian watched her go back to the house and disappear through the doors. He crept closer to the edge of the grove and, through his spyglass, watched until the light in her room came on. He breathed a sigh of relief and hurried to his horse.

As he rode to Vincent's cottage, Julian couldn't stop his grin from stretching wider. Fate had turned out better than he had hoped since he first planned to steal the duchess. At the time, he was determined to do anything to get the woman to confess her husband's misdeeds. He had never harmed a woman before, but he was willing to be a little rough with the duchess. Instead, he'd kidnapped the sister, and she was a godsend. She would be able to do something her older sister probably wouldn't do—find him the proof he needed.

Julian rode fast and soon reached the cottage. As he walked in, he noticed that Vincent had added more to the place. A few more chairs sat next to the fireplace, and an Afghan quilt lay across the sofa. Julian shook his head. Why hadn't his friend done this *before* Julian brought Miss Templeton? Nevertheless, the scent of something delicious cooking in the kitchen filled the air and made his stomach grumble, making him remember he hadn't eaten—and also that he'd forgotten Alexandria had brought him some of her dinner.

He headed for the kitchen, untying the sack around his waist that held the food. Vincent glanced up from the pot over the fire and gave him a nod.

"I hope you are hungry, good man. I'm making my famous stew."

Julian chuckled. "I'm hungry, but I'll eat what Alexandria brought me."

"Alexandria?" Vincent arched an eyebrow. "You are on a first-name basis now?"

"Actually, no. She has yet to give me permission to call her by her given name."

Vincent gave him a cheesy grin. "You don't say. And yet you hold to customs regardless."

Julian rolled his eyes. "It's the least I could do, since I wrongly kidnapped her." He strode to the table and sat on the chair, laying his feast on the flat surface. His mouth watered just from the scent before he could even take a bite. Thankfully, his friend had brought more things for the kitchen as well.

"Tell me what happened today." Vincent moved closer and stopped by the cutting table. Julian was a head taller than Vincent, but that hadn't stopped them from becoming fast friends, since they had so much in common. As they matured, they had realized how much they loved cooking, and even competed a time or two.

Vincent cocked his head. "I'm dying to know how you kidnapped the wrong sister, especially when I gave you specific details about what the duchess looks like."

Shaking his head, Julian scratched his chin. "Therein lies the problem, my friend. You did not tell me her younger sister has the same blonde hair and loveliness."

"She does?" Vincent arched an eyebrow. "I thought the younger sister was a wallflower."

"She is a wallflower, but only because she is shy. She is certainly a very lovely flower."

"Tell me what transpired today," Vincent said. "This sounds like a very interesting tale."

As Julian explained, his friend's smile grew until he finally laughed. Although it really wasn't a laughing matter, especially since Alexandria was the victim, Julian had to admit it was humorous, only because the situation made him look like a fool.

"Are you about finished?" Julian asked in irritation.

Vincent's laughter subsided, and he turned and walked back to the boiling pot over the fire. "I'm happy to hear that she has agreed to help, although…"

"Although what?" Julian asked.

"I really doubt she'll be much help."

"Why do you say that?" An odd sense of defensiveness came over Julian. "Of course she will. She can search through Martin's rooms to find evidence."

Vincent sighed heavily as he removed the pot from the fire, brought it over to the cutting table, and set it on top. "Unfortunately, my good man, I'm sorry to say I haven't had any luck in my search."

Julian's heart threatened to sink, but he'd hold on to hope until he heard his friend's story. "Why?"

"I visited all the pubs your cousin frequents, and the men he consorts with tell me that Martin was in town during the middle of March." Vincent shook his head. "I went to several taverns, and the men there said the same thing: if Martin was gone at all, it was only one day, not a sennight."

Groaning, Julian smacked his hand on the rickety table, causing it to wobble. "That can't be right. It was him, I know it. He is the only one who would want my family dead. Besides, when I asked Alexandria about it, she recalled he was gone for a while not long after Martin married her sister."

"I don't know what to tell you. All I know is that the men at the pub said differently." Vincent spooned some stew into a chipped bowl. "But this only proves that your cousin isn't an imbecile. He is covering the evidence too well, and it's going to be the devil trying to find proof."

Julian leaned his elbows on the scarred table and rested his head in his hands. His mind scrambled through all that Alexandria had told him. She might not have seen Martin leave, but she knew he had been gone for two weeks in the middle of March. At least her sister knew. If only her sister wasn't so ill and could talk to him.

He snapped his head up and looked at his friend. "Did you tell me my father and brother died of the plague, yet nobody in the house had the same symptoms?"

"Yes, why?"

"Because"—Julian pushed away from the table and stood, hope growing inside his chest once again—"Alexandria mentioned that her sister has been very ill for the past five days."

"The duchess is ill?" Vincent asked with a raised voice. "How ill?"

Julian frowned. "Alexandria did not say how ill, just gave me the time frame." He studied his friend, who appeared more worried than normal. "Why does it bother you so?"

Vincent shook his head. "It doesn't bother me. However, what if this means Martin is trying to kill another person?"

Julian smiled, feeling victorious. If that were indeed the case, they would catch Martin this time. "Now you're thinking. Although it sickens me to think he wants to kill his wife, we will ensure it doesn't happen and catch him doing it in the process."

CHAPTER ELEVEN

S LEEP WAS IMPOSSIBLE!

Alexandria had lain in bed tossing and turning for an hour with no hope of resting. How could she when her mind wouldn't relax? Many times, she found herself smiling, giggling, and rolling to her side, hugging her pillow. Thoughts of Grey wouldn't leave her head. And really, she didn't want them to. Sleep wasn't that important, was it?

Finally, after an hour, she climbed out of bed and sat at her desk. She readied her quill and ink and a fresh page. Her attention dropped to the passage she had written this morning before her life drastically changed—for the better—and she brought it under the lamplight and read through it again.

She had left off with the heroine hiding in her bedchamber from the man who'd killed her family. In the character's hand was a dagger, and she waited for Mr. Blackwood to break down her door and come after her.

Pausing in thought, Alexandria scratched her chin. What this poor heroine needed was someone to give her encouragement and strength from within. Someone like…*Grey.* As thoughts tumbled in her head, she dipped her quill in ink and started writing.

The footfalls on the floor in the hall grew nearer. Her heartbeat hammered so fast that she breathed slower to try to calm herself before she died of heart palpitations. Who could help her? By now, Mr. Blackwood had probably killed all her servants so that they couldn't come to her rescue.

She glanced toward the window. Should she climb out the second-story window and jump to freedom? As a young girl, she had accomplished this feat many times. Tonight was different. Tonight, someone was after her, and her limbs shook uncontrollably. It would be almost impossible to climb down a tree with unsteady arms and legs.

However, it was something she must do. She must be brave, just as Nicholas Loveland had encouraged her to be. As her neighbor, the handsome widower had taken her family under his care. She had gone on many walks with him, and he was a beacon in the storm, giving her confidence she never thought she had.

With the decision made, she ran toward the window and shoved it open. Outside, the wild wind thrashed through the trees scattered throughout the yard. Perhaps her unsteady limbs wouldn't be the thing making her fall from the tree after all. The wind would carry her away, to be sure.

Then again, at least she would be away from this place when Mr. Blackwood broke down her door. By the sound of his boots hitting the floor, that moment would soon be upon her.

As carefully as she could, she slid the dagger into the pocket of her apron, since she had no other place to carry it. Just as she scooted on the window ledge, a thundering noise echoed through the night, overriding the sound of the wind. In the distance, someone shouted her name.

She peered into the shadows, searching for the person calling out to her. The clouds in the sky parted briefly, showing the full moon. She was able to glimpse a horse and rider approaching—a very muscular man with his dark hair flapping in the wind. Her heart leapt with joy. Lord Loveland! As always, he was there for her. Perhaps now would be the right time to give him her heart.

Alexandria's smile widened as she wrote about Grey. In her

story, she called him Lord Loveland, an appropriate name for a fitting hero.

Somewhere in the house, a door slammed, bringing her out of her thoughts. She jumped in her chair and swung her gaze toward her bedchamber door. The villain in her story might be fictional, but the evil man her sister had married was very real.

Alexandria sneaked to the door and pressed her ear against the thick wood, but she didn't hear anything. Carefully, she opened the door and peeked down the hall, listening to the sounds inside the house. Muffled voices floated through the air, and for a moment, Alexandria thought one of them came from her sister.

Concern flowed through her, and she wrung her hands against her middle. What could have upset her sister? It was probably Martin. Alexandria hesitated to leave her room to investigate, but now was not the time to be fearful. If Charlotte needed her, she would be there.

She tiptoed out of the room and down the corridor toward her sister's bedchamber. As she neared the corner of the hall, she slowed her steps, listening more intently. The voices were raised in anger, and Alexandria recognized Martin's voice.

She peeked around the corner and paused. The door to Charlotte's bedchamber was closed. Dare Alexandria intrude upon a husband and wife's quarrel? So far, it hadn't sounded as if Charlotte was in danger. In fact, a few times it sounded as if Martin was the one being scolded.

Suddenly, the door swung open, and Martin marched out, scowling. Panic gripped Alexandria, so she withdrew back around the corner and flattened herself against the wall. Squeezing her eyes closed, she held her breath and prayed her brother-in-law wouldn't come her way.

Within seconds, she detected a foul scent. *Liquor!* Martin had been drinking again. Inwardly, she groaned. There would be no reasoning with the drunken lout tonight.

Why hadn't she done as Grey instructed? She should have

stayed in her room. Now, she was vulnerable to her insane and murderous brother-in-law.

Alexandria held her breath and listened for his heavy steps. Would he come to her room? There was really no reason for him to head down this corridor, since her room was the only one in this part of the manor. But he had been so insistent about finding her a husband and washing his hands of her that she wouldn't doubt the man would come to her in the middle of the night, threatening her again.

As Martin's footsteps headed in the opposite direction, she released a pent-up breath. Thankfully, the drunken fool wouldn't bother her tonight. Charlotte wouldn't be in danger tonight now that Martin was out of her room.

Alexandria remained against the wall until she couldn't hear his footsteps any longer. Slowly, she tiptoed back to her bed-chamber. There was no need to check on Charlotte now, and of course, she didn't want to explain to her sister what she was doing up so late at night. There was no way she could tell Charlotte about Grey.

After Alexandria closed the door, she leaned against it and sighed heavily. Hopefully, she could tell Charlotte about the newest man in her life soon. She didn't know how much longer she could keep this excitement to herself.

She forced herself to return to bed, hoping she could sleep this time. Within time, her eyelids became heavy, but as she drifted off to sleep, Grey was on her mind.

It seemed as though it had only been a few minutes, but soon the morning sun shone through the window and onto her face. Groaning, she turned away from the light, wanting to climb back into her dreams of Grey. Yet she couldn't sleep in. She had a job to do today, and she would not shirk her duties. For the first time in her life, she would play the part of an investigator.

Alexandria quickly dressed and then waited patiently—well, maybe not so patiently—for Martin to leave the estate. She stood by her bedroom window and parted the curtain slightly, glancing down toward the stable. He had already left the house and gone to get his horse. Any minute now, he would ride out of the stable toward the path heading for the main road.

Impatiently, she tapped her foot. Blasted man! What was taking him so long? He had never chitchatted with the stable hands before, so why hadn't he mounted and left by now? Then again, she had never taken the time to watch him when he left the house before, so she really didn't know how long his routine was.

Finally, his horse trotted out of the stable. Martin adjusted the riding crop in his hand before urging his horse faster.

She exhaled a relieved breath. It was time to search his study.

Finding all the courage she had, she crept out of her room, down the hallway to the stairs, and then stepped softly toward the lower level. She listened for any sounds from the servants, but they were abnormally quiet this morning. She didn't dare take the time to wonder why. Then again, at this hour of the morning, she was usually up in her room just waking up and ringing for the maid to bring her breakfast.

Her body shook with nervousness as she crept on shaky legs toward Martin's study. She held her breath until reaching his door. Slowly, she placed her trembling hand on the doorknob.

Alexandria's palm moistened to the point that she couldn't even turn the blasted doorknob. Grumbling under her breath, she swiped her hand on her dress and tried once more to open the door. This time it worked, and she hurried inside, closing the door before anyone noticed.

She pressed her ear against the hard wood, listening for the servants again. Fortunately, none were moving about in this part of the house.

Letting out a heavy sigh, she turned into the room. There were many expensive pieces of furniture, chairs, and lounges placed in the spacious room. Against the far wall sat his large oak desk. She hoped he kept documents of importance in there.

She hurried to the desk and knelt on the floor, carefully opening one drawer at a time. The first one didn't hold anything that appeared to be secret, so she moved to the next. A few letters were inside. She took one out and carefully opened it. Thankfully, Martin had already broken the seal, so he wouldn't know she had been in here snooping.

She skimmed the handwriting. It wasn't precise, as most women she had known, so Alexandria assumed it was by a man. She turned the page and glanced at the signature. Sure enough, it was written by Lord Fenley, whoever that was. The details inside the letter didn't make any sense to her, and the contents mainly talked about a trip that Lord Fenley had just returned from in Scotland. Nothing—not even a hint—about wanting to kill anyone. She folded the letter and placed it back in the drawer.

The second missive was from Martin's mother. Alexandria rolled her eyes. Naturally, the man wasn't going to tell, or involve, his mother in murderous affairs. Just as Alexandria was about to place it back in the drawer, an idea struck her. What if the old woman was greedy and unscrupulous like her son? Perhaps Alexandria should read what was inside after all.

My dearest son,

I have heard gossip of late, and I fear if this is true, then your days as Duke of Linden are numbered. The word around town is that your cousin, Julian Stratford, wasn't killed a few months ago after all. However, his body has yet to be found. Although I don't wish your cousin to be dead, I hope the authorities can find his body as soon as possible so that this utter confusion can be over. A man working for the magistrate, Mr. Franklin, is looking into this matter for me. I shall keep you informed.

Alexandria arched an eyebrow. How very interesting. Would this kind of news be the reason Martin had been irritable lately?

After searching through three more missives, she found one written by a woman, and the contents of the letter were extremely personal. Gasping, Alexandria covered her mouth as she scanned each word. Embarrassment filled her and scalded her cheeks. Good heavens! How could a woman say these words to a married man? Apparently, the woman and Martin must have been close at one time, perhaps even lovers. The woman wrote how much she missed him and wanted to see Martin again—amongst other things.

Alexandria took a glance at the date, which was last week. Irritation grew inside her. Could her idiot brother-in-law possibly be thinking of cheating on his new bride? Or perhaps he was having an affair right now. That could explain why he rode into town every day instead of staying home with his wife. The cad! He had better not break Charlotte's heart, or Alexandria would have to...have to...

She frowned. Who was she fooling? She would do nothing because she couldn't even talk to the man without stuttering. And heaven forbid she would do anything violent toward him, even if her mind conjured up many ways to torture the imbecile.

The letter was signed *your beloved Mary*. Alexandria shook her head. There were too many women named Mary, and it would be impossible to track her down.

Voices drifted from out in the hallway, and she froze. Listening closer, she tried to decipher who was speaking. When Martin snapped instructions to one of the servants in his familiar bark, her heart dropped. The blood in her body turned to ice.

He was going to catch her in his study. He would kill her for sure.

Frantically, Alexandria glanced around the room, searching for someplace to hide. One of the sofas was near the window and pulled away from the wall enough for her to squeeze behind.

Hurrying, she scampered toward the piece of furniture and slipped behind it. Just as she crouched, the door to the study opened. Martin's heavy footsteps pounded on the floor, heading straight for his desk. She held her trembling hands together and prayed he wouldn't find her.

She didn't dare peek around the sofa to see what he was doing, but it sounded as if he was shuffling through the papers on his desk. He grumbled low, making it difficult to tell what he was saying.

Two very long minutes later, he finally marched out of the room, slamming the door behind him. She remained hiding, listening for signs that he had left the estate. Finally, she heard his voice outside the window and then the thundering from the horse's hooves on the ground.

Relief swept over her, and she breathed easier. Why had he returned? But she prayed he wouldn't come back so quickly next time.

Being as quiet as she could, she moved from behind the sofa and walked back to the desk. There were papers scattered on the top, and she carefully moved them around, looking for evidence of his misdeeds. So far, she had seen nothing—except the letter from the woman. But that didn't prove he was a murderer, only that he was a dolt for possibly cheating on his wife.

She finished looking through his desk but didn't find anything of importance. There weren't many other places to look in his study, so she quietly left. As she hurried away from the room, her heartbeat slowed considerably. Now she should look through his bedchamber. He and Charlotte didn't share the same room, which Alexandria thought was odd, since she remembered her parents had shared a room. Nevertheless, this way was better because Charlotte wouldn't ask what she was doing.

It still worried Alexandria that Charlotte's health wasn't im-proving quickly. Exactly what was her illness? Nothing had been explained well.

As Alexandria neared Martin's bedchamber, a thought struck her, stopping her in her tracks. Martin was getting rid of people he didn't want around—either killing them or finding a husband. Did he not want his wife any longer? Did he want this woman, Mary, instead? If so, would he sink so low as to try to murder his own wife?

Alexandria's gut twisted as bile rose to her throat. Grey be-lieved Martin was capable of murder, so she must also believe that. And that meant she needed to take her sister away from this place, and very soon.

She glanced toward the nearest window, wondering if Grey was hiding and watching her. She really needed to speak to him about assisting her with getting Charlotte out of here. But without the proof they needed to have Martin arrested, what good would it do to take Charlotte someplace different?

Alexandria straightened her shoulders and rubbed the ache in her forehead. All of these jumbled thoughts confused her even more. What she needed to do was find evidence.

Making the decision, she walked into his room. The musky scent that had always been with Martin suddenly surrounded her. Chills ran up her arms, and she shivered. Yet, at the same time, confidence grew inside her. She was determined to find something. Her sister needed her. Alexandria *would* save Charlotte.

As she looked around at Martin's personal items, she tried not to feel embarrassed. After all, she was in a man's bedchamber, which was highly improper. Trying to put the feeling aside, she imagined herself as one of the investigators she had written about in her novels. Her duty was to find evidence, no matter how she obtained it. With this in mind, the embarrassment left, and her determination grew.

First, she went to the armoires. As she searched through them, she checked in pockets or anywhere a piece of paper or missive could be hidden. Nothing was found.

Frowning, she scanned the room, studying each chair and sofa. There would be no place to hide secrets in pieces of furniture. Still, she checked underneath each one just to be certain. Once again, she found nothing.

The side room was his bathing chamber, but nothing of consequence was in there, either. As she left his room, her hopes were low and dragging behind her. She had failed. The only thing she could report to Grey was the letter from Martin's mistress. Oh, and the missive from his mother, too.

Either Martin was very crafty in hiding the evidence, or he'd destroyed it.

Disheartened, she walked toward her sister's room. She needed to check on Charlotte to see if she was making any sort of recovery. But then, if Martin was gradually killing her, was it too late for Charlotte?

Taking caution, Alexandria opened the door and peeked in. Her sister sat up in bed, reading a book. Immediately, a smile stretched across Charlotte's face.

"Xandria. You are here."

Alexandria's heart lifted. "Yes. I was hoping you were up for a visit."

"Indeed I am." Charlotte motioned with her hand. "Please come sit and talk to me. I've been so bored."

"You appear to be feeling better," Alexandria said.

"Indeed, I do have a little more strength today."

"Tell me, Charlotte," she said, sitting on the chair next to the bed, "when did you start feeling so ill? Have you eaten something or drunk something? Or did it come upon you suddenly?"

Charlotte's forehead creased. "I'm not certain. I suppose it came upon me slowly. I had a bout with the common cold, that is all. Why do you ask?"

Alexandria shrugged. "I'm just trying to figure out why you have been sick for so many days without improvement."

"Oh, but my dear Xandria, I *am* improving." Charlotte smiled, but then another cough shook her body. It took a few more moments, but then she was able to stop the coughing. "See, I told you I was feeling better."

Why was it so difficult for Alexandria to believe her sister?

"Please, Xandria, do not fret. It's not your duty to look after me, but mine to look after my younger sister." Charlotte reached over and grasped Alexandria's hands.

Alexandria shook her head. "But *you* are the one who is ill, not me." She squeezed Charlotte's fingers tenderly. "So, allow me this one time to care for you."

"Oh, Xandria. You are sounding like my husband now."

Alexandria hated being compared to that mongrel. "Why do you say that?"

"Because he is smothering me with his concern. Can you believe he wants the physician to put leeches on me?" She shivered. "Forgive me, but I refuse. Last night I argued with him until he stormed out of here. I told him I would not have those *things* on my body."

Sadness crept over Alexandria. "Are you really that ill? Why else would he suggest it?"

"No, I'm not that ill. I have a passing malady, and as I told you, I am starting to feel stronger. I will beat whatever is inside me and return to my fun-loving self once more." Charlotte winked.

"I pray you are correct. You and I have been together for so long, I don't know what I would do if something happened to you. Please allow me to help in any way you need me."

"You are so sweet." Tears sprang to Charlotte's eyes, and she reached over to grasp Alexandria's fingers. "I've been so blessed to have a sister like you."

A knot formed in Alexandria's throat. She was the one who'd been blessed, but now she had to repay the Lord by taking care of Charlotte and keeping Martin from killing her.

CHAPTER TWELVE

JULIAN SHUFFLED FROM one foot to the other as he peered through the spyglass. His nervousness grew the longer he watched, and he couldn't stand still. Martin had left the estate hours ago, yet Alexandria still hadn't come outside.

When Martin had briefly returned home, Julian prayed Alexandria wasn't caught. He suspected she had already begun her search. However, the longer it took for Alexandria to walk outside, the more he worried something terrible had happened to her.

Even after Martin left the estate again, Alexandria hadn't appeared. What could have happened to her? Had Martin tied her up somewhere? Was she unconscious and bleeding?

Julian couldn't stand it any longer. Although he would risk being seen by servants who had worked for his father, he knew he had to go inside to see if Alexandria was harmed.

He set the spyglass down and left the security of his hiding spot. Ignoring the throbbing in his leg, he hurried toward the manor. He had almost reached the house when one of the side doors opened, and out walked Alexandria. Relief washed over him. When her eyes met his, panic crossed her expression, and she shook her head. She motioned toward his hiding spot as she glanced between him and the grove of trees.

Understanding her silent instructions, he turned around and

hurried back to his hiding spot. It only took a few more minutes before Alexandria joined him. She looked so lovely today wearing a light green dress. Her hair was styled as it had been last night, and he wished she would leave it long and hanging around her shoulders. She had such glorious blonde hair that he wanted to stroke its silkiness again.

"Thank the good Lord you are all right," he said as he took her hands in his.

"Yes." She smiled brightly.

"When I saw Martin return, I thought for sure—"

"I hid behind the sofa in his study. He didn't even know I was there."

"Splendid." He stroked his fingers across her skin. "I cannot believe you did it, but I'm proud of you for doing it even if it frightened you."

She chuckled softly. "I must admit, I've never done anything so bold. I've never thought about attempting to sneak into a man's room, let alone one that belongs to my mean brother-in-law."

"Did you find anything?"

Her smile disappeared. "Not really. However, I did find a letter from his mistress." She rolled her eyes. "It said nothing about the murders, but I could definitely tell this woman, *Mary*, was his mistress or had been at one time."

"A mistress, eh?" Julian shook his head. Why wasn't he surprised? "But nothing about plans to kill his uncle for the title?"

She paused as confusion crossed her features. "Unfortunately, no. However, there was a missive from his mother. Apparently, Martin's cousin, Julian Stratford, is assumed to be alive because the authorities cannot find his body. Martin's mother mentioned that her son might not hold the title of duke for much longer."

Julian froze, his mind whirling with worry. If Martin suspected Julian was still alive, he would only be more determined to find Julian and end his life. There was no way he could show himself now. Not until they had proof.

"That is very interesting indeed," he said, not wanting to give Alexandria any hint that he was the man in question.

Yet the longer she studied him, the more the light of awareness sparked in her eyes. Slowly, she shook her head as her eyes widened.

"I'm wondering how you know Martin killed his uncle for the title." She sucked in a quick breath. "In fact, I think I know just how you are connected with Linden Hall."

Groaning aloud was not an option, even though in his mind, he was doing that very thing. It was too soon to tell her the truth. The less she knew, the better.

"Word travels fast in this area," he said, then mentally kicked himself for such a foolish answer. Why did his brain refuse to work whenever he looked upon her loveliness?

"What I meant to say was," he added, "I know Martin well enough, and he has made some uncouth deals before. Besides, the circumstances leading up to his obtaining the title are very sketchy."

Hopefully, she would believe him. He couldn't have her doubting his word now.

ALEXANDRIA'S MIND REELED with the possibilities. But of course Grey would know Martin, or the others involved. That was how he knew where to hide on this estate. If Grey was a friend of one of the Stratford men who'd been killed, that explained why he was so anxious to see her brother-in-law arrested for murder.

This amazing man who had first kidnapped her and then rescued her in so many ways was more than he presented himself. That was probably why Grey didn't want Martin discovering he was alive.

"Grey, by chance, are you friends with the Stratford men?"

He remained stiff, and his expression was unreadable. After a few moments of silence, he nodded.

"You guessed correctly, Miss Templeton. I was good friends with both Forbes and Julian, along with their father." He cleared his throat and shifted from one foot to the other. "I want to see their killer hanged for his crimes."

"That is very understandable. I would want the same if I were in your place." She grinned, feeling victorious after discovering a little bit more about Grey.

Groaning, Grey closed his eyes and rubbed his forehead. "I didn't want you to know how close I was to them," he muttered.

She touched his shoulder. "I understand, but I promise I shall not tell anyone."

His head snapped up, and his eyes met hers. "Will you keep our secret? I don't want you to tell your sister either, not until we find evidence against Martin. If the servants ever overheard you saying anything of that nature, my secret would be out. Until we have the proof, I need to stay hidden."

"Forgive me," she whispered, slowly pulling her hand away.

He grasped her hand. "Please, Miss Templeton, I did not mean to insult or doubt your words. It's just very important—"

"Yes, I know. You may rest assured that I shall do as much as I can to help you." She released a sigh. "I just want to do more. I wish I could have found something in my search this morning."

"I wish you could have as well." He shrugged. "We shall have to look elsewhere." He released her and walked farther into the grove of trees. A blanket lay on the ground with a sack of food.

As she followed closely behind, her mind tried to piece together Julian's story just as she would when writing her novels. "How soon after the deaths of the duke and his sons did you suspect Martin?"

He took her hand and helped her down on the blanket. Once she was seated, he linked his hands behind his back and paced in careful, measured steps around the blanket. He remained quiet for longer than Alexandria expected, which made her slightly nervous.

Finally, he stopped and looked at her. "I didn't suspect Martin at first. However, I was curious to know why the physician's diagnosis was that Forbes and his father died from symptoms of the plague, and yet none of the servants had contracted this disease." His face grew hard as he stared at the ground and paced again. "I had just received word of their deaths and was on my way back home."

"Home from where?"

"I was the major in the military."

"The military? I had heard that Lord Julian was also in the military. Was he one of your men?"

His expression relaxed as he stared at her. She loved it when he looked at her this way. The fluttering of her heart was so uncommon, but since meeting him, it had happened quite often. She rather liked feeling this way.

"Yes. You see, Lord Julian wanted to travel with me, so he came along with a few of my men from the regiment. We were headed to the next town over to search for a missing soldier. Out of nowhere, I heard the squeal of a cannonball flying through the air. My men and I had very little time to scramble out of its path before it hit."

"Oh my." She gasped, placing her hand on her bosom. "Was this where Lord Julian was killed?"

He hesitated before he nodded. "We actually couldn't find his body."

"That is just awful." What a terrible way to die. She couldn't even imagine how his family would feel if they were still alive.

Grey scratched his chin and peered off into the distance. "My men were closer to the blast than I was, so I wasn't knocked unconscious right away. I struggled to sit up, and I looked to where the cannonball came from and saw three men running away. Although my leg was cut up badly, and I was not only losing a lot of blood, I was fading into oblivion. Yet I still had the strength to grab my pistol and fire at those responsible for the blast. As the unknown men scattered, I tried to hit at least one of them. Finally, one fell to the ground, but he soon stood and continued running. He was clutching his left arm." He turned his focus back on Alexandria. "I don't know if this man was Martin, but I'm certain he was part of the few who shot the cannon toward my men and me." He lowered himself to the blanket beside her and then rubbed his leg. "I cannot prove that Martin was behind it, but I have a sickening feeling he was. There is no logical reason that someone would try to kill me and my men with a cannon, but it makes sense that someone would want to kill Lord Julian for his title, since he was the remaining son who would inherit everything."

"Indeed, that is a rational explanation." She didn't dare touch him again, but it was hard. Touching him was so enjoyable. "I'm just very relieved Martin wasn't able to kill you in that cannon blast. He needs to be arrested. I don't think he makes a very good duke, anyway. I have never met a more disagreeable man in my life."

Grey chuckled. "I don't think he is suited to become a duke, either. Then again, he was never raised to take that title."

"So perhaps we are going about this search all wrong. We need to look for a man with an injured arm," she said.

Grey's eyes widened. "Alexandria, you are brilliant!" He grasped her shoulders. "That's exactly what we need to do."

Happiness grew inside her. She hadn't given him permission to be so personal with her name, but she wouldn't reprimand him for not asking to use it. She wanted them to become better friends and, hopefully, much more.

She loved how he made her feel so smart, special, and needed. Nobody had ever said such things that uplifted her spirit, except for her parents, of course. Her face grew warm from his compliment, and her cheeks hurt from smiling so wide.

"I wouldn't say I was brilliant, Grey."

"You're not the one saying it. I am." He winked. "But you are exactly right about looking for someone with a recent arm injury."

"In his left arm?"

"Correct again." He pulled her closer and kissed her forehead. "Oh, Lexie, I'm so very fortunate to have found you."

Lexie? Her heart melted. Charlotte had always called her Xandria, but she actually liked being called Lexie even better.

She lifted her head and stared deep into his dreamy eyes. "I'm the one who has found good fortune," she said softly. "Because of you, I'm gradually coming out of my shell, something I never thought I would do."

His warm gaze caressed her face, took her in, and devoured her in slow, measured increments, finally coming to rest on her mouth. Suddenly, the mood between them altered, and her throat grew dry. Anticipation made her heartbeat quicken, and the urge to kiss him became overpowering. She prayed he would make the first move. They were so close. All he had to do was lean in just a few inches.

When he licked his lips, she swallowed hard. He leaned forward, and she closed her eyes, waiting…hoping…

CHAPTER THIRTEEN

ALEXANDRIA COULDN'T STAND the wait. If he didn't kiss her soon, she would go absolutely mad! Perhaps she needed to make the first move.

Just then, Grey's lips brushed against hers. She closed her eyes and sighed with happiness. He wrapped his arms around her and pulled her closer. When her bosom made contact with his hard chest, she melted. Never in her wildest dreams had she imagined such a wonderful feeling. The longer he kissed her, the more her strength was sapped, but she didn't mind.

At first, the kiss was soft, but soon his hold became tighter, and with a small groan, he tilted his mouth over hers. *There's more?* How could she have known there would be more to the kiss besides two sets of lips pressing against each other? And yet there *was* more. The way he moved his mouth over hers, nibbling in certain spots she never thought could make a woman squirm with anxiousness.

Breathless, she clung to him, wanting more, wanting their kiss to last longer. Forever. Nothing in her life had made her feel so alive. Did all women feel this elated? She never wanted the emotion leaping and expanding inside her to end. So many feelings assaulted her all at once, and the sheer volume threatened to sweep her away. Where? She was not sure, nor did she care.

Her whole world tilted, going down…down…down…until her back pressed against the ground. Then she realized Grey had laid her on the blanket and now loomed over her, moving his mouth with hers. This was so very personal, but she liked it.

When his hot tongue slid inside her mouth, she gasped. The shock of the sensual feeling slipping over her made her breathless, and yet her heavy breathing told her she was still alive and relishing every moment. She was consumed by his teachings, and she thrived on the foreign feelings inside her.

She wound her arms around his neck and ran her fingers through his hair, which was remarkably silky, and she never wanted to stop touching. The pressure of his upper body on hers made her feel safe and protected. Strange how she would feel this way now, when in the beginning, he'd frightened her. *Frightened?* She must have been insane to think such a thing. Being with Grey made her feel alive in ways she couldn't describe. Just thinking about it made her blush.

"Oh, Lexie," he muttered against her lips, "I shouldn't be doing this. I cannot have these feelings."

Her heart skipped a beat. If he felt anything like she did right now, she understood him perfectly. "I know, Grey."

He groaned and tightened his hold on her, kissing her urgently at first and then slower, more meaningfully. She copied how his mouth moved with hers, even the way his tongue swept through her mouth. Although this was highly improper, she couldn't tear herself away from what they were sharing. She never wanted to leave his side.

His hands wandered up to her neck and then to her hair. The pins holding her coil together fell out one by one until he combed his fingers through her hair. Sighing with pleasure, she thoroughly enjoyed how he touched and caressed her as if he couldn't get enough. She knew she would never be able to get enough of this amazing man.

Just when she thought she was lost forever in her pleasure, Grey gradually pulled his mouth away from hers and rested his face in the crook of her neck. His hot breaths touched her skin, sending tingles of delight through her. His irregular breathing matched hers perfectly.

"Oh, Lexie, forgive me…"

"For what? Stopping?"

His body shook with silent laughter as he lifted his head and looked into her eyes. "Well, certainly for that, but mostly for being unable to control myself. I should not have let the kiss become so intense and passionate."

"I enjoyed it very much. You should not be apologizing. You are extremely good at it."

His grin stretched as he ran the pads of his fingers across her cheek. "You are so lovely, my Lexie, and I'll be eternally grateful that you were not offended by my kiss."

"Why should I be?"

"I'm assuming that was the first time a man has kissed you?"

She shook her head. "No."

His eyebrows creased together. "It wasn't?"

She chuckled. "Are you forgetting the brief kiss you gave me last night?"

His smile widened. "No, my sweet Lexie, that was not a kiss. That was a mere sample. What we just shared now was indeed a kiss."

"Oh, well…then yes, that was my first."

He gently traced her lower lip with his thumb. "I usually don't kiss innocent women such as yourself, and I really shouldn't be so daring."

"Even if I liked it, and learned from your example?"

He laughed. "Oh, my sweet Lexie, you are so endearing. I never want you to change."

She loved hearing his nickname for her and how he said it with a sigh. "I never want you to change, either."

He kissed her again but kept it brief and pulled away. He moved completely off her but leaned on his elbow next to her, gazing into her eyes. Grey was such an intoxicating man that she could stare at him forever. By the way he stayed in that position, she wondered if he was thinking that he just wanted to stare at her. Hopefully, she could convince him to do more.

JULIAN SHOULD MOVE, but he couldn't. Being this close to her was pure torture, only because he knew he must behave like a true gentleman. Meeting in private was very improper, and if they were caught, it would certainly ruin her reputation. Yet he didn't want to leave the coziness they had shared these last few earth-shattering and blissful moments.

At times, guilt flowed through him for lying to her. She'd nearly guessed his true identity, and although he would love nothing more than to hear his real name from her lips, he still worried for her safety. If Martin ever discovered Lexie was helping him, she would be in grave danger. It pleased Julian so much to think she was so selfless in her endeavors. And now, after sharing that magical kiss with her and seeing the twinkle in her eyes, he suspected she had some feelings for him as well. It was hard to believe she had already captured his heart.

Could he possibly feel this strongly about a woman he had only met yesterday? Impossible! He reasoned that it had been too long since he was with a woman. Yet his insanely beating heart and the pleasure flowing through him right now told him he was indeed falling hard.

She licked her lips. "What should we do now?"

He couldn't stop the grin tugging on his lips. She would certainly slap his face if she knew what he wanted to do now. "I'm actually just enjoying this coziness. Aren't you?" He slid his arm around her waist and scooted closer.

Alexandria's face reddened. "Yes, I think this position makes me very relaxed. However, what I meant to say was, what should we do about Martin?"

Get your mind out of the sewer, Greystone. Embarrassment washed over him, which didn't happen often. He should scoot away from her, but curse his hide, she was just too soft and cuddly for him to leave this position. "Good question. If you say you didn't find any information leading toward Martin's guilt, then he is shiftier than I first suspected. Where else would he hide the evidence?"

"Do you think he has an office in town?" She hesitantly slid her hand over his arm, caressing his limb as it lay over her.

"Lord Trenton has followed Martin into town several times, and the only thing he has found is that Martin frequents the taverns, I'm afraid."

"There must be something we're missing."

"I agree, but I'm encouraged after you mentioned the arm wound. That will narrow our suspects down a bit." He trailed his fingers up her arm and to her neck, softly caressing her skin. "Have you noticed Martin rubbing his left arm in any way?"

"Like the way I've seen you rub your injured leg?"

He nodded. "Yes."

"No. I haven't noticed, but then, I don't look at him that much. I have never really taken the time to study my brother-in-law. Perhaps that is what I'll do at dinner tonight. Maybe I'll purposely bump against his left arm."

"See if he stretches his arm in a certain way. The ache from a bullet wound lingers months afterward, so if Martin was the man I shot, he would still hurt."

"I'll be certain to watch him closely tonight."

"Just take care not to make him curious."

"Indeed. He would surely know something was amiss then." She chuckled. "He is not used to me watching him."

"I would hope not." Julian shifted, suddenly feeling very possessive. He knew Alexandria would never think of Martin in such a way, but he wanted to make certain he was the only man on her mind.

As he drew small circles on her neck, he had the incredible

urge to see if her skin was as soft on his lips as it was beneath his fingers. She was just too tempting, and he couldn't resist any longer. He lowered his mouth to her neck. When his lips touched her skin, she sucked in a breath and stiffened.

"I hope I'm the only man you want to watch from now on," he whispered as he placed tender kisses along her throat. Slowly, she relaxed, tilting her neck and giving him better access—which he didn't hesitate to take advantage of. Indeed, her skin was silky smooth and tasted scrumptious.

While he devoured her neck, he rubbed her shoulder and gradually pulled the material of her gown to expose more skin. Her fast breaths caused her bosom to rise and fall quickly, drawing his attention there instead of her bare shoulder. There was so much more skin to partake of.

Warning bells rang in his head, reminding him this was not something he should be doing to such an innocent woman, but heaven couldn't stop him. Only she would be able to cease his actions this time. He almost hoped she wanted this as much as he did.

Chapter Fourteen

PLEASURE POURED THROUGH Alexandria like hot liquid. Just when she thought she had experienced everything she could with Grey, he proved her wrong. Her chest ached, and her breathing came much too fast. His kisses had thrown her emotions in different directions, yet they were still all heading toward one place. Paradise.

The confusion inside her head and the excitement shooting through her body made her squirm and sigh with pleasure. Small moans escaped her throat several times, and she was helpless to control them. Her skin burned with awareness, and the more he exposed the skin on her shoulder, the higher the temperature inside her grew. She needed to stop his improper actions, yet at the same time, she never wanted him to stop.

But they weren't married. They weren't even engaged. He had mentioned earlier that he wasn't used to kissing innocent women, which meant he was used to more experienced ladies. Alexandria was definitely not in that category, and she never would be. No way did she want him to believe she was like one of those *fallen* women.

She must stop him. She must find the strength to say the words. But when she managed to speak around her swollen tongue, the only word that escaped her was his name in whispered gasps. *Grey*. She couldn't stop saying his name. The phrase *don't stop* tumbled from her thoughts toward her mouth, but thankfully, she did not speak them aloud.

His mouth put her mind in a different place, and his soft caresses calmed her fears. Within moments, she didn't care anymore. All she wanted now was his love. Her mind whirled in a confused daydream, and the earth moved beneath her.

Actually, the earth was indeed moving beneath her!

She snapped out of her dreamlike state and became more aware of her surroundings. Why was the ground shaking with the rumbling of horse hooves...several horses' hooves, in fact?

Grey jerked his head up and looked around. Before she could ask what was going on, he jumped to his feet and ran toward the edge of the grove of trees.

She struggled to stand, but it took a few moments to gain her strength. His kisses had sapped it from her. Once she stood upright and steady, she hurried after him, pulling up the sleeves of her dress to cover her shoulders. Heavens, had he pulled down that much of her dress? She should be embarrassed, but at this moment, that wasn't the emotion rushing through her. Many men riding horses were entering the estate's grounds.

Grey stood at the exact spot where she had met him earlier, holding a spyglass to his eye as he surveyed the uproar toward the house.

"What...what is happening?" she asked breathlessly. She couldn't see the men riding, but several horses were moving toward the manor. This group didn't appear to be the cavalry. However, by the way the ground had sounded a few moments ago, she wouldn't be surprised that these men were soldiers.

"I don't know." He continued to peer through his small spyglass. "Martin is with them, and he just went into the manor. I don't know who the other men are. None of them are familiar to me."

"Are they nobles?" she asked.

"I cannot be certain."

"How are they dressed?"

"Like well-to-do gentlemen. But they aren't anyone I remember associating with before I enlisted."

"How many are there?"

It took him a little longer to answer, and she figured he was counting.

"Twelve." He lowered the spyglass and looked at her. "Did Martin mention having any of his friends over today?"

"Not to me. I believe he would be foolish to have a social gathering when his wife was ill."

Grey lifted the spyglass back to his eye. "Well, it appears he's going to have one now. At least with his friends. There are no women in this group. I wonder why he invited only men... Oh, wait. Martin is coming out of the manor."

From a distance, her brother-in-law called her name. She sucked in a horrified breath, the energy inside of her quickly draining. "Oh no!" Her voice broke as dread washed over her. "I think I know why they are here."

"Why?" Julian lowered the spyglass as his focus came back to her again.

"Martin is going to sell me to the highest bidder. And it looks like he intends to do so today."

ANGER FLARED THROUGH Julian, hotter than he had ever experienced before. He would not allow this to happen. Even if it meant coming out of hiding and declaring he was the rightful Duke of Linden. If that happened, he and Trenton would have to figure out a different way to find the evidence needed to jail Martin.

He pulled Alexandria into his arms and pressed her head against his chest. His heart squeezed with emotion as helplessness flowed through him like an angry river. He could not let her go.

"I won't let this happen," he said tightly. "You are going to stay right here with me."

"No." She sobbed into his waistcoat and cravat. "Martin will come looking for me, and then he will discover you are alive."

"It doesn't matter any longer. I promised I would keep you safe, and I shall."

She lifted her head and met his eyes. Tears streamed down her cheeks, wrenching his heart even more.

"Nothing will happen immediately with Martin and his friends. Even if one of them offers marriage, it is still going to take a couple of weeks. Meanwhile"—she gently stroked his cheek, giving him a weak smile—"we shall keep searching for evidence. I'm confident we'll find something soon."

"Oh, Lexie," he whispered, cupping her face in his hands and kissing her soundly. Mixed emotions grew inside of him. He wanted to protect her with every fiber of his being, even if it messed up his own plans. But she was right. Coming out of hiding now was pointless.

"Alexandria. Where are you?"

Martin's voice made the hackles rise on Julian's back. He wanted to take his cousin out to the dueling field at this very moment. If only he had Lexie's faith that everything would work out. But she was correct in assuming nothing would happen immediately.

She pulled away from him and wiped the tears from her eyes. Taking a deep breath, she squared her shoulders. "I must go before he comes searching for me."

"I know, but before you go, let us fix your hair."

She gasped, and her hand flew to her hair. She hurried back to the blanket and collected the pins. Between Julian and Lexie, they wound her hair back in the coil. Even though it wasn't perfect, it would do.

"I shall return tonight after the evening meal and let you know what has happened," she told him. "I shall do all I can to dissuade these men. I certainly do *not* want them to offer marriage."

"Please be careful." He stroked her cheek. "Remember, I'll be watching you."

Nodding, she turned and walked away from him toward Martin and the other men. Julian tightened his grip on the spyglass as he watched. If his cousin allowed his friends to lay one hand on her, Julian would certainly lose his temper, and those men would soon believe they were in hell.

TRYING HER BEST to relax in her steamy bath, Alexandria closed her eyes and relived the day's events. A smile tugged on the corners of her mouth, and she giggled. How daring she had been with Grey today…how forward. Not even the women in her stories had the courage to say—or do—so much with a man. Yet Alexandria enjoyed the newfound awareness buzzing through her. She wanted to explore her feelings more, and oddly enough, she wasn't frightened of the unknown. Grey would be there to give her assistance and even encourage her. He had certainly changed her life for the better.

Smiling, she trickled water over her arms with the sponge. Unfortunately, Martin had ruined her wonderful afternoon with Grey. Her idiotic brother-in-law had indeed brought his acquaintances to the manor to meet her. Martin knew that would be the only way for them to see her, since she rarely attended social functions.

This afternoon had been a disaster. Not only was she embarrassed beyond belief by Martin's actions, but she was also so upset at him that she wanted to slap him across his face. He had turned her from a kind person to a violent person within a few days.

Alexandria punched her fist into the bathwater, splashing it over the tub. Nevertheless, she'd rarely met the men's eyes while Martin made the introductions, and she mumbled her responses when the men asked her questions. She received the impression that most of them were put off by her lack of enthusiasm, but there were a couple that still appeared overeager to sit by her or fetch her a drink.

How much would Martin pay these men to marry her? She prayed she would never have to find out. Yet the tender way Grey had taken her into his arms and the catch in his voice when he told her he wouldn't allow the marriage to take place made her believe that she was safe. He would protect her. Always.

Grudgingly, she climbed out of the bath and dressed for supper. It irritated her that she would be the only woman at the table tonight. All of Martin's friends would be watching her, and her brother-in-law knew very well how uncomfortable that made her. Nevertheless, she decided that when she entered the dining room, she would not be herself. As her sister once suggested, Alexandria would be one of the characters she had written about in her story.

Indeed, she would be clever and witty, but not overly so. She would have the sharp tongue her sister was known for when putting a man in his place. Alexandria had been around her sister enough times to see how it was done. She was certain that stepping into the role of a viper wouldn't be too difficult.

Above all, she would show Martin's associates tonight that she was *not* the woman they wanted to marry.

Dread swept through her, and she sighed, leaning against the bedpost. Could she accomplish such a feat? This was something she had never done before. Then again, the past few days had been firsts for her as well, and she had come out of the situations unscathed.

An hour later, she was dressed in a rose gown with white lace trim around the wide neck and hems of the short sleeves. A maid had curled her hair in ringlets, but Alexandria made certain there was nothing fancy about how her hair was styled. Although she had planned to come across as a hardheaded woman this evening, she wanted to look as plain as she possibly could. In other words, she would look like she did on most days.

Her hands shook slightly as she made her way down to the

lower level of the grand house. Men's boisterous voices echoed from the sitting room. She slowed her steps, and her heart hammered with panic. Taking a deep breath, she reminded herself, *I can do this!*

And yet it was the other voice inside her head that told her, *No, you can't,* that had her worried. She feared tonight would be a disaster.

CHAPTER FIFTEEN

TAKING A DEEP breath of courage and strength, Alexandria continued toward Martin's gathering. Before she reached the sitting room, another room caught her attention. She quickly stepped into the empty blue room to collect her thoughts. What would she say? How could she act? And more importantly, could she become the strong-willed women in her stories?

She moved to the window and peered out. The estate grounds were so lovely, manicured, and eye-catching. Of course, now she realized this wasn't Martin's doing at all. It was the former Duke of Linden who had taken care of the estate.

Was Grey out there watching her right now? He had told her to stay by the windows so that he could keep an eye on her. She glanced toward the nearest cluster of trees. Lanterns had been lit outside the estate tonight, probably because Martin expected one, or more, of his friends to take her for a stroll in the moonlight. Her stomach churned. She would have to avoid that at all costs.

Right away, she detected movement on one of the lawns. She studied the shadows, and within seconds, she noticed a man coming her way. *Grey!* Her heart sang, yet at the same time, worry tightened her chest. She must stop him from coming any closer.

She quickly closed the door to the blue room before hurrying over to the window and opening it wide. She waved her hand. As he came closer, she realized there were two men. Grey and the other man rushed to the side of the house near the window.

"Why are you not hiding?" she whispered, leaning out the window.

Grey grasped her hand and squeezed. "Lord Trenton came earlier this evening"—he motioned his head toward the other man—"and he recognized some of the men here tonight."

Lord Trenton stepped into her view. This was the first time she could see him clearly. He wasn't as tall as Grey, and neither was he as muscular, yet he was handsome nonetheless. His wavy blond hair was a lighter shade than hers.

"Good evening, Lord Trenton," she said with a smile. "It is a pleasure to see you again."

He bowed. "It's a pleasure to see you, as well. You are looking lovely this evening."

Grey nudged his friend with his elbow and scowled. "There's no time for flirtatious bantering right now. Tell her what you told me earlier."

She tried not to grin at Grey's jealous antics, but it was hard not to feel giddy.

"Forgive me," Lord Trenton said as he threw his friend a glare. When his eyes met hers again, the irritation had left his handsome face. "Miss Templeton, I'm acquainted with three of those men, and I know their sordid reputations. I thought you might like me to tell you before you meet them. Perhaps you can use this information to your advantage while trying to ward off their advances."

She nodded. "Indeed. Please tell me. Anything will be helpful."

"Lord Eugene Fairfax is the eldest son of an earl. He's not much into religion, and his family hasn't attended church in quite some time. Fairfax visits the gaming tables and brothels more frequently than most men."

Heat flamed in her face. It was quite improper for a man to discuss this subject with a lady, but she was glad he had told her this tidbit of information anyway. "I shall remember that."

"Mr. Fisher Lyttle is the third son of a viscount. He loves hunting more than life itself, and he has a room full of his trophies."

She arched an eyebrow. "Trophies, my lord?"

"Yes. Heads of the animals he kills."

She shivered in disgust. "I understand."

"Lastly, there is Mr. George Finch. His grandfather is a baron, and the family has no money because Finch is addicted to gambling. Naturally, he is looking to find a woman with a large inheritance."

She snorted and rolled her eyes. "Then why would he be interested in me?"

"My blossom"—Grey patted her hand—"I can assure you that Martin plans on offering money to the man who asks for your hand."

Her stomach churned again. "That is what I had surmised."

"I have confidence in you." Grey smiled. "I know you will convince these men they do not suit, and you'll turn in a splendid performance."

Chuckling, she shook her head. Never before had a man been so caring and supportive. Then again, she had never acted this way, either. It was then that she realized she hadn't stammered in front of Lord Trenton. Perhaps her shyness had been cured. She could only hope.

"I thank you, Grey. You don't know what that means to me." She wanted to lean down and kiss him, but it wouldn't be proper. Besides that, he and Lord Trenton needed to return to their hiding place. "You two need to leave before someone sees you."

"I know." Julian squeezed her hand again. "Remember, stay by the windows so we can keep an eye on you."

"I shall."

She watched them until their shadows merged into the cluster of trees. Taking a deep breath, she left the blue room and wandered into the grand room. As soon as she walked inside, the men's voices silenced, and all turned to look her way. She curtsied and gave a nod. "Gentlemen."

All at once, they came toward her, giving her greetings and flirtatious compliments. She wanted to roll her eyes in disgust. Meaningless words were thrown at her, and she didn't believe them. For certain, Martin had promised these men some kind of reward for marrying her. She didn't have a trousseau, but she was certain her brother-in-law would pay a pretty shilling to get her off his hands.

She moved her attention to Martin, who stood by the hearth with a drink in his hand. It was probably sherry, which was his drink of choice. He watched her with a critical eye as he smirked. She wanted to slap that expression off his face. But no. She wouldn't give him the satisfaction of seeing her anger. Her main purpose was to irritate him tonight, as well as most of his friends.

"You certainly look lovely this evening, Miss Templeton," Mr. Finch said.

His whining voice grated on her already frazzled nerves. Since she had met him earlier this afternoon, he always seemed to have a bead of moisture on his upper lip and forehead. He was a slightly large man, and she wondered if he was constantly hot.

"I thank you, Mr. Finch."

"May I fetch you a glass of punch?"

She quickly recalled what Lord Trenton had told her about this man. "Punch? Heavens no. My brother-in-law is wealthy. I'd prefer a glass of his finest wine." She forced a chuckle. "I shall have to ask Mr. Higley, the butler, if he could locate me a bottle of one of the wines His Grace smuggled in from France. I have absolutely become addicted to the taste."

The poor man's face paled. "Addicted?" He gulped and dabbed his handkerchief to his moist forehead.

"Oh yes. I fear my future husband will have a hard time breaking me of that habit."

"Uh, indeed he will." He nodded.

She glanced around the room as if searching for someone.

"Let me go find Mr. Higley now." Without waiting for his answer, she left Mr. Finch. Once she had turned away from him, she couldn't stop her grin. The man's shocked expression was priceless.

"Ah, Miss Templeton, you are finally alone," Lord Fairfax said as he stepped in front of her.

She stopped and stared at the rude man. Then again, she was sure all these men were nice—it was Alexandria who had the bad temperament.

"Yes, for the moment," she answered, hoping her tone didn't reveal her irritation.

"I thought we could get to know each other." He waggled his eyebrows.

"That would be nice." Fairfax seemed like a pleasant gentleman. He was of average height and had average looks, but he was balding even at his young age. Now, what was it that Lord Trenton said about this man? Oh yes, he was not a churchgoing man. Far from it, in fact.

"Your brother-in-law tells me you do not attend many social gatherings." He shook his head. "I find that impossible to believe, since you have presented such charm and grace already this evening. You don't appear as the wallflower the duke made you out to be."

She flipped her hand in the air. "Oh, His Grace tends to exaggerate. Truly, it's a vice he must overcome. If my brother-in-law doesn't stop lying, he shall have quite a bit of groveling to do in front of our Lord on Judgment Day."

"Groveling, you say?"

His expression was laughable, but Alexandria refused to show the humor in the situation. At least in front of him.

"Indeed. His Grace tells everyone I'm a wallflower, but I'm not. What the duke doesn't like to confess is that his sister-in-law would rather spend time reading the Good Book and in prayer than socialize with a bunch of gossipmongers and liars." She huffed and folded her arms, trying to appear vexed. "My brother-in-law doesn't realize how much I love the Lord, and I shall devote my life to Him."

"How very advantageous of you," he said in almost a snicker. "I'm certain God will appreciate such a fine servant."

She steepled her hands and nodded. "Amen."

"Yes, well…" Lord Fairfax glanced around the room. "Oh, look. There is Sir Tolland. I need to have a word with him. If you'll excuse me."

"But of course." As he walked away rather quickly, she bit her bottom lip. Again, she felt like laughing. Although she was still uncomfortable about being the only woman in this roomful of men, she found it easier to turn them down. If only Grey could see her now.

FOR THE PAST hour, Julian and Vincent had traded off using the spyglass to watch Alexandria. Anger built within Julian. The same anger he had felt since he realized his cousin must be the one who tried to kill him and succeeded in killing his father and brother.

When had Martin become so heartless? Julian didn't remember his cousin being that way when they were lads. Greed had ruined many people, and obviously, it had worked through Martin's now uncaring soul.

Julian zeroed in on his cousin, who wore a grim expression. From what he could see, Martin was keeping close watch over Alexandria as well.

Grumbling, Julian stopped his pacing and peered toward the manor once more. "There has to be something more I can do."

"Calm yourself, Greystone," Vincent said. "Miss Templeton is fooling those idiots inside. She is wonderful."

Julian grinned. "She has outdone herself this time. No longer is she a shy wallflower."

"I quite agree." Vincent chuckled. "And I must admit, she is quite a beauty. It is no wonder you mistook her for the wrong woman. She does resemble her lovely sister."

The way Vincent's smile softened made the green monster of jealousy sneak through Julian. "Tell me, Trenton, have you ever had feelings for Alexandria's sister?"

Vincent shifted on his feet. "I must admit, at one time, I thought of her and no other."

"Indeed? Why did you not pursue her?"

"As I explained to you before, she was the type of woman who made a man want to beg for mercy. Her tantalizing eyes, along with her charm and wit, could seduce most men."

"Yet you also told me she had a tongue of a viper."

Vincent nodded. "Indeed, she does, but only if she is vexed with that person. I've heard her put men in their place, rendering them speechless. I decided then and there not to be the man who upset that particular woman."

"That doesn't explain why you didn't pursue her," Julian said.

"Because she had eyes only for Martin."

Julian snorted. "But Martin didn't have a title at the time."

"True, but she acted like she was in love with him and wanted only him." Vincent held up his hands in surrender. "I can't compete with that. A man will do anything to protect the woman he loves."

Julian rolled his eyes. "So I've been told." He lifted the spyglass to his eye. "I hope Lexie will be able to convince those men that they don't suit."

"I'm sure she will."

"What worries me more is if Martin becomes suspicious as to why none of his colleagues are offering marriage. I fear for Alexandria's safety if that happens."

"I have no need to fear if that happens," Vincent said nonchalantly.

Julian swung his focus to Vincent. Although shadows grew within the trees, the bright moon outlined his friend's frame. "Did I hear you correctly?"

Vincent chuckled. "Indeed you did."

"Explain yourself before I call you out for being so rude."

Vincent shrugged. "I don't fear for her safety because I know you won't let Martin lay a hand on her."

"Not one finger," Julian snapped.

"My point exactly. You have grown quite fond of this young lady in a short amount of time."

"No, I haven't," Julian mumbled. Yet he really had, although he didn't want to admit it. If he admitted it, that would mean he really cared for her, and he knew exactly where that emotion would lead—somewhere he didn't want to travel.

Vincent laughed louder but still kept his voice from carrying. He took the spyglass away and peered through it toward the manor. "There is no use denying it. Falling for a woman this fast isn't like you. This wasn't your behavior around women before you left to join the military. In fact, you were quite a scoundrel back then."

Julian relaxed slightly. "Very true. I wasn't like this before."

"Admit it. You are enamored with Miss Templeton." Vincent turned and put his hand on Julian's shoulder.

Exhaling deeply, Julian took the spyglass from his friend. That was something he would never admit, only because he knew it wasn't true. The only reason he felt this way about her was because he had set his sights on charming her so she would cooperate and help him.

"Will this dinner party never end?" he muttered as he looked toward the lighted room.

A movement from one of the manor's side doors caught his attention, and he swung the spyglass in that direction. One of the servants stumbled out, holding a bottle of wine. Julian rolled his eyes. Another one of Martin's servants had been in his cousin's collection again. Actually, Julian was certain this was probably the wine that his father had gathered over the years.

When the servant slumped by the side of the house, an idea popped into Julian's head. "Trenton, I'm going inside."

"Are you addled?" Vincent asked.

"Hear me out first." Julian pointed in the direction of the servant who had passed out. "I need you to assist me as I change into that man's clothes so I can go inside and help serve Martin's guests. You see, with me in there, I'll be able to spread some gossip around about Martin, and in doing so, this will make the other men believe he is not a respectable man. I'll say he is losing money or something along those lines. I'll also be able to sway some men away from my Lexie." After realizing he had labeled her *my Lexie*, he shook his head and added, "I mean, Miss Templeton."

"Indeed, you *are* addled." Vincent shook his head.

Perhaps Julian was not thinking straight, but he felt helpless doing nothing but watching. Thankfully, within a half-hour, Vincent had helped him undress the servant and Julian was clothed in the man's attire. Julian even wore the servant's spectacles. Of course, he had to squint a little in order to see through them, but at least it altered his appearance slightly. Unless someone really studied Julian, they wouldn't know his true identity.

"I wish you the best of luck, my good man, because I honestly don't see this ending well." Vincent slapped Julian on the back. "However, I'll be here watching you and praying you don't get noticed."

"I shall do my best to blend in."

"Why do I not believe you?"

Vincent's laughter followed Julian as he made his way toward the house. He didn't understand what his friend thought was so comical. Julian couldn't wait until a woman caught Vincent Trenton's interest. Then Julian would see what strange and ridiculous stunts his friend would accomplish to protect a woman.

Julian must make everyone believe he was a servant. If even one person recognized him, he would be in serious trouble, and he would have to come clean with his identity, especially with

Lexie. Was he ready to tell her the truth? He still feared it was too soon. She certainly wouldn't forgive him. Before that could happen, he needed to make her fall in love with him, just as he knew his heart continued to soften for her.

But only time would tell.

CHAPTER SIXTEEN

T RYING TO ACT like a servant, Julian kept his attention
downward most of the time, only glancing up occasionally.
He moved through the kitchen to collect a tray of champagne
glasses before quickly leaving to enter the room where Alexandria
and the others were gathered.

He took his time, moving from person to person. Just as he
had assumed, none of them looked directly at him. He did
recognize some from his early years before joining the military,
and he prayed they wouldn't remember him.

Three men were grouped together, whispering about something as they cast glances toward Martin, who was chatting with a
man across the room. Julian moved to the group of three and
held out his tray of champagne.

"And I heard," one of the men said, "that he had something
to do with the deaths of his cousins and uncle just to obtain the
title."

Julian tried not to grin. Perhaps coming to the party to spread
false gossip was futile after all.

"Indeed, my good man. It's a touchy subject around Linden,
to be sure." Another man nodded as he took a flute of champagne
from Julian's tray.

"Forgive me for interrupting," Julian said in a low voice. "But
would you be interested in another little tidbit about the duke?"

At first, the expressions on their faces let Julian know they were rather shocked that a mere servant would speak so boldly, but within seconds they nodded.

"Some of the staff are saying that he is low on funds."

The tall man snickered and shook his head. "That is ridiculous. I've seen him at the gaming tables. He acts as if his coffers have no limit."

Inwardly, Julian seethed. That was supposed to be *his* money. "My point exactly," he continued. "He doesn't do well at the gaming tables, so he is losing money fast."

The three men traded glances in silence. Julian knew he had planted the seed of doubt in them, which was worth the risk of being caught.

"If you will excuse me." Julian bowed and moved away from them. He tried not to grin, but it was hard. He figured those three men would tell others, and by the end of the evening, nobody would offer for Alexandria's hand.

He paused, covertly scanning the room, hoping to see her, but he couldn't. Panic engulfed him, and he snapped his head around, doing another quick search. Finally, he saw her in the corner of the room talking with Mr. Lyttle. Julian quickened his step and headed toward them. Just as he reached the two, he heard her lovely voice, which calmed him greatly.

Lyttle was a small, pudgy man who always appeared nervous. Lyttle and Alexandria had champagne flutes in their hands.

"I would enjoy taking you hunting with me," Lyttle said with a smile.

She tilted her head slightly and narrowed her eyes. "Why? Did my brother-in-law hint that I enjoyed hunting?"

"Indeed he did."

"Hunting *animals*?" She gasped.

Lyttle chuckled. "But of course. What else is there to hunt?"

She placed her hand on her throat. "Oh, Mr. Lyttle. How inhumane of you to hunt for mere sport." She shook her head. "I suppose my brother-in-law meant well, because I do love animals.

However, I love them as pets, not to hunt as mere objects for prizes only."

"Pets?" He smirked.

"Indeed. When I go riding every morning, I love to feed the deer and the birds." She added to the dramatics with a heavy sigh. "I enjoy all types of animals. In fact"—she tapped her finger on her chin—"if I could figure out a way to remove that terrible scent from a skunk, I would love to have that as an indoor pet. They are such lovely creatures."

Julian quickly put his hand to his mouth to keep a laugh in. He couldn't believe Mr. Lyttle wasn't laughing too. But thankfully, the middle-aged man took Alexandria seriously.

"That is the most ridiculous thing I've ever heard," he snapped.

"Oh," she said. "Forgive me, Mr. Lyttle, but that was quite rude of you to say."

"I speak what's on my mind, Miss Templeton."

"As do I." She gave him a sharp nod. "And with that being said, I can see that you would not make a very good husband at all, so if you will excuse me, I won't waste any more of your precious time."

"Indeed, my time is extremely precious." He bowed and left her side so fast that one would think dogs were nipping at his heels.

Alexandria blew out an exasperated breath and rolled her eyes. Her cheeks were red, and her mouth was pinched in a fine line. Julian could see she was tired of this evening already. So was he. Too bad they couldn't figure out a way to end it quickly.

"More champagne, Miss Templeton?" he asked, holding out the tray to her.

"I thank you." She glanced at him before placing her empty flute on the tray and taking another. "You cannot fathom how much I need this right now." She sipped the drink.

"I could tell you did, Miss Templeton."

She passed him a smile before looking away. His hopes sank.

In a way, he'd wanted her to notice him, but it wouldn't be good if she had.

He frowned and prepared to step back, but then she inhaled abruptly and snapped her attention back to him. Gradually, the color in her face faded, and she shook her head.

"You should not be here," she whispered.

Gladness filled his heart. "I couldn't stay away."

She scoped out the room. "What if someone notices you? What if Martin—"

"Shh," he said, and gently touched her arm. "If we don't make a scene, nobody will believe I'm not whom I present."

"How long have you been here?"

"Only a few minutes."

"You need to leave." She sipped her drink.

"Can you sneak out of the room for a moment?"

"Don't be silly," she said with a forced chuckle. "Being the only woman in this room, I think I would be missed if I left."

"Tell Martin you are going to use the chamber pot."

Alexandria's face turned dark red. "Grey," she whispered. "I highly doubt this is a proper conversation—"

"Just do it." He winked. "I'll meet you down the corridor just before you enter the music room."

He turned and made his way out of the party, not looking back to see if Alexandria was coming, only because he knew she would.

THE HEAT IN Alexandria's face grew to the point of making her head throb. Sometimes Grey could say things that would catch her unawares and leave her tongue-tied. However, she couldn't deny that she enjoyed his company, and she loved how he could make her smile and laugh.

Although it embarrassed her greatly, she informed Martin

that she was stepping out to visit the chamber pot. Once she was out of the room, she hurried down the hall. Taking a deep breath to compose herself, she moved in the direction Grey had indicated. With each step, her heart hammered faster, and she became more anxious.

When she neared the music room, she slowed, listening for any sounds around her, especially voices from Martin's acquaintances. Thankfully, no one took it upon themselves to follow her.

"I'm in here."

She swung her head toward the door of the music room. It opened enough for her to see a section of Grey's face. She hurried inside and closed the door behind her. When she finally was able to get a good look at him, she nearly laughed. He was dressed as a servant, minus the glasses he wore earlier, but not any servant she had ever encountered. The taut material of his shirt outlined every muscle of his shapely physique even as his every movement threatened to burst the seams of his pants most indecently. To think none of Martin's guests even questioned why a servant would wear such ill-fitting clothes.

"This has got to be the worst decision you have made since we met." She shook her head. "Grey, do you know how dangerous it is for you to be here?"

He grasped her hands and pulled her closer until she had to tilt her head back to look at him. "Lexie, I thank you for being so concerned about my welfare."

"How can I not be concerned? You have done so much to try to protect me. It is only natural I should return the gesture."

He caressed her cheek with the backs of his knuckles. "I watched you from outside, and your performance was spectacular. When I overheard you talking to Mr. Lyttle, I wanted to laugh. I believe, my blossom, that you were throwing the men off quite nicely without my help."

She ran her palms up and down his arms. "As much as it thrills me to hear you say that, I'm still worried you will be discovered. I think you need to leave. I don't want you caught."

His dark eyebrows rose. "In the music room? Pray, how am I supposed to get caught when no one knows we are in here?"

"You never know who will want to sneak through the house. Perhaps one of the servants, or it could be one of Martin's very intoxicated friends who becomes lost." She shrugged. "I don't want to take that chance."

He nodded. "Then I shall take my leave, because I don't wish to worry you." He touched a finger to the tip of her nose. "But before I go, I want a kiss that will last me throughout the night."

Her heart melted as she slid her hands around his neck, leaning closer. "An enduring kiss you shall have, my dearest Grey."

Their mouths joined, and as before, excitement shot through her. She didn't know if it was because this incredible man was kissing her again or if it was the prospect of being discovered. Yet it didn't matter. She prayed nothing would disrupt her happiness right now.

In the other times before, he'd started their kisses soft, but now he kissed her as though he was hungry for more. A spark of desire and longing took over her soul, and she wished she could keep him with her all night. Forever, in fact.

His hands moved with urgency over her back, and she suddenly wanted to touch him the same way he stroked her. Hesitantly, she slid her hands over his back and then around to his chest. Her hands had rested against his wide chest a few times before, but she had never really caressed him. She couldn't stop herself from doing so now.

When her palms met with his tight muscles, she sighed in awe. Tingles erupted throughout her, and instead of wanting to push him away in embarrassment, she embraced the overpowering feeling.

Keeping his mouth on hers, he withdrew slightly to give her hands more room for exploration. This shirt was too small for Grey's body, and when she brushed her fingers across the top buttons, they immediately came apart. Her fingertips connected with his warm skin and the dusting of hair across his chest.

Oh, good heavens! This was so wrong, and yet the excitement pouring through her only intensified. As she touched him, it seemed to stir some kind of urgency inside Grey, because his kisses turned wild.

Improper ideas filled her head, and she tried to push them away. Being intimate with him like this would create such a scandal, and if they were caught, it would ruin her reputation for good. Titled men like Grey usually jumped such disgraces with ease, but there was no way a woman could avoid the gossip.

Before she could muster up the courage to break the incredible kiss, the floor outside the music room squeaked, and the door swung open. A loud gasp hit the wall, ricocheting around the room.

Alexandria jumped in Grey's arms, but he didn't remove his hold. Instead, they both faced the intruder, ready for battle.

CHAPTER SEVENTEEN

JULIAN'S HEART RACED. At this moment, he didn't know if it was from the pleasure he felt while kissing Lexie or because he had just been caught in a very intimate embrace…not to mention his shirt had come undone.

As he focused on their unexpected visitor, he regulated his breathing and mind. He needed a clear head in order to figure out a way to get out of this mess.

"What is going on here?" Lord Senwick exclaimed angrily.

Silently, Julian groaned. Of all people to catch them, why did it have to be this man—a man from Julian's past he hadn't ever wanted to see again. And why hadn't he known the lord was at Martin's party? Julian knew for certain he hadn't seen him earlier.

Before he could get any words out, three more men entered the room. More gasps bounced off the walls.

Julian cursed under his breath. For certain, he and Alexandria had been ruined. All because of his lusty impulses.

"*Lord Julian?* You are…alive?" Lord Senwick's voice rose over the mumbles in the room.

Alexandria gasped and stiffened. She snapped her head up to look at him, but he couldn't meet her eyes. Not yet. Of course, she would now realize he had lied to her. But once he explained his reasons for deceiving her, he was certain she would understand.

Julian cleared his throat and straightened. "Actually, no, my lord. I'm the Duke of Linden, if you must know."

The older man huffed. "I don't care who the devil you are," he snapped. "I can see you have ruined yet another woman."

Alexandria inhaled sharply, her eyes widening more by the second. Julian gritted his teeth. How could he shut this man up before he said too much?

"Lord Senwick, I think you need to let the past rest," Julian growled.

"Why should I? You were the reason my sister's name was dragged through the gossip circles, and you are the reason she has not yet married."

"I'm certain that is *not* my problem," Julian said, realizing Senwick had said too much already, "but as I mentioned before, that has nothing to do with this current situation."

"I beg to differ, *Your Grace*. Ruining her good name is not how you treat a woman you are betrothed to."

Julian didn't like the way Senwick snickered the title.

"This just proves that you will never change," Lord Senwick continued. "You are still a disgrace to your family and an insult to other nobles."

Anger rushed to Julian's head, and he moved away from Alexandria. In two large steps, he stood in front of the insipid man. "Enough, I say. I will not be insulted in my own home. If I weren't a gentleman, I would call you out to the dueling field for my satisfaction. As it is, I realize you have been drinking too much, and you don't know what you're saying."

"Oh, tosh! I have just arrived and haven't been drinking at all."

No wonder Julian hadn't noticed him before. If he knew this particular lord had been invited, he wouldn't have come in to check on Alexandria.

"What in the devil is going on here?" Martin's voice boomed through the room as he hurried inside. The moment his focus landed on Julian, his face lost color. "Julian?"

"Indeed, it is I, cousin." Julian moved away from Lord Senwick and walked to Martin. "And I'm here to take back my title as the rightful Duke of Linden. As for my first order of business"—he glanced at the intruders—"I want all of your friends out of *my* home immediately."

"Yes, Your Grace," Martin muttered as he ushered his friends out of the room.

"Martin?" Julian said sternly. "Once they are out, I want a meeting with you."

"Of course, Your Grace."

Julian waited until Martin had left and closed the door before he turned to Alexandria. She appeared to have crawled back into her wallflower shell, because she stood with her hands clutched together, pressed against her bosom, and her eyes were downcast. He'd known this wouldn't be an easy thing to explain to her. He also needed to repair the damage to her reputation, if only he could figure out a way.

He approached her cautiously. The tears trailing down her pale cheeks made his chest hurt, and all he wished to do was brush them away and see her smile. He placed his hands on her shoulders and squeezed. "Lexie, my blossom—"

She pushed his hands away and turned her back to him. "Leave me alone," she said in a choked voice.

"I cannot, my dear. I must make this right."

"You can't. It is too late."

"Nothing is ever too late." Hesitantly, he touched her back. "I will do everything I can to repair what happened a few minutes ago."

"I'm not referring to that," she snapped, swinging around.

"You aren't?"

"No, *Your Grace*. I want you to explain why you thought it necessary to lie to me all this time. Why didn't you tell me who you really were?"

"It's complicated—"

"And let us not forget about what Lord Senwick said, either.

Why did you not tell me? Is there any further information I need to know that you are purposely keeping from me?"

A pain of remembrance throbbed in his forehead, and he rubbed his skull. He would rather not talk about it. "'Twas nothing that happened with Senwick, my dear. The man was muttering foolishness that wasn't even important."

She arched an eyebrow. "Indeed? Well, it certainly sounded important, and obviously, he thought it was imperative, or he wouldn't have mentioned it."

"The reason he mentioned it was because he thought I had wronged his sister."

"Who was your betrothed at the time, apparently."

He nodded, feeling more and more frustrated. "That was long ago, before I entered the military." He took hold of her arms again, and this time, he wouldn't let her break free. "Lexie, what happened in the past doesn't matter."

"It does to me. I feel as though you kept the truth from me on purpose." She dropped her gaze to his chest again.

"Forgive me for not telling you my real name, but I was only trying to protect you. I couldn't tell you everything about my life."

"And why not? I told you everything about mine."

He held his breath, trying unsuccessfully to control his frustration. She was overreacting, and he didn't like it one bit. He also didn't like how she looked at him now. Before she'd stared at him as though he was her hero, but now…there was loathing in her expression. It made him feel less than a man.

"You really expected me to tell you everything? Why, Alexandria? We just met a few days ago. I was taking the time to get to know you and hoping you would be patient in getting to know me."

"How could I get to know you when you weren't honest with me?" She covered her face with her hands and shook her head. "Forgive me, Your Grace. I thought you felt something more as I did. I thought…I thought…" She pushed away from him and hurried out of the room.

He took a step to go after her but stopped himself. She was too distraught right now. He would wait until she calmed herself before he discussed this with her again. She'd had quite an upset tonight, and rightly so. It was not every day a wallflower was caught in a man's embrace while sharing a steamy kiss.

And what a kiss that was. He had almost forgotten how it had shut down his mind to where all he could think about was kissing her endlessly. And when she caressed his chest, he thought he had died and gone to heaven.

Yet it certainly felt like hell right at this particular moment. He had wronged her, yet he didn't know what to do about it.

The door opened, and Martin strolled in, his shoulders drooping. His frown made lines appear around his mouth and on his forehead.

"I'm here, as you requested, Your Grace."

"Please close the door."

Once Martin had done as instructed, Julian crossed his arms behind his back and paced, allowing the silence of the room to weigh uncomfortably on his cousin. After a few moments passed, Julian decided to take control of the situation.

"I'm sure seeing me alive has come as quite a shock to you."

Martin nodded. "I had heard rumors that you might be alive, but the authorities hadn't found your body."

"As you can see, I am alive." Julian stopped directly in front of Martin and leaned closer. "And I don't expect to die anytime in the near future."

"I'm certain most of us feel that way."

"So, in light of what's happened, I want to resume my life, which of course means taking back my title and lands."

"I understand." Martin stared at the floor.

"I would like you out of the house as soon as the servants can pack your things. I trust you have someplace to go?"

Martin nodded. "Charlotte still has her family's house in Cornwall. I'm certain we can go there."

"Is your wife not ill?" Julian asked.

His cousin raised his eyes to Julian. "She has been laid up in bed for several days already."

"Then I suggest you leave her here until she is well enough to travel."

"What about her sister?" Martin asked with a touch of malice in his voice.

"Miss Templeton can stay to help care for her sister, of course."

Martin flipped his hand. "I had assumed that, but I was referring to the scandal you created tonight. Some of my associates tell me they found her in your arms in what appeared to be a very intimate embrace."

"Indeed they did." Julian realized once again that he really needed to fix this particular issue.

"What are you going to do about it? Or are you going to take care of this problem as you have done the last several women you've compromised?"

Julian bunched his hands into fists by his sides. The one thing he absolutely hated was feeling trapped. "What I plan to do about Miss Templeton is my own business, not yours."

Martin shrugged. "Considering she is my sister-in-law, I feel responsible for her because her parents are dead." He straightened his shoulders. "So, being that I'm her guardian, I insist you repair the damage you have caused tonight and marry her immediately."

Pain gripped Julian and threatened to suffocate him. This was the same emotion he had experienced when Lord Senwick demanded Julian do the right thing and marry his sister, Theresa. Julian had gotten out of that sticky situation easily enough, but he didn't think he would be able to worm his way out of this one.

CHAPTER EIGHTEEN

ALEXANDRIA RAN DIRECTLY to her sister's room. She prayed Charlotte was still awake. Without knocking, she rushed into the room and closed the door behind her. Charlotte was sitting up in bed, reading a book. A shawl was wrapped around her shoulders, and several pillows were stuffed behind her back and underneath her arms. Her eyes widened when she looked at Alexandria. Seconds later, she frowned.

"What happened?" she said in her protective big-sister voice.

Alexandria sobbed and rushed to the bed. She sat on the edge and laid her face on Charlotte's lap. Her sister stroked Alexandria's hair. Like it had when Alexandria was a child, her sister's touch calmed her.

"Tell me all about it," Charlotte said.

"Oh, Charlotte. I've never felt like this before." Tears fell faster. "I thought I was in love, but... He lied to me, and it hurts so much." Alexandria cried harder.

"You are in *love*?" Another fit of coughs attacked Charlotte, making her whole body shake.

Alexandria fetched a glass of water, which helped calm her sister's coughing so she could breathe better.

Charlotte sighed and cleared her throat. "Now, as I was saying... So, you are in love? Alexandria Margaret Templeton, you had better tell me what is going on this very minute before I get the vapors."

Nodding, Alexandria straightened to a sitting position and wiped her moist eyes. "There is so much to tell you, I don't know where to start. Two days ago, your husband informed me that he was going to marry me to one of his friends in order to get me off his hands."

As Alexandria explained the day-by-day proceedings, Charlotte never took her eyes off her sister, even during the many times she coughed uncontrollably. Alexandria didn't hold back from telling her sister about Julian's doubts—that he thought Martin had killed his family and tried to kill him. However, she did leave out the part about thinking Martin was slowly poisoning his wife.

"Oh my," Charlotte whispered as she covered her mouth. She coughed again, but it wasn't as bad as before. "Why didn't you tell me before now? I might have been able to help."

"I couldn't tell you. Grey...um, Julian—or actually, His Grace—didn't want me to say anything. The only reason I am saying something now is that it is all in the open. Your husband knows his cousin is alive, as well as the guests at his dinner party." Alexandria's tears returned as her heart ached.

"Xandria, dear...you still have not told me why you're crying."

"I thought he loved me," she confessed brokenly. "But he certainly didn't act like it a few minutes ago. I thought he felt the same as I did. I was so very wrong."

"Shh," Charlotte hushed her. "I'm sure he will do the right thing."

Blinking, Alexandria again wiped tears from her eyes. "What do you mean?"

"He has ruined your good name. It is his duty to marry you now."

Duty? Although Alexandria had thought of what it'd be like to be his wife, she didn't want him to marry her because he *had* to. "Oh, no, Charlotte. I couldn't marry him like that."

Charlotte shook her head. "You don't have a choice. You were caught alone with him in an intimate embrace. You must marry him."

"But what if he doesn't ask for my hand?"

A small smile touched Charlotte's face. "I'm sure he will. He seems like an honorable man."

"What about those things Lord Senwick said?"

Charlotte coughed hard again and placed her handkerchief to her mouth this time. Once the coughs subsided, she took a deep breath and exhaled slowly. "Give His Grace time to explain. Men don't express their feelings as easily as women." She leaned back into her pillows. "My worry is what he is going to do about us."

"What do you mean?"

"Well, we are living in his home now."

Alexandria couldn't believe she hadn't thought of that. "You are correct, dear sister. But I'm certain he won't throw us out."

"He will if he still believes Martin has something to do with his family being killed."

Deep sadness encased Alexandria, making her want to cry all over again. "True. However, I shan't allow him to move you until you feel better. He knows you are ill, so I believe I can convince him to keep you here until you have recovered."

"I hope he listens to you," Charlotte said weakly. "I'm not in any condition to move."

Alexandria touched her sister's hand. "I'll make certain you stay here until you are fully recovered...even if I have to fight him."

A lazy smile lifted the corners of Charlotte's mouth. "You are too sweet, my darling sister. What would I do without you?"

"Not to worry." Alexandria gently squeezed her sister's fingers. "You shall never find out."

ALEXANDRIA STAYED IN her room for two days straight, too afraid to confront Julian. What upset her most was not that she had fallen in love with a man who wasn't real or that he had yet to explain himself or offer marriage, but that she had turned back into a little mouse. She'd quite enjoyed her new role as a woman who stood up for herself and didn't allow others to take advantage of her. So why had she gone back to being a meek wallflower once more?

For two days, she had cried out all her tears. She had no creative energy to write, either, and to her, that was unthinkable. Now she was determined to get out of bed and confront her future.

If she had one at all.

She moved to her desk and sat. Writing stories had been in her blood since she was a young girl, but as she stared at the blank pages, she couldn't conjure up any words to finish writing her story.

She scowled. *Thanks for ruining me, Grey!*

Charlotte had always been around to talk with, but since she was sick, Alexandria needed another friend. A friend who would understand what she was going through right now.

Maxey! The face of Alexandria's favorite cousin popped inside her head. Her nerves calmed slightly as she thought of the cousin who was one year younger. As children, they were inseparable. Then Maxey's father moved the family to Wales. Alexandria had been so lonely that she thought she would die. That was when Charlotte became her best friend and confidante.

Words swirled in Alexandria's head. She picked up the quill and dipped it into the ink to begin her letter.

Dear Maxey,

So much has happened, and I wish you were closer so that we could talk in person. I miss those days with all my heart. I hope things are well with you and your father in Wales. If I could, I would find a conveyance and head to that destination today.

My heart is broken. Actually, it is shattered, and I need your wisdom and love to help me repair it. Charlotte has a terrible ailment, and she sleeps most of the day. I fear the man I thought I was in love with has ruined both my mind and reputation, and I don't know how to repair the damage.

As Alexandria poured her heart out in her letter, tears filled her eyes. Maxey couldn't help. Not even her wisdom could fix Alexandria's problem. The burden weighed heavily on her shoulders, which discouraged her more.

She ended the letter and prepared it for the post. God willing, this letter would reach Maxey soon.

Alexandria pushed away from her desk and moved to the armoire to search for a dress to wear, one that would make her feel like a strong, confident woman. She frowned. Apparently, she needed to go shopping. She couldn't see one gown that would make her convincingly feel such emotions.

A knock came upon the door. She jumped and swung around, her hand flying to her bosom. Could it be Julian coming to talk to her finally? She tried to steady her breathing as she hurried to get her wrap. "Who is it?"

"I'm your new maid, Miss Templeton."

New maid? Martin had never given her a maid of her own. Then again, her brother-in-law wasn't in charge any longer.

Cautiously, she stepped to the door and opened it enough to see who was on the other side. A young woman, perhaps only a few years older than Alexandria, stood facing the door, wearing the dark brown dress with a round white collar and the matching apron of a maid's uniform. Her blonde hair was a shade lighter than Alexandria's curls.

"Good morning, Miss Templeton." The maid smiled and curtsied. "My name is Miss Johnson."

Alexandria nodded. "Good morning." She licked her dry lips. "Who hired you?"

"His Grace did, just last night. He said I was going to be your personal maid."

How thoughtful. She realized her heart was softening toward him. No, she must not forgive so quickly. At the moment, he wasn't exactly on her list of favorite people.

"It is nice to meet you, Miss Johnson. Please come in." She opened the door wider. "Do you have a first name?"

Miss Johnson nodded as she entered and closed the door behind her. "Dawn."

"What a pretty name." Alexandria realized she would finally have someone to talk with now.

"Thank you, Miss Templeton. Would you like your breakfast now? Or would you like me to assist you in dressing?"

"Actually, I would like my breakfast and then a bath, if that is all right."

"Of course, Miss Templeton." Dawn curtsied and left the room.

Alexandria walked back to her bed and sat on the edge, trying to figure out why Julian would get her a personal maid. She suspected her brother-in-law had already moved out, and thankfully, she hadn't had to fight Julian to keep her and Charlotte here, so naturally, the servants would have left with Martin.

Yes, that was probably why a new maid was assigned to her.

During the next two hours, she ate, bathed, and dressed. Dawn proved to be a very skilled lady's maid, and Alexandria was grateful to Julian for being so thoughtful. But that was the only thing she was grateful to him for.

As Alexandria sat in her chair in front of her vanity table, Dawn styled her hair. Alexandria stared at her reflection in the mirror with a frown. Although she might not have a gown or the hairstyle that made her feel confident, she needed to break out of her melancholy and continue with her life. She couldn't hide away in her bedchamber forever. It didn't matter if Julian had ruined her reputation—she must remember that he hadn't forced her to follow him into the music room. She could have stayed in the grand room with Martin and his friends. She could have resisted when Julian kissed her, too.

However, she would never forgive him for lying to her.

But that was all in the past. The deed had been done, and she needed to keep going forward as if nothing had happened. If only that were possible.

Alexandria lifted her gaze in the mirror to Dawn. The pretty woman was cheerful and friendly. Alexandria was certain they would eventually become good friends.

"Tell me, Dawn, how long have you been a lady's maid?"

"Only a few years, Miss Templeton." Dawn smiled. "I served Miss Chambers before she married the Earl of Worthen two months ago."

"Oh, yes. I have met Miss Chambers. I'm happy to hear she is married now."

"And she is very happy."

"Then I assume you have lived in this area for a while."

Dawn nodded. "North Devon has been my home."

"I'm certain you have known the duke's family or at least heard of them."

"I have heard about this family. Who in North Devon hasn't heard of Linden Hall?"

"It was tragic to hear about the duke's father and brother dying. How did the family act a few years ago? Were they well respected?"

"Indeed, it was terrible what happened to the father and his eldest son, to be sure. But I remember the duke and Lord Forbes were very sociable. Everyone liked them. They were good to their servants, and many of my friends wanted to work for them."

Perhaps Alexandria shouldn't ask, but curiosity overrode her shyness. "What about Julian Stratford? What was he like during that time?"

Dawn fidgeted as she concentrated on aligning the ringlets around Alexandria's head. For a moment, Alexandria wondered if the servant had even heard her, but then she realized Dawn had and was just avoiding the question.

"It is all right, Dawn. You can tell me. I'm not one to spread gossip. At this point, I'm not very fond of the new duke, anyway. Whatever you tell me will be helpful, I assure you."

Dawn smiled bashfully. "Well, to be perfectly honest, Lord Julian didn't have the best reputation. He was quite a scoundrel in his younger years."

Alexandria couldn't stop her heart from crumbling even more. She would bet money that he had lied to those women, as well. "That is the rumor I have heard, too." She sighed. "Do you know anything about the woman he was betrothed to?"

"All I know is that her name was Miss Theresa Dickson. Her brother is Lord Senwick."

"That is all you know?" Alexandria asked. "You don't know the particulars? After all, servants know most everything, do they not?"

Dawn giggled. "We know quite a bit of what happens in most homes. I had heard that Miss Dickson made a spectacle of herself in front of Lord Julian. Of course, what unmarried young woman wouldn't? As it were, she was obviously trying to sink her claws into him because of the family's wealth. Julian was sweet on many women, and as I mentioned, his reputation with the ladies was deplorable. Nobody knows what really happened, except for them, of course, but they were caught together in a very intimate position." She paused, leaning closer to Alexandria's ear. "And he wasn't wearing a shirt, and her gown was hanging off her shoulders."

Alexandria tried not to let the image cloud her thoughts. Although she hadn't seen him without a shirt, she had glimpsed his bare neck and a little portion of his chest…and what a fine, muscular part that was. When heat started climbing in her face, she quickly grabbed her cup of tea from the vanity and sipped. "Is that all you know?"

Dawn shook her head. "Lord Senwick tried to get Lord Julian to do the right thing and marry his sister, but not long after that scandal, Lord Julian enlisted in the military."

Interesting. Alexandria wondered why Julian didn't do the right thing. Wasn't that what gentlemen were supposed to do after compromising a lady? "Tell me, Dawn, did anyone see Miss Dickson and Lord Julian in the intimate position?"

"Let me think." Dawn scratched her ear. "If I recall the story correctly, I think that Lord Senwick was the only one who caught them."

"Then who knows how true the rumors are?"

Dawn nodded. "We all accept the rumors as fact, since there was nobody to deny them."

"Those are my thoughts, as well." Then again, if Julian had that kind of reputation, Alexandria was certain he had been caught with Theresa, just as he had been caught with her.

Would history repeat itself?

Yet, at the same time, she didn't want to force Julian into doing what he didn't want to do.

"There you are, Miss Templeton." Dawn stepped back and eyed her handiwork.

Alexandria had to admit that the maid was very skilled. It had been quite some time since she looked this nice. "I thank you, Dawn." She pushed away from the vanity and stood. "I think I shall check on my sister and see how she is faring."

"Oh, before I came to check on you, I talked to her maid. She said the duchess…um, I mean, Mrs. Hinsdale was sleeping."

"Do you know if her coughing is still really bad?"

Dawn nodded.

Alexandria's hopes dropped. "All right then, I shall go riding." She motioned to her day dress. "Would you help me change into my riding habit?"

"Certainly, miss."

Thirty minutes later, Alexandria made her way to the stable and realized the last time she had ridden Buttercup was when Julian kidnapped her. Tears stung her eyes, and she tried to blink them away. The wonderful memories would be with her forever, along with the heartache. If only she could think of this as another chapter in her book, perhaps it wouldn't seem so real.

But it was real, and the pain in her heart was unquestionable. Why had she believed him to be so sweet? Why hadn't she doubted him at all? She had right at the very beginning, but it was only because he thought she was someone else. But, truth be told, it was actually Julian who had been someone else.

She walked into the stable and noticed a groom throwing hay into one of the stalls. "Excuse me, but could you ready my horse, Buttercup?"

He stepped away, swiping the back of his gloved hand over his sweaty brow. "I'm sorry, Miss Templeton, but your horse has thrown a shoe and is out of commission for now."

She didn't dare ask what else could go wrong in her life. "Fine, I shall walk around the grounds, then. The exercise will do my legs good, I'm sure."

"Yes, Miss Templeton."

Disheartened, she left the stables, trying hard not to step on her droopy spirit as she walked toward the same path she took whenever she rode her horse. The weather was perfect, and she was grateful for that small pleasure. Not a cloud marred the sky, and only a slight wind teased her ringlets. She didn't even need a shawl.

Julian's face wouldn't leave her thoughts, no matter how hard she tried to usher out his image. They had grown so close in a short time, and it would be difficult to forget about him completely. Yet what was she going to do about the scandal? Did she even have a choice? She had lived most of her life as a wallflower, and had been satisfied continuing on that path, except now that she had experienced a man's hungry, wild kisses, she wanted more.

The question was…could she ever let another man into her heart? For certain, she would not trust him right away for fear he would lie to her and eventually break her heart. The pain was too grueling to bear.

"Alexandria, stop!"

A familiar voice rang through the air, pulling her from her thoughts. She stiffened and closed her eyes, groaning. What was *he* doing out here?

She didn't want to see him. What were her chances of running away from him…and his letting her go?

Slim to none, she was sure.

CHAPTER NINETEEN

ALEXANDRIA STOOD FROZEN as she watched Julian come toward her. Why couldn't she run from him? Yet she knew the answer. His injured leg wouldn't allow him to run. As much as she was upset at him, she couldn't be the reason he damaged his leg again.

"Alexandria," Julian said, breathless, catching up to her. "I'm glad I caught you before you could get too far."

"Why?" Worry quickly escalated inside of her. "Is something wrong with my sister?"

"Not that I was told about—however, I cannot allow you to go for a walk by yourself."

Anger ignited inside her. "And why not? Has it slipped your mind that I have done this several times already, and I have been just fine before? Have you forgotten that I'm a wallflower and I'm invisible to most people?"

He released an exhausted breath. "It has not slipped my mind, Alexandria. I don't want you to go alone because I fear for your safety. We still haven't found any evidence against Martin, and that man could still want me dead, and in doing so, he could harm you." He shook his head. "I promised you once, and it still stands until my dying breath. That man will *not* harm you."

For a moment, she wondered if he was telling the truth about being in danger. Could all of this with Martin have been in

Julian's imagination? Perhaps he had gone insane and conjured everything up. It was certainly easier to believe.

But then she remembered his father and brother had died of a questionable malady, and Julian had been injured. And her sister was very ill. Although there was no evidence, Martin was still a suspect.

She sighed heavily. "Forgive me, Your Grace. I had forgotten." She turned and walked past him, going toward the manor.

"Hold up, Lexie." He grasped her arm, stopping her. "I think I've left you alone for too long. Now it is time to talk."

She stared into his glorious green eyes, feeling herself falling for him all over again. Shaking off the feeling spreading over her, she pulled her attention away and looked at the ground. "If you that is your command, then I shall do as you require, Your Grace."

He reached out and lifted her chin with his fingers until she met his eyes once more.

"Lexie, don't look down. I miss you peering into my eyes. I miss a lot of things about you. And I would love for you to call me Julian. Won't you please talk to me?"

Tears burned her eyes, and she quickly blinked them away. She couldn't cry in front of him again. "Yes, I think we should talk. However, I might not immediately trust what you say. I've already learned my lesson with trusting someone so easily."

"I didn't want to hurt you. I still don't want that to happen."

"I fear it is too late. My heart has already been injured."

He caressed her cheek. "Is there not any room in your heart to forgive me?"

"Why should I? After all, I believed every word you said. Every word!"

Closing his eyes, Julian dropped his hand back to his side. She could see her words upset him, but right now, she didn't care. Part of her wanted him to feel as much pain as he had inflicted upon her. How could she explain that trust was ruined when someone they thought they loved lied to them?

"Lexie, why are you doing this?" he muttered.

"Doing what?"

"Making things so difficult?"

"Difficult for whom? You are not any different from the way you used to be, so I've heard. However, I'm the one who has the problem, not you. You were someone I had created in my mind—a larger-than-life hero, if you will. You were a man who could do no wrong, who I thought was being truthful to me. You were the first man to kiss me and make me feel a woman's desires. It is no wonder I pictured you as a knight in shining armor in the fiction books I have read. But the other night in the music room, my dreams vanished. I'm no longer living in the fictitious world I created. I'm living in a very painful reality."

By his changing expression and the sadness encasing his face, she knew her words had injured him. Strange, but she didn't feel victorious at all in the discovery. In fact, her heart ached even more.

She waited for him to say something, but when he remained silent for several awkward minutes, she walked past him, intent on reaching the manor and its sheltering shadows. This time, he didn't stop her. He followed but didn't say a word.

The silence was deafening.

JULIAN DRUMMED HIS fingers on the desktop as he stared out the window. His servants had cleaned out many of the rooms in the last three days, and he was grateful for their speedy assistance. He didn't want to have anything of Martin's in his home. Yet two things still remained…Charlotte and Alexandria.

Sighing, he leaned his head into his hand and rubbed his forehead. He had heard that Charlotte was on the mend from her maid, even if her coughs echoed in that section of the wing. Some days she was strong and walking around her chambers, and other days she was as weak as a newborn lamb. He wished he knew how to get her healthy and keep her that way. Then again, if her husband had been secretly poisoning her, perhaps it was best for Charlotte to remain under Julian's protection.

Until he and Vincent found evidence against Martin, they were all in danger. Vincent had assured Julian that he would continue to watch Martin, and the earl even hired several detectives to constantly spy on Martin. Yet it had been three days since Julian kicked his cousin out of the manor—three very long and agonizing days—and still, nothing had been discovered.

What made matters worse was seeing Alexandria and knowing that he had damaged her spirits so severely that she wouldn't even look at him. When she did peer his way, she quickly looked in the opposite direction. He wanted to see her smile, hear her laugh, and especially gaze at him with her lovely sapphire eyes. Every time he saw that color, he immediately thought of her.

Another thing that weighed heavily on his heart was the fact that he'd sullied her name and hadn't done anything to repair it. Of course, he had been busy completing the legalities so he could officially become the Duke of Linden, but he realized he couldn't keep putting this off. He needed to do something soon. Really, there was only one choice to make.

Marry her.

Although the idea of marriage had always made him run the other way, for some reason when he thought about it now, he wasn't frightened. In fact, deep inside his heart, he looked forward to making Lexie fall in love with him again.

Decision made, he pushed away from the desk and left the study. The first servant he saw, Julian asked, "Pardon me, but have you seen Miss Templeton?"

"Yes, Your Grace." The man bowed. "She is in the library."

Julian headed for Alexandria's favorite room, and with each step, excitement built inside him. He should calm his enthusiasm a little because he was certain she would be hesitant about the marriage. She wasn't going to suddenly change her attitude and love him again.

Although she'd never said those three little words to him, he could tell she held strong emotions for him. Her lovely eyes stared at him with such admiration, and the way she responded to his kisses…

Tingles crept over his body as he recalled how he had felt during those times. He couldn't wait to feel that way again.

He took great care to ease the library door open and peek within. Alexandria sat on a sofa with her feet tucked under her, reading a book. She twirled a loose curl about her finger as she lost herself in the story. The emotions that played across her face as she read failed to hide how deeply engrossed in the story she had become. She didn't hear him enter. Julian didn't want to scare her, but he couldn't stare at her for very long without wanting to take her in his arms.

He softly cleared his throat, startling her. She nearly dropped her book.

"Forgive me for disturbing you, but I needed to talk to you about an important matter."

Nodding, she sat up straight and moved her feet to the floor, discreetly slipping them into the slippers beside the sofa. "That is fine." She placed the book by her side before smoothing the wrinkles out of her skirt.

"May I?" He pointed to the space next to her.

"But of course, Your Grace. This is your library, after all."

Inwardly, he fumed. Would he ever hear her say his given name? Whenever she had said it before, it was like angels singing. Within time, he knew he could soften her. He must have patience.

He sat and turned toward her. Her body remained stiff as she looked straight ahead.

"Lexie, I want to tell you how sorry I've been for my busy schedule of late. I've been meaning to have this talk with you for a few days, but other things kept getting in the way."

She glanced at him and nodded. "I understand."

"I want to talk about what happened the night in the music room."

Her attention snapped to him. "I thought we had already discussed this."

"Not completely, no."

"What else did you want to add? I thought we had already expressed our feelings."

"Actually, we hadn't. Only *you* had." He reached over and took her hand. She tried to pull it away, but he wouldn't let her. "Now, if you don't mind, I would like the chance to express mine." She arched an eyebrow, so he quickly continued before she could interrupt him. "But know this—it doesn't matter if you do mind. I'm going to have my say."

"Fine." She sighed in defeat.

Taking a deep breath, he tried to calm his jittery nerves. He wasn't used to conveying his thoughts to women, but he felt the urge to do so with this particular woman. "When I first kidnapped you, I didn't think I could trust you, so naturally, I wasn't about to tell you my real name. Remember that one time when you nearly guessed my identity? I almost confessed, but then I realized I still couldn't tell you because I worried that Martin would discover I was alive and do something awful to you for helping me." He waited for her to say something, but she remained silent, looking at him with inexpressive eyes. "Anyway, I want you to know how much you mean to me. You are unlike any woman I have ever met. You make me smile more and laugh, which was something I hadn't done for a long time." He stroked her knuckles with the tip of his thumb. "The past few days, I've realized I want you by my side. Always. I want to marry you, Alexandria Templeton."

He studied her expression, but she remained blank. For a moment, he thought her eyes would water over, but she rapidly blinked, and the liquid was gone. Little by little, his heart broke. He tried reasoning in his head. She was still hurting, which was why she acted in such a way. Perhaps he should take it one day at a time with this amazing woman. He wanted their relationship to return to how it had been before they were caught in the music room.

Determination surged through him. He *would* change her mind and make her fall in love with him.

Of course, right now, he needed to get her to marry him.

"I thank you for your offer, Your Grace. Because of the scandal that happened, I will accept. My sister will be relieved to know you have stepped up to do the right thing."

No! He didn't want her to think he offered marriage because of the scandal. Yet she wasn't going to believe him. Not yet.

Nonetheless, he would start to soften her heart after they were married. One way or another, he would get her to say, *I love you.* And hopefully, by then, he would be able to say the words to her as well…and mean them.

CHAPTER TWENTY

ALEXANDRIA KNEW THE wedding wasn't going to be large and extravagant, only because they needed a quick ceremony to help drown out the rumors that were already in an uproar. But why couldn't she be a little more excited about it?

She was actually going to marry a duke—and a handsome one at that. Not many ladies could say they had accomplished such a dream. She should be happy, ecstatic, and so nervous she could hardly concentrate. But she wasn't. Less than a month ago, she had no inkling of even wanting to marry, much less a man with such a grand title, and now she would soon be the Duchess of Linden.

Her sister couldn't assist in planning the wedding. Some days Charlotte felt good, but most days, she didn't. Alexandria wondered why her sister hadn't overcome her malady. With Martin out of the manor, wouldn't Charlotte start feeling better as each day passed? Alexandria prayed her sister wasn't worse than everyone had first thought.

The maid and the housekeeper helped Alexandria plan the wedding. Julian had told her that he wanted her to wear the most beautiful wedding gown, and he hired a seamstress to have it made quickly. A small part of Alexandria jumped with excitement, knowing she was getting something so lovely, yet at the same time, she squashed any hopes of being truly happy with him because she couldn't trust him.

They would be married, but in name only. She didn't plan on giving herself to him on their wedding night, or any other night, for that matter. He had to prove to her that he had changed, and right now, she wondered if he could ever accomplish that.

After the seamstress left, Alexandria finally had some time to herself. She wandered outside to partake of the fresh air. It wasn't fair that Julian wouldn't allow her to ride Buttercup, but she supposed he was right to worry about Martin. Julian had mentioned the other day that Lord Trenton still had people looking into the case, but no evidence had been found against her brother-in-law.

She walked to the edge of the curved drive. Neatly trimmed bushes edged the drive, complemented by the beauty of the colorful flowers. The scent surrounding her calmed her greatly. Closing her eyes, she breathed in the heavenly aroma.

From up the road, the clip-clop of horses' hooves startled her, and she spun around. A woman approached, perched regally on her horse. Her haughty demeanor suggested everyone should bow to her. As the lady neared, Alexandria could see she was quite lovely. Dark brown hair escaped her bonnet and bounced about her head in rhythm with the horse's trot. She wore a maroon riding habit with a white blouse. When she reached Alexandria, she stopped.

"Good day," Alexandria greeted her, and curtsied.

"Good day to you. I'm looking for Miss Templeton. Can you get her for me?"

"I'm Miss Templeton."

"Splendid." The woman motioned for one of the groomsmen to come and assist her with dismounting. Once she was off the animal, she strolled closer to Alexandria with her nose lifted haughtily in the air. "I was told you were engaged to Lord Julian...um, I mean the Duke of Linden."

"You heard correctly."

"When is the wedding, may I ask?"

Alexandria instantly disliked the lady's attitude. "In a few days. Why do you inquire about the date?"

With a sigh, the lady presented a pitiful frown. "When I heard that Lord Julian—er, His Grace, was engaged again, I thought it was my duty to come and talk to you to prepare you for heartbreak."

Curious, Alexandria took a step closer. "Go on."

"Let me first introduce myself. My name is Miss Theresa Dickson. My brother is Lord Senwick, whom I was told you have already met."

Immediately, Alexandria stiffened, and her heart broke all over again. She had heard a few rumors, but to actually confront the woman involved in the scandal was something she thought would never happen. "I have heard of you."

"Splendid." Theresa smiled. "Then I assume you know that Julian and I were once engaged, but he broke off the engagement at the last minute."

Alexandria nodded. "Yes, I heard."

Theresa smirked and arched an eyebrow. "Allow me, if you will, to clear up the rumors going around." She folded her arms. "A week before we were to marry, he realized he didn't want the responsibility of becoming a husband, so he broke off the engagement and joined the military. He begged me to call off the wedding plans first so my reputation wouldn't be ruined, but I refused. I was in love with him, and I wanted him to be my husband. Because I wouldn't call it off, he did, which I'm sure you know. Indeed, he ruined me for other marriage offers." She breathed deeply and frowned. "Men see me as someone who wasn't good enough to marry a duke's son. Because of Lord Julian, I will forever be a spinster."

Alexandria swallowed hard. "I thank you for bringing this to my attention, Miss Dickson."

The pitiful expression returned to Theresa's face, and she touched Alexandria's arm. "I came to see you because I wanted to prepare you for what might happen. His Grace has no feelings because he has no heart. Believe me when I tell you I'm not the first woman who has had her reputation destroyed."

"Yes, I have heard that tittle-tattle as well," Alexandria said in a tight voice. "Again, I thank you for informing me of his true character. However, I cannot back out of the marriage. As I'm sure you have heard by now, he and I were caught in an improper embrace, and my family insists I marry him."

"I understand, but just know he may find some excuse to back out. Whatever you do, keep your heart from getting involved. Upon my word, it will only cause a lifetime of misery."

Too late for that. Alexandria wanted to cry again, but she held on to her courage. "I shall heed your wisdom, Miss Dickson."

"That is all I ask." Theresa turned to the stable hand, and he assisted her on top of her horse.

"Have a pleasant day," Alexandria called as Theresa rode off.

Anger burned inside of her. Would Julian do the same thing to her? For some odd reason, she didn't think so. After all, he was now a duke. He had an obligation to fulfill because of his title, and marriage and having heirs came with that.

However, the doubt still hung inside her for the days that followed. Would he marry her or turn and run away?

THE MORNING OF the wedding, Alexandria was a bucket of nerves. She couldn't get Theresa out of her mind.

As her sister sat in the cushioned chair issuing instructions, several maids rushed around Alexandria's room, trying to ready her for the ceremony. Dawn styled Alexandria's hair differently this time. Instead of ringlets, she coiled Alexandria's hair in sections, so it piled higher on her head. The veil was a simple azure jeweled tiara attached to the white lace cascading down her back. White baby's-breath flowers were stuffed in the bun, making her appearance angelic.

When she finally slipped into the gown, she nearly lost her breath. Never in her wildest imagination would she have put together such an elegant creation. She doubted a princess would have owned a garment so lovely. The white satin gown had an overdress in striped gauze and trimmed with Brussels lace. White pearls were sewn into the bodice, the sleeves that hung off her shoulders, and the ruffled border of the dress, giving the gown a touch of elegance. The garment fit her body perfectly. As she stared at herself in the full-length mirror, she couldn't believe that the image staring back was her, Alexandria Templeton, the wallflower.

Self-conscious about showing so much of her shoulders and bosom, she tugged on the sleeves to lift them higher, but Dawn gently tapped her hands on Alexandria's knuckles and shook her head.

"Miss Templeton, don't be so modest. You are so incredibly lovely in that dress. It would be a shame to cover anything up."

Part of Alexandria couldn't wait for Julian to see her, and yet the other part of her was scared of watching his reaction. She remembered the look in his eyes when he kissed her passionately, and especially when he desired her. Seeing his green eyes turn darker was her weakness. She wouldn't be able to refuse him for anything.

For finishing touches, she slipped on elbow-length white gloves and then picked up the bouquet of lavender roses mixed with freshly cut pink lilies lying on her vanity.

The maids stood back and gazed upon Alexandria, wearing satisfied smiles. Charlotte slowly maneuvered from her chair and weakly walked to her. She had donned one of her lovelier powder-blue gowns with long sleeves but wore a white shawl around her shoulders and arms.

Charlotte patted Alexandria's cheek. "You are very beautiful, my dear sister. Our parents would have been so proud."

Tears formed in Alexandria's eyes, and she nodded. "I wish they were here."

"As do I." Charlotte looked at Dawn. "Please help me downstairs. We are ready to begin."

Alexandria walked behind her sister, and the maids slowly followed down the stairs. Her limbs shook, and her heart knocked crazily against her ribs. Breathing slower, she tried to steady her nerves, but it was no use. She had never been more anxious than she was at this moment.

It shall be over soon. But not soon enough, unfortunately.

She waited in the hall just outside the ballroom until it was her turn to enter. She clutched the bouquet harder, and her palms grew moist inside the gloves, yet her body was cold.

Finally, Dawn motioned for Alexandria to enter. She wouldn't be surprised if she swooned at any moment. Her legs were going to collapse beneath her, she just knew it.

As she looked about the room at the few guests, one person stood out more than the others. Julian was placed right by the clergyman, and his intense gaze was directly on her. *Oh dear...* Just as she figured, the way he looked at her made her weak in the worst way. It was as though his eyes devoured every part of her.

His appearance took her breath away. Never in her wildest dreams would she have imagined it possible for him to become *more* alluring, but he had. He wore a white waistcoat with a blue double-breasted coat with a velvet collar and black cashmere trousers. His fine-striped cravat was fixed perfectly around his throat, and the black top hat made him as regal as a prince.

The closer she walked toward Julian, the harder it became for her to breathe. Her vision narrowed, and she couldn't see anyone but him. The tender expression on his face as he reached his hand out to her calmed her fears, especially when she slipped her palm against his. Warmth spread through her, and she was more peaceful than she had ever felt before.

As the clergyman read from the Book of Common Prayer, Alexandria didn't hear a word he was saying. All that she heard was her own crazy heartbeat and her irregular breaths. Julian stared at her the whole time, as well. As each second passed, his expression became more tender, and soon desire shone in his eyes. Heavens, she hoped she didn't look at him the same way, even though she felt it.

To have and to hold from this day forward…

She finally heard the clergyman's words, and she pondered them briefly. *From this day forward.* She would have Julian from this day forward. Her heart flipped. If only she could start to trust him again.

Therefore, I plight thee my troth.

Julian nodded. "I will."

When it came time for her to repeat the words, she gently cleared her throat. "I will."

Then it struck her. She had just pledged to be completely loyal and faithful to her husband and the marriage contract. And of course she would. Was there any doubt?

And yet she didn't think Julian could do the same.

CHAPTER TWENTY-ONE

ALEXANDRIA TRIED TO focus on the clergyman and what he was saying, but nothing registered in her mind. Whatever he said made Julian grin and take her hand, pulling her closer. Panic gripped her chest, making it difficult to breathe. Was she really expected to kiss him in front of these people? Why hadn't she thought of this before now?

She swallowed hard and licked her suddenly dry lips. Holding her breath, she waited until Julian took her into his arms and placed his mouth over hers. She kept herself stiff, not wanting him to know that tingles ran amuck through her body, and several times she felt her legs grow weak.

Cursing the effect he had over her body, she vowed he would not be in control any longer. She could harden her heart and command her body to behave. She couldn't have these swoon-attacks happening. And right now, she was *not* going to show him how much she enjoyed the moment. Thankfully, the kiss didn't take long, and he withdrew first.

Exhaling slowly, she turned to greet the guests as they wandered up one at a time. Charlotte stayed in her chair with tears in her eyes and a smile stretching across her face. Alexandria waited until everyone had congratulated her before going over and hugging her sister.

"I'm so proud of you," Charlotte said.

It made Alexandria's heart soften that they were both finally married. However, she worried that Charlotte's husband was still a murder suspect.

Everyone congregated in the dining room, where Julian had arranged to have a large meal prepared. He pulled out a chair for Alexandria at one end of the table, and she sat, then he moved to the other end of the table to take his rightful place as lord of the manor.

As everyone else sat, she searched for Charlotte but couldn't see her. When she saw the butler, she stopped him. "Excuse me, Mr. Higley, but have you seen my sister?"

"Mrs. Hinsdale is up in her room, Your Grace. She was not feeling well."

Alexandria's heart dropped. Her sister was still not well. And yet a different emotion grew inside of her. The butler had called her *Your Grace*. It did sound rather nice, but certainly a change, since not even a week ago, people were calling her sister by that title.

"I thank you, Mr. Higley."

"You are very welcome, Your Grace."

She tried not to grin as he walked away. She could definitely become used to hearing that. Too bad she couldn't bring herself to forgive Julian. They might actually make a happy couple.

If only she could truly believe that.

JULIAN PACED BACK and forth in the hall, waiting until the right moment to enter his bedchamber, which was now occupied by his wife.

He hadn't asked her to sleep in his room, but in his mind, there was no way around it. His wife *would* occupy his room alongside him. Julian had instructed her lady's maid to move Lexie's things into his chambers. Since he hadn't heard any argument from his wife, he wondered if he would hear her objections when they were alone. After all, he didn't ask what she thought, just assumed she would know he wanted their relationship to be very intimate for now and always.

Now and always...

He still couldn't believe he had finally married. She was a beautiful bride, to be sure. Tonight would be full of adventure, that was certain, only because he still didn't know how she was going to act lying next to him all night.

Excitement shot through him, and he couldn't believe how nervous he was. All evening he had worried she would refuse his husbandly rights. He had never been a forceful man, and he wouldn't start now. If she told him no, he would stop.

Off and on throughout the evening, he caught her staring at him with a gleam in her eyes, but she quickly withdrew her attention before he could really study her. Although the kiss they'd shared in front of their guests at the conclusion of the ceremony wasn't as heated as he hoped it would be, she still participated. Unfortunately, when he tried to slip his arm around her throughout the evening, she acted as if she was repulsed by his touch.

Tonight would be different. He would be tender with her and show her how loving and understanding a husband could be. However, he wouldn't understand if she told him no. This was their wedding night. Would she be so cold-hearted on such a special occasion?

Finally, the door opened, and out walked the lady's maid. She curtsied. "Your wife is ready for you now, Your Grace."

"I thank you, Johnson. You may retire for the rest of the evening."

"Yes, Your Grace." She curtsied again and hurried down the hall.

Gearing himself for what was to come—whether good or bad—he entered. The lamps were low, and a few candles were lit near the bed. In the shadows, he could see the lump in the blankets, but he couldn't quite see his wife.

He walked closer to the large bed that had been in his family for years. An overmantel framed the top of the bed, with blue velvet curtains draped on each corner and sheer white curtains hanging in between. A sweet smell lingered in the air. He closed his eyes and breathed deeply. Lilacs. Alexandria's scent had been permanently marked in his memory.

He parted the sheer curtain nearest to him. Alexandria lay in bed with two pillows stuffed behind her, propping her up slightly. Glorious waves of blonde hair cascaded over her shoulders, and his fingers itched to stroke her silky locks. The white gown she wore ruffled in the mid-arm sleeves and was tied with a pink ribbon above each elbow. The wide neck had thin lace bordering the bodice, and a pink ribbon weaved in and out along the edge.

Gazing upon such beauty took his breath away. Urgency surged through him, and he couldn't wait to take her in his arms and make her his wife in the Biblical sense.

But when he looked upon her pale face and wide eyes, he paused. She was frightened. Of course she was. She had probably heard horror stories of how husbands had no concern for the woman's sensibilities. Although he couldn't wait to make her his, he wasn't about to hurt her in any way.

He had already hurt her enough.

"You're so beautiful," he said softly.

"Th-thank you."

He grinned. "There is nothing to be afraid of, my dear. I assure you, I am a gentle man."

She nodded as her gaze dropped to the blanket she clutched around her bosom.

He moved closer and sat on the edge of the bed. Cautiously, he stroked one of her hands. "And I thank you for joining me in my room this evening."

"Was it not required of me?"

"It's expected, yes, but I have many friends who've married, and their wives did not join them on their wedding night."

"I didn't know I had a choice."

He chuckled. "You did, actually."

She stared at him for a few moments in silence. "Then can I change my mind?"

His laughter grew as he shook his head. "Indeed, you can always say no, but I pray you do not."

He lifted his hand higher and stroked her cheek. She inhaled sharply but didn't pull away, thankfully.

"I…I suppose I can try," she whispered.

"That's all I ask." He leaned over and kissed her forehead before pulling away and standing. "I'm going to undress now."

She gasped and closed her eyes. Julian held in a laugh as he moved to the other side of the room. With the low lighting, he doubted she would be able to see him in the shadows. Then again, she was probably the kind of woman who didn't peek.

He stripped off his clothes and hesitated in going to her wearing nothing at all. Although he didn't usually wear nightshirts to bed, perhaps he should just this time so as not to frighten Alexandria.

He located a nightshirt and slipped it on before returning to bed. Her eyes were still closed, but he knew she wasn't asleep. She was still too stiff for any kind of rest. He climbed in between the sheets and scooted next to her. Lying on his side, he propped himself on his elbow and looked upon her again. As before, her beauty made it hard for him to breathe.

"You can open your eyes now," he told her.

Her lashes flickered as she looked at him. Immediately, her focus dropped to his chest, and she sighed, her shoulders relaxing. He held back a laugh. Apparently, she had expected him to be naked.

Gradually, her attention came to his eyes. Her throat jumped.

"See, my blossom. There is nothing to fear."

One side of her mouth rose. "Not yet."

"Not from me. Not ever." He cupped the side of her face. "I know I have hurt you, but it was unintentional. Please, Lexie, I want you to forgive me. I *need* you to forgive me for not being honest with you."

He studied her sad expression. She kept silent for a few moments, but at least she wasn't arguing with him. That was good.

"Lexie, I need you to believe in me again. I'll do anything to bring back the bright smile to your lovely face. I would give anything to see that happy twinkle in your eyes when you look at me."

She licked her lips. "Your Grace, I shall try to forget all that has happened and see you as a new person."

"That is all I ask. Because I assure you, I'm not the man you heard rumors about."

She nodded but didn't say anything.

He leaned closer and brushed his lips across her cheek, inhaling her sweet scent. Scooting closer, he slid his hand around her head, holding her next to his face as he moved his mouth down her neck. She shivered, but she had yet to push him away.

Encouraged, he continued his seduction, wondering how far she would let him go.

CHAPTER TWENTY-TWO

WARMTH SPREAD THROUGH Alexandria faster than she had expected. Yet this man had always made her heart beat quickly and left her gasping for breath. He knew how to numb her mind until all she could think about was him. Julian's mouth traveled down her neck, proving that he hadn't lost his touch and that her body couldn't forget the thrills of excitement that shot through her every time he did this.

Her body cried, wanting to experience his tender and sweet ministrations, but her mind argued. Not more than a couple of minutes ago, she had told him she would *try* to forget. So, why had it taken her so little effort to completely forget?

Unfortunately, no matter how hard she tried, her mind couldn't convince her body to stop melting in his arms. Her mind shouted at her to push him away, but all she could do was grasp the blankets around her bosom and enjoy. She wanted to tell him to stop, but it was as though her mouth didn't want to speak the words.

"Oh, Lexie," he groaned, pulling her fully into his arms as his mouth connected with hers.

Her heart hammered wildly. No, she must stop this. Panic grew inside of her. "Please, Your Grace—"

"No, my Lexie. Call me Julian. I beg you," he muttered against her lips. "I want to hear your sweet voice say my name…my real name."

She couldn't help it. Her heart soared. "Julian," she sighed, loving the way his name sounded.

He must have enjoyed it as well, because his kiss turned more eager, as though he wanted to please her. This man didn't have to work very hard at pleasuring her because he always seemed so flawless.

Hesitantly, she slid her hands up to his neck, and she found it strange that she quite liked touching him. But as her palms encountered his taut muscles, she was delighted for not having the strength to cease her actions. When she hooked her hands around his neck, he pushed her back on the bed, lying half on top of her. Breast to breast, mouth to mouth, heart to heart.

Her mind softened. She mentally fought it just as she had been fighting these feelings so far, and yet nothing had worked. Obviously, her mind was not in control, and her body was going to get what she had been longing for since she first met this man. His kisses were too tender, and the way he caressed her arms and back thrilled her beyond words.

Alexandria was lost in a dream…a dream she never wanted to end. She finally succumbed to his lovemaking. She needed to relax and enjoy every minute, every kiss, and every stroke of this man's sensual touch. He would take her to paradise and back if she let him.

"Oh, Lexie." He broke the kiss long enough to gaze into her eyes. "I feel as though I'm the luckiest man alive. And I promise you, I shall prove to you that I'm a different man. More than anything, I want you to love me."

Love him? He really wanted her to love him? Her heart skipped, and she was ready to tell him yes, but then a woman's face appeared in her head. Through the blissful haze in her mind, she recalled the visit from Theresa and what terrible things she'd said about Julian. She had assured Alexandria that Julian would never change.

"Julian," she said softly, "more than anything, I want you to be a different man. You cannot possibly be the type of man Miss Dickson warned me about."

He choked on his breath and blinked several times. "You spoke to Miss Theresa Dickson?"

"Yes."

"When?" His voice grew edgy.

"A few days ago, she came to visit me here at the estate."

His expression turned hard. He withdrew his comforting touch and lifted off her, sitting straight on the bed. Grumbling, he pushed his fingers through his hair.

"Julian? What's amiss?" she asked, afraid to move.

"Why did you not tell me this before now?"

He wouldn't look at her. Her first instinct was to cower and apologize, but then she remembered that she had nothing to apologize for. Julian was the one who hadn't told her about his life in the first place.

"At the time, I did not think it was important," she replied briskly.

He turned his head and peered at her through angry eyes. "Why not, pray tell? You had heard the rumors."

"I had, but then I heard it from the lady herself."

"Lexie, Theresa is *no* lady."

"No?" Alexandria tilted her head. "I thought she was related to a noble."

"She is, but I assure you, that woman is not a lady."

"Regardless," Alexandria muttered, "I don't understand why this news is upsetting you now."

"Because you brought up this subject while I was trying to make love to you."

Although the feelings he had instilled inside her were still fresh, the mood had been ruined, and her mind finally started working properly. "I agree that this was not the best place to bring up one of your lovers, and because I have destroyed our moment of passion, perhaps it is time for me to tell you that I'm not quite ready for our joining. It is still too soon."

She quickly moved from the bed, but he grasped her arm, stopping her.

"Lexie, you cannot be serious."

"Oh, rest assured, Your Grace, I am very serious." She yanked her arm away, grabbed her wrap from the nearby chair, and hurried out of the room.

Once she reached the hall, tears burned her eyes, and she rushed down the corridor toward her room, afraid that the tears would fall freely before she could reach the shelter of her bedchamber.

THE FOLLOWING MORNING, Julian sat in the coach with his wife as they traveled toward town, but instead of feasting on her beauty, he watched out the window. When he'd first seen her coming down the porch stairs toward the vehicle this morning, she looked absolutely lovely in her light blue gown and matching bonnet. However, her expression let him know she would have an irritable mood during their journey. It hurt his heart to see her this way.

Last night's disaster had kept him awake most of the night. Disappointment washed over him as he remembered everything that had happened, and especially what hadn't happened. Yet it wasn't just feeling upset about the turn of events that kept him restless throughout the night—it was knowing that he had hurt her, and he didn't know how to repair the damage.

During the night, he tried recalling his and his elder brother's talks about women. The only thing Julian could recall Forbes telling him was that in order to earn a woman's forgiveness, a man must buy them trinkets, gowns, or women's accessories. Forbes promised that was the only way to win a woman's heart. So, first thing this morning, Julian had instructed Lexie's maid to get the duchess ready so he could take her into town for some shopping.

He hadn't seen his wife until they met at the coach. He'd tried to charm her with light banter, but she chose to ignore him.

Sighing heavily, he tapped his foot impatiently on the vehicle's floor and drummed his fingers on the seat. What else could he do to soften her heart? He wanted her forgiveness and couldn't wait another day to get it. Yet it had seemed the more he tried, the harder she pulled away.

The coach's wheel hit something large and jerked them to the side. Lexie squealed and flailed her hands for protection. Immediately, Julian reached out to her, steadying her on the seat.

"Are you all right, my dear?"

"Yes." She adjusted herself back in the corner and turned her attention out the window again.

This silence must cease before he went insane. "Are you thinking about what items you will purchase today, my blossom?"

She shook her head. "No. Was I supposed to be thinking about that?"

"Of course, my dear. Are you not excited about purchasing new clothes?"

She shrugged. "Not entirely."

"Why not, may I ask?"

"I don't think I need more clothes."

"But, my dear"—he leaned forward and touched her hand—"you are now a duchess. It's expected that you will have nicer things. Since my wife is lovelier than any other woman I've met, I would like her to have all her heart's desires."

Gradually, the corners of her mouth lifted, but not into a full smile. Still, he took that as a good sign that her heart was softening.

"I thank you for thinking I'm lovely. I assure you, I don't deserve the compliment."

He took one of her hands in his. "You, out of anyone I know, deserve the compliment. You are lovely, not only in your appearance but in your style and grace. You are one of the kindest women I know, as well."

She released a light chuckle. "Kind, Your Grace? I'm surprised you would say that after what happened last night."

"Believe it or not, your actions last night have proven how kindhearted you are. I hurt you, yet you showed me that changing your feelings toward me won't happen overnight. You tolerated me for a little while last night. That quality makes for a wonderful woman with a tender heart."

She nodded but didn't say anything. He wished she would talk to him about this.

They were quiet for the remainder of the ride. When they reached the town, she perched on the edge of her seat, staring out the window with wide eyes. He grinned. She appeared excited about her shopping trip even though she had said differently. Seeing the enthusiasm dancing in her eyes made his heart leap. Perhaps he'd made the right choice by bringing her here after all. With any luck, she might come into his bed tonight so he could finally make her his wife.

As soon as the coach stopped and the footman opened the door, Julian jumped down and turned to assist Lexie. She took his hand and climbed down. With her hand still in his, he hooked it over his arm as he strolled down the street. His chest burst with pride, as he felt like the luckiest man in the world to have such a lovely creature as his wife.

He ran his fingers softly over her hand. "Which shop would you like to visit first, my dear?"

"Oh, Your Grace, there are so many of them," she exclaimed cheerfully. "I couldn't possibly choose one." She tugged on his arm and looked up at him. "You pick one."

He loved seeing the giddiness on her face. "I think we should start with this shop"—he nodded to the closest one—"and continue down the street. What do you say to that suggestion?"

"Splendid idea." She beamed.

It did his heart good to see her smile. As they strolled from shop to shop, she became more talkative, and she touched him often. He wondered if she even realized she was doing that. Yet he enjoyed sharing the warmth of her body, no matter how slight it was.

Within an hour, Alexandria had returned to the woman he got to know before she discovered his identity. She laughed and appeared to thoroughly enjoy herself. When acquaintances came up to him, he introduced his new wife. He wondered how Lexie would handle things, and like a true duchess, she smiled politely and was very friendly. She was making everyone believe they were the perfect couple and that she adored her husband.

He suspected she was doing it all for show, but deep in his heart, he really wanted her love and forgiveness, as he worshipped her completely. The realization that he felt this way brought a smile to his face. Perhaps she would share these feelings in time.

They walked into a shop that made and sold bonnets. Although she studied each one, she didn't seem satisfied with the work for some reason. As she moved from one table to the next, he stood back and watched her. Strange, but she appeared to be looking for something in particular. Were all women this precise when shopping for a mere head covering?

The bell on top of the door chimed, announcing another prospective buyer. Recognition slammed Julian in the face as though a brick had hit him. Pain rushed through his head as his temper mounted. Fisting his hands, he bit the inside of his cheek to hold back the vulgar words he was ready to spout. Keeping his thoughts to himself would be hard considering what this particular woman had done. And pray, what could she have possibly said to Lexie? They were lies, to be sure.

But what bothered him most was how Lexie would react.

CHAPTER TWENTY-THREE

JULIAN HELD HIS breath when Miss Theresa Dickson met his glare. She arched a haughty eyebrow and lifted her chin, walking past him as if he wasn't even standing there. But when she headed for his wife, he had to intervene. There was no way he could allow this to happen.

Theresa stopped in front of Lexie. "Miss Templeton, it is a surprise to see you in town."

Lexie's eyes widened, and her focus jumped between him and Theresa.

"Miss Dickson, good morning," Lexie said breathlessly. "Nice to see you again."

"Pardon me, Miss Dickson," Julian interrupted, stopping beside his wife and slipping a protective and possessive arm around her waist, "but she is no longer Miss Templeton. She became Duchess of Linden yesterday, so I expect you to address her properly from now on."

Theresa's face paled slightly. "You actually…married her?"

"Indeed I did." He stroked Lexie's cheek. "And I wish I had married her sooner. Is she not lovely beyond compare?"

Bright pink highlighted Lexie's cheeks, and she rolled her eyes. "Your Grace, you are over-flattering—"

"Nonsense, my dear. I cannot stop saying endearing things about the woman I married."

"I...I..." Theresa cleared her throat before exhaling roughly. "I'm very happy for both of you, then."

"Thank you," Alexandria said. "I do believe I married a wonderful man."

Her words warmed him all over. He was certain she didn't mean them, but she would eventually. He had to make certain of it.

"Ah, my love," he whispered. "I'm only wonderful because you made me this way."

He had almost forgotten about Theresa, but when she huffed indignantly, he realized he must have really upset her this time. He didn't care. He had Lexie's attention and wouldn't trade it for all the money in the world, especially now that the twinkle in her eyes had returned. She looked at him as she had done those few days before his identity came out. This moment he would treasure always.

"Well..." Theresa cleared her throat again. "If you will excuse me, I shall leave you two alone."

He didn't know when Theresa left because he couldn't take his eyes off his wife long enough. She smiled at him, and thankfully, she didn't look away. He stroked his knuckle across her cheek, slower this time.

"I love seeing that beam in your eyes. Indeed, you will make the sun envy your radiance."

"Come now, Your Grace, you don't have to keep up the pretenses," she replied in a low voice.

"What makes you think I'm pretending?"

A blush reddened her face again. "Then perhaps I should say you must stop complimenting me so much in front of your acquaintances. I don't wish them to get the wrong impression."

He chuckled. "What if I want them to think I'm happily married to the most beautiful woman on earth?" He lifted her hand and brushed a kiss on her fingers.

Her smile widened, and she rolled her eyes. "Really, Your Grace. You can be so wicked sometimes."

She pulled away and moved to the next table. Hope grew inside him, and he prayed she would stay this way throughout the day. Perhaps tomorrow, she would have a different outlook toward him.

"Tell me, my blossom"—he moved beside her as she studied yet another bonnet—"what are you looking for, exactly?"

"If you must know, I'm making certain the bonnets don't have any straw in them." She picked one up. "See this one right here?" She pointed inside the bonnet. "There is a small amount of straw, and I don't want one with straw because it bothers my ears."

"Ah, yes. That does present a problem. Do you wish me to help you look?"

She chuckled and turned back to the table. "Not at all. I can accomplish this on my own."

Fifteen minutes later, they finally left the shop—without a new bonnet. Julian ushered her into another shop, and then another. For lunch, they dined at the best hotel in town. Julian had been here before and knew this was the place to take a woman to impress her.

Their meal consisted of fish, chicken, sweetmeats, vegetables, cheese, crackers, dry cakes, trifles, and chocolates. He enjoyed watching her eat as she tried to figure out which dish she liked the most.

By the time they were in their coach, ready to journey home, both were overstuffed with food and wine and tired from a morning of shopping. Drowsiness consumed Julian, and Lexie appeared to be having the same problem. Most of their purchases were tied to the back of the vehicle, and only a few boxes were inside with them. He used this as an excuse to sit next to her on the seat, as the packages occupied the other seat.

After they had been traveling a few minutes, she released a heavy moan. Relaxing back into the seat, she laid her head on the coach's wall. After a few seconds, she adjusted herself, looking as though she couldn't get comfortable.

"What is wrong, my dear?" he asked.

"My bonnet is bothering me."

"Then let us remove it, shall we?" He didn't wait for an answer and hastily pulled the ribbons under her chin, loosening the bonnet before removing it from her head.

She smiled and sighed. "Yes, that is much better, Your Grace."

"Lexie, we are alone. I think you can call me Julian." He turned on the seat to face her better. "I would like it better if you did, actually."

"Fine." She grinned. "Julian, I thank you for removing my bonnet and making me more comfortable."

"I shall be your servant any time you wish."

She closed her eyes and rested her head against the wall again. All he could do was stare at her, wishing he could caress her face and neck. He longed to kiss her, to resume where they had left off last night, but this time he had to be certain to continue. He wouldn't make the mistake of talking again. As long as he kept her mouth busy, her mind would be occupied as well.

Perhaps the time for talking and discussing their problems was in the daytime and *out* of the bedroom.

"Lexie?"

"Yes?" she answered without opening her eyes.

"If it is agreeable with you, I would like to discuss Miss Dickson now."

Alexandria's eyes popped open. "You would?"

"Yes. I think it's time to tell you what really happened with her."

She nodded and straightened. "I would like that very much."

Collecting his thoughts, he traced his finger along the edge of her sleeve. Her skin looked so tempting to caress, but he resisted. This was the moment to be honest with her, and he prayed she would believe him.

"Before enlisting in the military, I was an accomplished rogue."

She didn't look surprised at all. Then again, if she had heard the rumors about him, she would know this.

"Most ladies were innocent, so I avoided them at all costs."

"Then whom did you seduce?"

"Wealthy widows. They were easy prey because they were not looking for a husband to support their lifestyle."

She nodded. "Go on."

"Then there were the calculating women who wanted to sink their claws into me and turn me into marriage material."

"Like Miss Dickson?"

"Exactly like her."

"But she was innocent when you met her, correct?"

He shrugged. "So I had thought, but some of the things she said and some of her actions made me suspect she wasn't the woman she presented to society." He licked his dry lips. "I wasn't courting her. I saw her on occasions at gatherings, and she would *accidentally* run across me while I was out riding. Soon, I noticed she was purposely trying to put us in a situation where we were alone."

"She did?"

"When I finally realized what she was trying to do, I stayed far away from her. I wasn't ready to marry, especially to someone like her."

"Then how did you get caught in an intimate position?"

"One evening, I was attending a dinner party for one of my friends. I left earlier than planned, and when I walked to the stable to retrieve my horse, I heard a woman screaming. It sounded as if someone was attacking her. I first thought that a stable hand was trying to rape one of the maids." He shook his head. "When I rushed into the stall, I saw a woman whose dress had been torn from her body; she wore only a petticoat and stockings. Her hair was mussed and hanging in her face, and she was crying. But there was no man around. Out of concern, I hurried to her, hoping to discover who had attacked her. I was determined to find this man and turn him in to the magistrate."

"You didn't know it was Miss Dickson?"

"No. As I mentioned, her hair was hanging in her face. Not only that, but her hands were rubbing at her eyes."

"Oh dear. That's not good."

"I still thought her to be one of the servants. When I finally came close enough to her, she fell into me, sobbing against my chest. Of course, I was going to console this poor woman, so I put my arms around her. Just then, her brother walked inside the stable and caught us."

Alexandria remained silent for a few seconds. She tilted her head, narrowing her eyes on Julian. He waited patiently for her to say something. He prayed she would believe him, since nobody else had.

"Did you not think it was coincidental that her brother would happen by right at that precise moment?"

"I did, but he would never tell me why he was out there at that time." Julian frowned. "When Lord Senwick started making threats and telling me I must do the right thing and marry her, I knew it was wrong. I had not compromised her. Although, in a way, I had. I just happened to be there at the wrong moment and took the blame. I was determined not to marry her, no matter how it made me appear in society's eyes, and I certainly didn't give one iota about how it ruined her name."

"Do you think," Alexandria said, "that she had staged all of this? Perhaps she hadn't been attacked after all."

He nodded. "That is what I thought. You see, mere minutes after her brother caught us and demanded I marry her, her attitude changed. No longer did she appear like the victim of a near-attack. Just the opposite, in fact. She wanted to cuddle next to me, and her sweet words sounded planned. After that, I wondered if her brother was somehow in on the charade. It felt like I was being set up."

He raked his fingers through his hair, staring down at his lap as he again experienced the frustrating emotions that had altered his life five years ago. During the week after the incident, he felt like a sinking ship. He had discussed the issue with his father and brother, and thankfully, they believed him. They both decided on a course of action. If only Theresa would have called off the wedding, as he suggested, instead of letting it happen the way it had, perhaps she could have repaired her reputation. Yet she was at fault, so he shouldn't feel guilty about how her life turned out.

"Julian?"

Alexandria's heavenly voice brought him back to her, and he met her kind sapphire eyes. "Yes?"

"I believe you."

Although they weren't the exact three words he wanted to hear from her, at this moment, they were the greatest words she had ever said to him. Happiness sprang inside him, making his heart flip. He grasped her hands and pulled them to his mouth, kissing her knuckles.

"You do?"

"I do."

"Why? Only a few people believed me. Almost everyone trusted that she was telling the truth."

She smiled tenderly. "When I met her for the first time, she didn't appear as a woman with a soiled reputation. She was far too haughty for that. Miss Dickson was the one who came to see me. I, of course, happened to be on *your* estate. A broken woman wouldn't have done that."

He rested his mouth against her fingers, enjoying the warmth seeping into his body. "Tell me you understand why I didn't want to talk about it before. All these years, I was made to appear as a bad person for what I did. I knew the truth, but most people wanted to believe the worst in me because I'd been a scoundrel."

"Julian, I do understand now why you didn't tell me." Her smile faded. "Can you ever forgive me for being so critical?"

"Oh, my blossom. There is nothing to forgive." He released her hands to cradle her face. "It is I who needs to ask forgiveness. Will you ever be able to find it in your heart to forgive me?"

"Julian, I do forgive you for keeping this from me. However,

I'm still hurt that you didn't trust me enough to tell me your true identity."

He was relieved to know he had passed one obstacle with her. At least he was halfway there.

Just then, the coach slowed considerably. Mere seconds later, a crackling noise rent the air, and the coach turned sharply. Alexandria fell against Julian, but before he had time to wonder what was happening, the coach crashed to the side and they were rolling inside the vehicle.

As difficult as it was, he wrapped his arms around Alexandria and pulled her against him, trying to protect her with his body as the coach kept flipping over and over. Every time he slammed into something, pain ricocheted through him. When they fell again against his injured leg, a blast of pain speared him. He clenched his teeth to keep from screaming in agony.

Finally, the vehicle stopped. He lay on top of his wife. His head throbbed nearly as hard as his leg, and his body cried out. He breathed with difficulty, knowing he had bruised a few ribs.

"Lexie, are you all right?" he asked, trying to rise off her. When she didn't reply, panic grew inside him. "Lexie?"

He looked at the woman in his arms. The deep gash on her forehead bled profusely, and she was not moving.

His chest wrenched as a different pain rushed through him, directly to his heart. "No!" he cried out, touching her face, neck, and chest, hoping to feel some kind of heartbeat. "Lexie, you cannot die on me. I won't allow it!"

Tears formed in his eyes, but the sinking feeling of dread washed over him. Too many people he loved had been taken from him. Was she the next to go?

CHAPTER TWENTY-FOUR

D ARKNESS SURROUNDED ALEXANDRIA. It seemed she was floating on a cloud, but that didn't seem logical, since there was no way to make that happen. Yet she couldn't feel anything, so perhaps she was dead and drifting upward toward heaven. Would her parents be there to greet her at the pearly gates?

In the distance, she heard her name being called. It sounded like Julian, but his voice was too panicked, almost a tearful, pleading sound. What had happened to make him this way?

Within seconds, tingles of warmth seeped into her body, making her ache. The pain increased by the second until every part of her cried in suffering. She struggled to open her eyes because the pain and breathing made her chest ache. But she must identify whoever it was that kept encouraging her to look at him.

Good heavens, what had happened to her to make her feel this beaten and bruised? The last thing she remembered was traveling in the coach with Julian, falling and then spinning…

Moaning, she tried to turn her head but couldn't. It throbbed like nothing she had ever experienced, and a warm, sticky substance coated her hairline.

"Lexie, please don't die. I cannot go on without you." Julian's voice broke. "Please open your eyes and look at me."

Perhaps she should do what he requested, even though it

would be very difficult. His heartfelt tone was too much for her to bear. She concentrated on blinking, and although it pained her greatly, she was able to do it. Fuzzy vision coated her eyes when she finally opened them. Although she couldn't quite see him, she knew Julian's face was very near. It was then that she realized his strong arms were wrapped around her.

"Oh, my love," he whispered reverently. "You are alive. Thank the good Lord above."

She blinked again, and gradually her vision cleared. Julian's face came into view. Tears swam in his eyes, but he smiled.

"Oh, Lexie. I'm so happy..." His Adam's apple jumped as he swallowed hard. "Tell me how you feel. Are you hurting anywhere in particular?"

She didn't want to move, so it was hard to tell if there was one area worse than the others. "I—" She cleared her throat. "I don't know." She tried to concentrate. "What is this insistent pounding in my head?"

"You have a cut." He brought up a blood-spotted cloth and dabbed her head. "I've been trying to stop the bleeding."

"Is it very bad?"

"Thankfully, not anymore."

She tried to shift in his arms, but every muscle in her body screamed. She moaned and closed her eyes again. "Why do I hurt so much?"

"I'm going to touch certain places on your body to see if you have any broken bones. You tell me if the pain is unbearable."

She nodded, hoping he didn't find anything. His distress was evident as he slid his hands up and down her arms. Once in a while, his palm ran over something that hurt, but she could tell it was merely a bruise.

He administered the same examination to her legs. When he reached her right ankle, she flinched and a moan escaped her.

"Forgive me for causing you more anguish, my love."

Strange, but he had referred to her as *my love* twice now. Hearing those words caused her heartbeat to flutter in a silly way.

"I understand."

Carefully, he lifted her limb and felt the bones as he inspected her foot. "Can you move your foot like this?" He showed her, and she copied his actions. "Good. I don't believe it has been broken. You may have just a severe sprain."

She swallowed, but her throat hurt even doing that simple task. "I'm relieved to know that."

His eyebrows drew together as he moved his fingers to her ribs and poked around. It hurt, but not bad enough to inform him. He checked her neck and back before straightening and meeting her eyes again.

"Well, I'm not a physician, but I've been injured enough to know when something is broken. I believe the only serious injuries you have are your sprained ankle and the cut on your forehead." He blew out a breath. "I thought you were worse, especially when it took so long for you to respond. I had wrapped you in my arms to try to protect you as we rolled around in the coach, but when you were limp and unresponsive…" He blinked back the moisture in his eyes before kissing her cheek. "You don't know how happy I am that you're alive."

"You wrapped me in your arms?"

"I didn't want you to get hurt, though you did anyway."

Immediately, her mind pictured him cradling her in his arms. Perhaps she remembered what had happened after all. Her heart softened, and tears burned her eyes. He cared enough about her to protect her, risking his own life in the process?

A knot formed in her throat. Perhaps she had wrongly judged him all this time. She should re-examine her feelings and what she knew about him. Was he truly the same man she had fallen in love with before knowing his true identity?

"Thank you for doing that." She licked her dry lips. "I know not how to thank you."

"Let us not think of that now. We will have time later."

"Julian? What happened to us—to the coach?" She finally looked at her surroundings. They were still in the vehicle but now lying on the ceiling. The coach seats above them seemed to mock her. The contents of the boxes she had loaded in the coach after their shopping trip were scattered everywhere. The new beige shawl hung halfway out the window. Slippers she was eager to wear were crunched under Julian's legs, and a pair of lavender gloves she had purchased to match her riding habit was plastered against a portion of the roof, wet with the water that seeped through.

"I wish I knew, my dear. All I know is that the coach rolled. And because there is water inside the vehicle, I can guarantee we landed in a pond."

"Will we be able to get out?"

He nodded. "Now that I know you don't have any broken bones, I'll waste no more time."

He maneuvered to stand, balancing in the unsteady vehicle. When he grimaced and rubbed his previously injured leg, she knew something wasn't right. His jaw hardened as he slammed his shoulder against the coach's door, trying to get it open. The struggle he obviously was going through tugged at her heartstrings. He was probably in worse pain than she was.

"Julian, you are hurt." She tried to stand to assist him, but he quickly grasped her arm to keep her down.

"You need to stay still to keep your forehead from bleeding again, and I don't want you to do further damage to your ankle. I shall be fine by myself. I'll get us out of here, I promise."

She nodded, but she really didn't want to see him hurting so badly. When his face lost a little color, her stomach churned. He must be fighting intense pain, and she allowed him to do this for her, as much as she wanted to help him. Besides, how much assistance could she be with a sprained ankle and bloody forehead?

When the door finally opened and he pulled himself out, she breathed a sigh of relief. He sat on the edge of the vehicle as his legs dangled inside. She wished he would say something to let her know what kind of predicament they were in, but silence grew as he surveyed their surroundings.

Finally, she could stand no more. "Julian, where are we?"

"It appears we are at the bottom of a ravine. However, I don't see the horses or the driver."

Her heart dropped. "Oh dear. That cannot be good at all."

"And because they are missing," he continued, "that tells me the horses were not injured in the accident and they rode away, or they were unhitched from the vehicle before we went tumbling down the hillside."

Panic gripped her chest. Had she heard him correctly? "Are you saying that this accident was planned?"

He scratched his chin. "It appears that way, doesn't it?"

"Do you think Martin was behind it?"

Julian looked down at her and nodded. "That is definitely a possibility."

JULIAN GRUMBLED AND smacked his fist on the desktop. "This must stop. Now!"

It had only taken thirty minutes before they were spotted by another coach traveling that way, and the occupants had stopped to help, taking them back to his manor quickly.

He had been in his study since he and Alexandria arrived home and after the physician checked them both. Thankfully, she'd only sprained her ankle, as Julian suspected. He, however, had truly messed up his leg. According to the physician, if Julian stayed off his leg for at least a week, his limb would finally be able to heal and not give him any problems. Perhaps he should follow that advice. After all, he had not had a moment's rest since the day the cannon blast nearly took it off. But currently, he didn't have time to dally by tending to his injury the way the physician had advised. Finding the person responsible for trying to kill him and Alexandria was most important, and he could not wait another day.

Someone had planned this coach accident, right down to the missing driver and horses. Julian wondered if the driver was somehow involved. After all, Martin had hired that particular servant.

Groaning, Julian rubbed his forehead and closed his eyes. He couldn't just sit and wait for something to be done. He needed to do it himself, just to put his mind and heart at ease.

He stood and moved away from the desk. Before he made it to the door, someone knocked.

"Enter," Julian said.

The butler opened the door. "Pardon me, Your Grace, but Lord Trenton has sent a messenger with this missive." He held out the parchment. "I explained that you were not feeling well, but the messenger says it is an important matter."

Julian nodded and took the missive. "Thank you, Higley. I'll read it directly." He hobbled back to the sofa and sat, propping his injured leg on the coffee table.

As he scanned the urgent message from Vincent, excitement grew inside of him. Apparently, his friend had witnessed Martin talking to two men—their descriptions perfectly matched the blokes Alexandria had witnessed coming to the manor to speak with Martin a month or so ago. Vincent requested Julian's immediate presence at The Boar's Nest, one of the local inns. He would keep watch on the three until Julian arrived.

"Higley," Julian shouted, struggling to stand.

"Yes, Your Grace," the butler answered breathlessly, as if he had been running.

"Have my horse ready in five minutes."

"But Your Grace, your leg—"

"I don't care about my bloody leg right now. Lord Trenton needs me, and I won't let him down."

It didn't take Higley long to inform the stable hand to prepare Julian's horse. Thankfully, two stable hands helped him mount, since his leg was swollen and throbbing. He tried to will the pain in his limb away. There were more important things.

The ride into town was bearable, but he knew he would be in more pain tonight. Vincent was in front of the inn waiting for him, and assisted Julian with dismounting. The moment his foot touched the ground, he gritted his teeth against the increasing pain.

"Are they still here?" Julian asked.

"The two blokes are still here, but your cousin left about ten minutes ago."

Julian waved his hand. "That doesn't matter. I'm here to talk to those two men, not my cousin." He limped past his friend and toward the door, but Vincent stopped him again, grabbing his arm.

"Linden, you should know these men are with your driver."

Surprise shook Julian, and he gasped. "I should have known. After the coach rolled into the ravine, I discovered my driver had gone missing."

Vincent arched a thick eyebrow. "Your coach rolled? What accident are you referring to?"

Julian moved with Vincent to the side of the structure and briefly explained the accident earlier that afternoon. Recalling what happened and how his precious Lexie could have been killed fueled his anger. He *would* find the culprit—hopefully in The Boar's Nest.

"I believe it is time to ask some questions," Vincent said.

"Precisely."

Julian turned to move up the walkway toward the door again, but someone exited. When he recognized his driver, he flattened himself against the wall. Vincent copied his actions.

Although Julian couldn't see the middle-aged man's face, he knew this was his driver because of his black hair with streaks of white. The driver walked without any sort of impairment. Julian's anger intensified. Obviously, the driver had somehow jumped off the vehicle before it plunged into the ravine.

Julian would make certain this man was locked away for his

crimes. The question was, what else had he done? Julian had thought he could trust the driver. Now he didn't know whom to trust.

CHAPTER TWENTY-FIVE

J ULIAN WATCHED UNTIL the driver was out of sight before he and Vincent entered the establishment. The lighting in the room wasn't bright. He studied each man at the tables closely.

Vincent bumped his elbow to get Julian's attention and then pointed to the corner of the room. The two men sitting at the table were exactly how Alexandria had described them: early thirties with slender frames, wearing the clothes of the lower class. One had bright auburn hair and a scar on his cheek. The other man was blond.

Julian fisted his hands and marched directly to their table. He quickly took the empty seat as Vincent grabbed another chair and sat. The lower-class men jumped. Both wore stunned expressions, but Julian could tell they didn't recognize him.

"I hope you don't mind if we join you," Julian said.

"Uh, well…" The redheaded man shook his head.

"That's unfortunate," Julian snapped. "Because I'm not leaving until I get some answers."

The blond man's eyes widened. "What kind of answers?"

Julian leaned on the table. "First, I want to know what you were talking to my driver about just now."

"Yer driver?" The redheaded man shook his head. "We don't know yer driver, guv'na."

Julian exhaled, trying to keep calm, but it wasn't working. He pinched the bridge of his nose and inhaled slowly. "The man who just left your table was the driver for the Duke of Linden."

"Aye, the duke's driver, not yers."

Vincent chuckled. "Who do you think you're talking to?" He pointed to Julian. "This is the Duke of Linden."

The men stared at Julian for a few seconds before they laughed. The blond shook his head. "Yer not the duke. The duke is as blond as I am."

Julian rolled his eyes, trying to calm his temper. These two were idiots, and he didn't have the patience to deal with them. Why had Martin enlisted them to do his dirty work? They couldn't think for themselves very well.

"Listen closely," Julian began, talking slower so the imbeciles would understand. "I am the Duke of Linden. The man you are referring to is my cousin, Mr. Martin Hinsdale. He was duke for a few months because he thought I was dead. Now I have reclaimed the title."

Both men nodded.

"Now I'm going to repeat my question," Julian continued. "What were you and my driver talking about a few minutes ago?"

"Well, ya see, Yer Grace"—the redheaded man scratched his ear—"we were paid to make certain 'er Grace, Duchess of Linden, was in the coach when it runned off the road."

"Who paid you?" Vincent snapped.

"The Duke of—" The blond shrugged. "I mean, that other man."

Julian arched an eyebrow. "My cousin? Martin Hinsdale?"

Both men nodded.

Julian seethed. He couldn't wait to get his hands around his cousin's throat.

"What about the driver?" Vincent asked. "What role did he play in your scheme?"

"Well, we paid 'im to assist us. We didn't want the duchess to notice us, so that's why we paid off the driver to do the deed."

Julian couldn't think straight. The confusion in his head,

mixed with the throbbing pain in his leg, made it nearly impossible to focus. The only reason someone would want to kill Alexandria was to hurt him. He hadn't thought Martin would sink to such levels as to harm an innocent woman, but apparently, Julian didn't know his cousin very well.

He rubbed his forehead. "When did Martin pay you to do this?"

The two men exchanged glances before the redhead said, "A few weeks ago, Yer Grace."

Surprised at the answer, Julian sat up straight. Vincent gasped. Julian looked at his friend and slowly shook his head. "That doesn't make any sense. A few weeks ago, Martin was the duke. Why would he want his own wife harmed?"

"Actually, it makes perfect sense." Vincent leaned toward Julian. "Alexandria wondered if Martin was slowly poisoning her sister. A few weeks ago, the sister was still the duchess."

"You are correct, my friend. I'm relieved to know Martin didn't want my wife dead." Julian swung his focus back on the other two. "But why would Martin want his own wife harmed in such a way? What would he gain if she died?"

"Ya see," the redhead said, "Martin was unhappy with the duchess. He told us that she was an evil, controllin' woman who drove 'im insane." He snickered. "But if ya ask me, I think he wanted another wife."

"The mistress!" Julian said. "I would bet money that it was because of his mistress."

"Aye, Yer Grace." The blond nodded. "Now yer thinkin' straight."

Julian's mind scrambled to fit pieces of the puzzle together, but the continuous pain in his leg kept him from his task. Perhaps it was time to follow the physician's orders and get off his leg, at least for the remainder of the evening.

"How would the two of you like to earn more money than what my cousin paid you?" he asked.

Excitement lit their faces. "Aye, Yer Grace," the redhead said as the blond nodded.

"You are not to say anything to my driver or Martin about our meeting. Is that clear?"

They both nodded again.

"And, when the time comes, you will both confess to the magistrate that my cousin paid you. Is that understood?"

"We have an accord, Yer Grace." The blond held out his right hand to shake.

Before Julian left the inn, the two men wrote down their names and places of residence. He wasn't taking any more chances of losing this important information when they were so close.

⤜⤛⤛⤜

"HAVE YOU SEEN my husband?" Alexandria asked Dawn as she shifted in her bed, pulling some of the blankets away from her leg in the process. Already she was dreadfully tired of being in such a confined place, and she had only been here for a few hours. She wanted to move around and go outside to smell the fresh air and, especially, to talk to her husband. Unfortunately, the physician had denied her request.

"No, I haven't seen your husband, Your Grace." Dawn carried a cup of tea to the bed and handed it to Alexandria. "I have not seen him since right after you arrived at the manor. However, I did hear Higley mention that your husband had an errand in town, and he left not too long ago."

Alexandria frowned. "He really should follow the physician's instructions and stay off his leg." She sipped her tea.

"I agree." Dawn moved around the room, straightening the things the physician had messed up. "When I saw how badly your husband was limping, I knew he was in a lot of pain."

"Yes, he was, and yet he continued to pamper me just because I have a sprained ankle."

"Oh, but don't forget the cut on your forehead."

Alexandria gently ran the pad of her finger over the wound just below her hairline. "'Twas but a scratch, I assure you. My husband made my head injury out to be more than it was."

"I can see how much he cares for you." Dawn smiled. "I pray one day I shall find a man who takes care of me and loves me just as much."

Julian loves me? Alexandria doubted he loved her, but…

A smile gradually spread across her face. The way he looked at her and the tears in his eyes when he thought she had died were evidence that he held some strong feelings for her. Her heart softened. She hoped he did love her, because she couldn't stop loving him.

Clearing her throat, she set the teacup down on the side table. "Well, if he doesn't take better care of his leg, I will have to reprimand him. His health is most important right now."

"I agree." Dawn walked closer to the bed. "And because of the injury he had before today's accident, it is necessary to care for his leg so infection doesn't set in."

"The physician did mention that." Alexandria nodded.

"If infection sets in," Dawn continued, "you will need to treat it as soon as possible. It's very dangerous to have an infected wound. The longer the wound goes without being treated, the worse it will become."

"Are you certain?" Alexandria asked. She'd never heard about that before.

"Indeed, Your Grace. My cousin had an infection in her leg when she was young. The physician wanted to cut it off, but my aunt wouldn't allow it. Because the wound wasn't treated properly, the infection kept getting worse. Eventually, it killed her."

Alexandria sucked in a breath. "Oh dear. I'm very sorry for your loss."

"So, you must tell your husband to take care of his leg."

"Yes. I understand. Thank you, Dawn."

The maid returned to cleaning the room as Alexandria finished her tea. Julian was a stubborn man, but she must somehow convince him to stay off his leg. Now that she'd realized just how much she loved him and wanted to be his wife, she could not allow anything to ruin this for them.

Not too long ago, Charlotte had found that special love with Martin…or so Alexandria had thought. But now Charlotte was completely miserable in her marriage. Strange to think these past few days without Martin around had cheered her up quite a bit.

The more Alexandria pondered her feelings for Julian, the more her heart swelled with emotion. He had hurt her by not telling her the truth, yet that didn't bother her any longer. Not many men would risk their own lives to protect another person like Julian had done for her. From the day she met him, he had shown her that he was a tender-hearted man.

Now she couldn't wait to see him and talk to him. She hoped he would be receptive to her feelings, and more than anything, she prayed he returned them.

She needed to share this newfound feeling with someone. Since Julian wasn't around, the only person she could talk with was her sister. Although the physician had instructed Alexandria to keep off her ankle, she couldn't stay down. Besides, she would only visit with her sister for a few minutes. Not long at all. Once she was done, she would return to bed and prop her leg on a pillow.

She hobbled to the door, opened it, and peered down the hallway. Silence filled the corridor. She couldn't even hear any servants.

She moved toward her sister's bedchambers, relieved Julian wasn't here right now, as he would stop her. She understood his concern, but sometimes she needed her sister, and this was one of those times.

She knocked on the door and waited for a reply. Finally, her sister softly answered. Alexandria opened the door and walked in. As always, her sister lay propped up in bed with a heavy shawl that covered most of her arms draped over her shoulders. The once vibrant golden color of Charlotte's hair had faded to a dull yellow. Alexandria frowned. Why couldn't her sister recover from this unknown malady?

An odd scent drifted in the room, and Alexandria couldn't decide what it smelled like. It definitely wasn't food. Perhaps the maid was trying a new herb poultice to make Charlotte healthy again. No matter how much she told Alexandria she was recovering, her coughs were still very hard. It broke Alexandria's heart to hear them.

Charlotte smiled. "I'm delighted you are here. I wondered why you hadn't come to visit me in a few days."

Alexandria closed the door and moved toward her sister's bed. "So much has happened lately."

Charlotte's attention dropped to Alexandria's foot. "Why are you limping?"

Alexandria was certain the servants talked, but she prayed they hadn't said anything to Charlotte about the accident. She didn't want her sister worrying unnecessarily.

"Oh, it is nothing to fret about. I shall be walking just fine tomorrow, I assure you." She sat on the edge of her sister's bed. "But how are you doing? There is a little bit of color in your cheeks." At least, she thought there was. Then again, Charlotte's face was a buttery color.

Charlotte pulled the shawl tighter around her shoulders and arms. "I'm losing strength, I fear. And I'm tired more than I should be. If only I could get rid of my cough completely, then I would feel better."

Alexandria's heart ached. "I thought you were doing better, especially after Martin left the manor."

Charlotte shrugged. "I thought I was, but my body is telling me I'm not."

"When was the last time you saw the physician?"

"The day before Martin left. But I don't want him coming back just to repeat the same thing he said last time—that I need time to heal." Charlotte shook her head. "I'm not about to pay for something I already know."

"But what if it is something different—"

"Xandria, no. I've already had this argument with Martin. I'm stubborn, and I won't budge."

"Fine," Alexandria said. "I just want you well."

"And I will be in time." Charlotte weakly patted Alexandria's hand. "Tell me, what has been happening to you lately? A moment ago, when you entered the room, you had a certain gleam in your eyes. Dare I think you have fallen in love with your husband so soon?"

Chuckling, Alexandria nodded. "It's true, Charlotte. I was very upset when I discovered he had been lying to me, but he has proven his worth in a few short days. I have sorely misjudged him."

Charlotte shook her head and relaxed back against the pillows. "I don't want to dampen your spirits, dear sister, but men are fickle. One minute they are spouting words of love, and the next moment they turn into deceitful, selfish devils. Just as my own husband has done. I thought the sun rose and set on that man, but after we married, he turned into a monster." Tears glistened in her eyes.

"Were you truly in love when you married him, Charlotte?"

Charlotte shrugged and traced the flower pattern sewn in the fabric with her finger. "When I first saw him, I became infatuated. He was charming. He knew how to make me laugh. I had actually been interested in another man, but Martin made me think my world would be roses and rainbows if I married him." A tear slid down her cheek. "I wonder what would have happened if I allowed this other man's attentions instead."

"I'm so sorry, Charlotte." Alexandria caressed her sister's leg. "I wish I could change things for you."

"Oh, Xandria. You must always remember this one thing above all others—if you want to obtain something in your life, don't wait for it. Get it yourself. It will never happen if you wait for it to come to you."

Alexandria didn't know how to take her sister's advice. Obviously, Martin had turned Charlotte into a bitter woman, and rightly so after the kind of man he was.

Alexandria kissed her sister on the forehead before leaving the room and heading back to her own bedchambers. Her visit with Charlotte had left her feeling gloomy, and Alexandria realized the only way to brighten her day was to talk with Julian. She would speak to him tonight, no matter what obstacles she had to jump.

CHAPTER TWENTY-SIX

THE LOW-BURNING FIRE in the hearth relaxed Julian's body, but not his mind. He couldn't stop thinking about the day's events and how his wife could have died.

As difficult as it was to believe, he had fallen in love with her, yet he hadn't realized it until he thought he had lost her. Julian would have never forgiven himself if she had died without knowing his true feelings. He had wanted to tell her when he returned home from talking with the imbeciles at the inn, but Lexie's maid informed him that the duchess was asleep. Because of what had happened earlier today, he decided not to disturb her.

He moved his leg on the footstool, gritting his teeth, and adjusted himself in his cushioned chair. After returning home, he'd bathed and rested in his chair with his foot propped up, just as the physician had instructed him to do. Several times his valet had come to check on him, brought in a meal, and fetched a book, but Julian finally told his servant to retire for the evening.

Silence settled over the manor, and the room was oddly blanketed in the hushed calm. Only the occasional pop of burning wood in the hearth disturbed the quiet. He sighed. His bed beckoned to him.

He stretched his arms over his head and yawned. Reading hadn't kept his mind occupied. His thoughts strayed from the words on the page to replaying the accident and the knowledge that his cousin wanted to harm his sweet wife. He must find a way to have Martin arrested and convicted. He remained hopeful that their information about Martin would interest the magistrate to start a full investigation with the help of Walter and Sam—the two men from the inn. Julian would ask Vincent to accompany him tomorrow to bring this new development to the man of the law.

Julian rose from the chair and limped to the bed. The pain in his leg wasn't as severe as it had been earlier, thank the Lord. The physician had hinted about taking Julian's leg off after he was injured in the cannon blast. He was against it then, and he would *not* consider it now.

When he reached the bed, he shrugged out of his banyan and draped it over a wooden chair near his bed. Carefully, he climbed into bed and pulled the covers to his bare chest. Folding his arms behind his head, he stared up at the ceiling.

As his mind drifted to thoughts of holding Lexie as she responded urgently to his kiss, a smile stretched his mouth. He'd gradually made her trust him again, evidenced by the twinkle in her eyes when she gazed at him today. He would eventually win her over, and she would confess her love, just as he would confess his. If only it were sooner rather than later.

A floorboard squeaking in the hallway brought him alert. He jerked his attention to the door just as it opened. The only light in the room was the small lamp on the table beside his bed, so he couldn't see who had entered his chambers.

"Who is there?" he asked sharply.

"It is I, your wife."

He wanted to spring from the bed and rush to her side, curious as to why she had come to his room so late. Yet he dared not go to her, since he wasn't wearing a stitch of clothing. Seeing him in his undressed state would certainly frighten her away.

He sat up and stuffed the blankets around him in case more of his skin than she wanted to see was showing. "Are you well, my darling?"

"I'm doing better, thank you." Her shadow moved into the light, and he noticed she wore her pale pink wrap over a white nightgown.

When she reached the end of the bed, she paused, and her focus rested on his chest. She sucked in a breath, and her cheeks darkened.

"Oh, forgive me for intruding—"

"You are not," he interrupted her.

"I should probably leave."

He reached his hand out to stop her. "Please, don't. Stay and keep me company."

Her chest rose and fell quickly. Seconds ticked by before she nodded. "I actually came to talk to you about this afternoon."

"Do you wish me to meet you on the sofa?" he asked, but silently prayed she had wanted him to remain in bed.

She licked her lips and moved closer to the edge. "What I have to say shall only take a moment."

As she drew near, he took her hand and gently tugged her toward the bed. "Sit beside me, please?"

She nodded and perched on the edge of the bed.

Gazing upon her beauty, he nearly lost his breath. Long, flowing hair cascaded over her shoulders in an alluring manner, tempting his fingers to caress her locks. The lightness of her wrap against her skin made her appear innocent, yet at the same time very enticing. Perhaps he should convince her to meet him on the sofa after all. Making her his bride was upmost in his mind, and he didn't want to force her if she wasn't ready.

As he held her hand, he stroked the pad of his thumb across her knuckles. "What do you want to tell me?"

"Well..." Her throat jumped. "I want you to know how much I appreciate your protection today, first in the coach as you held me while we rolled and then when you carried me up from the ravine to the road. You were so very tender and considerate, even though I knew you were injured."

He smiled. "I hate to see you in pain, and I will do anything to protect you. I hope you know that now."

She nodded and touched his hand. "I realized that today. I also realized it doesn't matter if you hid your identity from me. You are still the man I came to know before the truth was finally revealed."

He wanted to sigh with relief or shout for joy, but he still worried there was a catch. "And pray tell, my darling, what kind of man do you think I am?"

Perhaps he shouldn't have asked that question, but he just had to know her feelings. He desperately wanted her to experience the same emotions as he was. He would do anything to make her feel that way.

A shy smile graced her lovely face, and her eyes sparkled. His heartbeat quickened, yet he still didn't dare believe she wanted to consummate the marriage. He had promised to give her time, and now he wondered why he was such a gentleman around her when he had never been before.

"You are the kind of man who puts others before his own needs," she said. "You cradled me in your arms to protect me from the accident, taking the brunt of the impact yourself. You ignored your own pain to see me safe. How could I not see you as the caring man I knew before? Though I was blinded by what I thought was your betrayal, I now see the truth. You have protected and cared for me from the start. I realize how much I enjoy your attention and the fact that you worry over me for small things. I believe you are the kind of man who I want worrying about me...forever."

Happiness burst inside of him, and it was all he could do not to pull her into his arms that very second. Once she was in his embrace, he wouldn't stop kissing her. However, first, he must confess his own feelings, or the moment would be lost.

"Oh, my love." He lifted her hand to his mouth and kissed her knuckles. "You don't know how I have longed to hear those words. Truly, you have made me very happy." His heartbeat thumped an irregular rhythm, and he suddenly found himself as nervous as a schoolboy, imagining how he could confess his love for her. Never in his life had he said those three little words to a woman.

He swallowed the lump of fear growing in his throat. No matter how anxious it made him, he must say the words. Now. "Lexie, I—"

"And because of how I feel about you now," she continued as though she hadn't heard him, "I feel it is time that…" She licked her lips again. "I feel I should now be a proper wife and share your bed."

Her startling announcement had him nearly jumping out of his skin with anticipation. He couldn't have heard correctly, could he? Yet the tender expression on her face as she stared at him told him he had.

Gingerly, she touched his bare chest. Shivers of warmth ran through him, igniting the feelings he'd had since meeting her but had never acted upon.

"Are you certain?" His voice squeaked, so he cleared his throat. "I won't take you if you're not ready."

"I'm ready, Julian."

He couldn't wait another second. His arms trembled with anticipation as he pulled her closer. She slid her palms over his chest and hooked her hands around his neck. A deep groan escaped him, one he had no wish to control. Her touch brought such sweet pleasure, and he wanted her to know it.

Their mouths came together. Alexandria was just as eager for him as he was for her. Sweeping her into his arms, he brought her across him and laid her on the bed. He leaned over and continued kissing her, urgency running through him. Yet this wasn't enough. Taking it slowly was not an option any longer.

He had to have more of her. Much more.

He moved his mouth from hers and trailed kisses down her neck. She threw her head back, arching for him to take more. The thunderous beat of his heart slammed in his ears, and against his lips, her pulse kept the same rhythm.

"Julian," she said repeatedly.

He wanted nothing more than to please her, so she thought of him as her hero again. He rose slightly and stared into her passionate face. "Lexie…love me," he said breathlessly.

"I do love you."

Once more, his heart burst with happiness. He caressed her face as he lay over her. "I love you, my darling wife." Her eyes enlarged in surprise. "I think I have loved you for a while now, but I did not dare admit it. I've never felt this way about any woman, and the thought of sharing myself with one woman for the rest of my life had terrified me and kept me from getting really close to any woman. I was a rogue, and I didn't care about anything except protecting my heart."

"And what do you think now?" she asked.

He grinned. "I'm eager to begin our marriage, my love. I'm eager to love you with all of my heart, my mind, and my soul."

"Julian, I have never loved any other man."

"Then our hearts will beat as one starting now."

"Now and always." She sealed their words with a kiss…a kiss that would last all night long.

CHAPTER TWENTY-SEVEN

ALEXANDRIA COULDN'T STOP smiling. A few weeks ago, if someone had told her she would find a man and actually *talk* to him and then become his wife, she would have believed that person insane. But now, peace and exhilaration settled over her. She'd never realized being in love could feel this glorious. She never wanted this emotion to end.

Last night with her husband had been magical. He had taken her to paradise and back. Recalling every moment made her cheeks burn with delight as a giggle sprang from her throat. He had asked if she would move her personal items to his bedchambers, because he wanted her next to him always. She'd agreed. She never wanted them to be separated again.

Just as she had done all her life, she had risen early this morning as the sun crowned on the horizon. She would allow her husband to rest. He appeared so handsome lying on the white pillow, which contrasted greatly with his tanned skin and day's growth of whiskers on his chin. His dark hair was tousled, but he looked adorable. She was tempted to crawl back into bed and wrap his arms around her, but she resisted. The poor man needed rest, to stay off his leg.

Just thinking about the wound festering and becoming infected made her stomach churn. Imagining the infection getting so bad he might lose his life brought a sharp pain to her heart. She didn't want him to be like Dawn's cousin.

However, with everything that was going on in Julian's life, her husband might not adhere to the physician's advice. So perhaps it was up to Alexandria to reason with him. She had to make certain he kept off his leg for at least a week, even if she had to keep him in bed all that time.

As quietly as she could, she dressed in her favorite deep blue riding habit and ventured downstairs for breakfast, realizing her ankle no longer hurt. Once again, she thought of the wonderful night. Another laugh bubbled up from her throat, and she covered her mouth. She didn't want the servants to know what had happened between her and Julian in his bed, although she feared they already knew. As she headed toward the dining room, many of the servants gave her a grin or a knowing wink.

As she ate her breakfast, she gazed out the window. Another beautiful day beckoned her to go riding. Although she shouldn't go without her husband, she didn't dare wake him and get him on his leg. But her husband was still asleep and would probably not wake until later. Her ride wouldn't be long, anyway. She would take a short ride just to get out and breathe in the fresh air.

She finished eating her breakfast, enthused to finally ride Buttercup again. But out the window, something caught her attention. A woman crept around the outside wall of the stable.

Setting her fork down, Alexandria peered intently in an attempt to determine who the intruder was. The woman wore a light green riding habit with a large hat that shadowed her face. When she stopped and threw a cautious glance over her shoulder, recognition hit Alexandria fully. What was Theresa doing here?

Anger fueled Alexandria, and she rushed out of the house and toward the stable. She would give that woman a piece of her mind. How dare Theresa think she could sneak on the estate without a proper invitation? And who in their right mind would invite the so-called *ruined* woman, anyway? Certainly not Alexandria, and she knew very well her husband wouldn't have invited Theresa either.

She slowed her steps when she neared the stable, listening for any noises inside. Theresa was in there, she just knew it. Where else would she have disappeared to?

Alexandria poked her head inside the open door of the stable and saw Theresa standing by Buttercup. Her back was toward Alexandria.

Taking quiet steps, Alexandria moved closer. She wasn't paying attention to where she was walking, and her foot bumped against an empty pail. The tinkling sound startled Theresa, and she swung around, facing Alexandria. In her hand was a chisel. She looked to the saddle on Buttercup. It appeared that Theresa was trying to damage the billet straps.

Alexandria gasped. "I would ask what you are doing here, but by the tool in your hand, I have my answer."

Theresa glanced at the chisel. Her expression changed. She straightened her shoulders and lifted her arrogant chin. "Indeed. Asking me about my presence would seem futile."

Alexandria was hit again with Theresa's rude demeanor. "I cannot imagine why you would want to damage my saddle"—she pointed to the chisel—"but since I caught you in the act, I shall report you directly to the local magistrate."

She searched the stable but couldn't see the servant that was usually there in the morning.

"John?" Alexandria called out, hoping he was close enough to hear her. Yet silence stretched throughout the stable as she waited for an answer. Even the horses remained quiet. Panic filled her, but she tried not to show any fear. "John? Where are you?"

Theresa released an evil laugh. "Unfortunately, he cannot hear you at this moment."

Alexandria did not like that tone of voice. Alarm rushed through her faster now, creating a painful throb in her skull. Frantically, she searched the stable again, praying Theresa was wrong about John and that he would make his presence known soon.

Near one of the stalls on the floor, she noticed legs lying very still. The rest of him was hidden by the wooden gate.

A sob caught in her throat, and she placed her fist to her mouth. Tears swam in her eyes. "Why…" She tore her focus away from John's unmoving body to glare at Theresa. "Why did you harm a defenseless boy?"

"He will be fine when he awakens. He shall only suffer a headache, I assure you."

Alexandria's hands shook as she pointed toward the stable's double front doors. "Leave now. You are not welcome at my estate."

Another evil chuckle came from Theresa as she moved from stall to stall leisurely, as though she didn't have a care in the world. "At one time, I had imagined all this to be mine, you know. I had captured the attention of a wealthy duke's son, and I was in hopes of marital bliss."

Alexandria arched an eyebrow. "I don't believe my husband shared the same feelings as you. In fact, he told me what *really* happened, and it is nowhere near what you would have others believe." She breathed deeply, trying to stay calm, if only outwardly. "You were trying to trap him into marriage, and he would not have that. Shame on you, Miss Dickson."

"*Trap* him? Oh, I think not. He wanted to meet me in secret, and he hinted at that every time we talked. I could tell that he wanted to kiss and hold me—just as much as I wanted him to. I wasn't blind, and I knew he was avoiding marriage." Theresa shrugged. "So, it was up to me to convince him otherwise."

Alexandria nodded. "Exactly my point. You had set out to trap him."

Huffing, Theresa stomped toward Alexandria, halting only a few inches away. "I was not trapping him, I tell you."

"Listen, Miss Dickson, we can stand here and argue all morning, but nothing will ever be resolved. You have your idea of what happened, and I know the truth."

With a growl, Theresa grasped Alexandria by the shoulders and roughly shook her. "You are very wrong, Miss Templeton.

Why can you not admit that your husband was once attracted to me?"

"Because he wasn't interested in you at all. He told me so himself." Alexandria pushed Theresa's hands away. "And you, Miss Dickson, may refer to me as Her Grace, the Duchess of Linden. Or as most people would address me, Your Grace."

"Ah! That title should have been mine." Theresa lunged, wrapping her fingers around Alexandria's throat.

Fear escalated inside Alexandria as she struggled to release Theresa's hold, but her grip was too strong. The more Alexandria struggled, the tighter Theresa squeezed.

Alexandria couldn't swallow, and breathing became more and more difficult. Her body weakened, and her lungs burned, needing air. If she couldn't break away soon, she would surely die. *No!* She wouldn't allow this to happen. Not when she had finally found happiness.

Become one of your characters...

Finding strength she didn't know she possessed, Alexandria fought harder, clawing at Theresa's hands, but that didn't faze the woman who had gone mad. As dizziness assailed her, Alexandria feared she wasn't strong enough.

Recalling one of her stories where her characters were attacked, she finally knew what to do. She lifted her leg and, using all of her strength, slammed her foot against Theresa's shin. The demented woman cried out, which, thankfully, loosened her hands. Alexandria used this moment to claw Theresa's face and continue to kick at the injured leg. Immediately, Theresa fell to the ground, clutching her leg. Her face bled from the scratches Alexandria had inflicted.

Sinking to the ground, Alexandria inhaled deeply, trying to refill her lungs. She focused on her hand where it was braced on the hay-scattered stable floor. Although dizziness continued to assail her, it wasn't as bad as before. If she closed her eyes now, she feared she would lose consciousness. Her throat burned when she swallowed, and her body ached. But at least she was alive.

A movement out of the corner of her eye made her aware of Theresa moving away. Alexandria prayed the woman would leave so she could alert the local magistrate and Theresa would be arrested.

"I'm sorry, *Your Grace*," Theresa said calmly.

Surprised at the apology, Alexandria dared look at her. Theresa stepped closer, hiding something behind her as she stared angrily at Alexandria.

"I'm sorry, but I just cannot allow you to take *my* place as the duchess. I belong with Julian. Not you."

Before Alexandria realized what was happening, Theresa pulled a wooden pail from behind her back and swung it toward Alexandria. The heavy bucket smacked the side of her head. Pain exploded in her skull. A flash of light streaked through her mind before she crumpled to the ground and surrendered to darkness.

CHAPTER TWENTY-EIGHT

JULIAN JERKED TO an upright position in bed, feeling disoriented. What had startled him and brought him awake in such a fashion? He had been sleeping so soundly, but now…

He shook his head and glanced at the space next to him in bed. Lexie was gone. Her absence must have been what woke him. Then again, he hadn't felt her leave his bed at all. He knew she was an early riser. Usually, he awoke with the sun, but not this morning. Exhaustion had taken over his body, and he'd slept so well last night.

Yawning, he stretched his arms above his head, releasing the morning kinks. He tried to think of what had woken him so abruptly. Was it a noise? Yet he didn't recall hearing anything. Something was in his mind and heart. Even now, he felt that odd sense that danger was afoot. Of course, until Martin was arrested, Julian feared he and his wife would never be safe.

Today he had to make certain the magistrate was informed of Martin's crooked dealings. Justice would be served. Then, and only then, would Julian and Lexie be safe. Full happiness was so close that he could taste it. Unfortunately, it wouldn't happen soon enough.

He climbed out of bed and wrapped a robe around him. Cautiously, he tested his leg. It didn't hurt as much as it had yesterday. That was a good sign. Perhaps he had been on his feet a little more than planned, but he would rest his limb if the pain increased.

Forty-five minutes later, bathed, dressed, and fed, he walked down the stairs, listening for the angelic sound of his wife's voice. Instead, the house echoed with emptiness. He hurried to the library, thinking she was curled up on the sofa reading, but she wasn't there. Every room he peeked into greeted him with emptiness.

When he passed her lady's maid, he stopped her. "Pardon me, Johnson, but is my wife visiting with her sister this morning?"

"No, Your Grace. Mrs. Hinsdale is still asleep."

"I thank you." He nodded and continued through the house until he reached the front door. When he walked outside, he immediately stopped on the limestone steps. Birds chirped, their songs drifting with the morning breeze, but he didn't hear Lexie's voice. His heart dropped. She hadn't gone riding, had she?

His worry heightened, pushing him toward the stable faster. Once inside, he stopped suddenly. Buttercup was still in her stall but wearing a saddle. Had Lexie already been out riding?

A boy's painful groan caught Julian's attention, and he swung his head toward the sound. John sat propped up against the stall's wall, rubbing his head. A spot of blood stained his hair.

Julian knelt by his side. "What happened?"

"Uh, I'm not sure, Your Grace." John touched his head near the spot of blood and flinched. "I think I was hit in the head with something. There's a big bump there now."

"Did you see who hit you?"

"No."

Julian scanned the stable again. "Have you seen my wife? Her horse is here and saddled. Do you know if she went riding already?"

"I don't know, Your Grace. I saddle Buttercup every morning for Miss Temple—um, I mean, Her Grace, because I know she likes to ride. But I didn't see her this morning."

"Stay right here, and I'll have a groomsman fetch my physician."

Julian hurried to find the groomsman, and his heartbeat quickened as questions swam in his head. Where had his wife disappeared to, and who would have hit John over the head? Deep down, Julian felt it was the same person responsible. He would bet money that his cousin was behind this.

When Julian finally found the man accountable for all this turmoil, the fool would wish he were dead. Julian would see to it that he got his revenge.

STARS SWIRLED IN Alexandria's head, accompanied by intense pain as she tried to open her eyes. Whatever piece of furniture she lay on felt lumpy and grimy, and a musty scent hung in the air. She dared not sneeze, only because she knew the agony it would bring to her skull if she did.

Her mouth was as dry as the air. She tried her best to moisten her mouth and lick her lips. At least she was still alive.

For now.

It took some difficulty to open her eyes, and when she finally gained her bearings, she glanced around the sparse room. She lay on a rickety bed without any blankets. Besides the bed, the only other piece of furniture was a small table next to the window with a lamp.

Familiarity pricked her. Why did she feel as though she had been here before?

Her memory returned, reminding her where she was. This was Lord Trenton's cottage, where Julian had brought her the day he kidnapped her.

Hope sprang in her chest. Had Lord Trenton somehow saved her from the madwoman? Yet, if he had, why did he bring her here? Why hadn't he just taken her inside the manor and summoned Julian's physician?

Her stomach twisted as another thought entered her mind. Was Lord Trenton somehow involved with Theresa? Why else would the woman bring Alexandria to his cottage?

Bile rose to Alexandria's throat. She must escape somehow. She would be able to do it this time, since she knew the cottage layout and grounds. And she knew that Linden Hall wasn't too far away.

She sat on the edge of the bed, holding on to the mattress. Dizziness assailed her once again, and she rode the wave of turbulence until it died down. She vowed she would not swoon. However, there was no way to know what kind of danger awaited her. If Theresa harmed people without feeling remorse, who was to say that she wouldn't try to kill Alexandria? After all, the woman was insane.

Once her dizziness stopped, Alexandria stood and stepped carefully toward the door. When the pounding in her head threatened to break her skull, she eased her footfalls, concentrating on her main goal of escape. Reaching the door, she fell against it and exhaled a relieved sigh.

With a shaky hand, she tested the doorknob. It turned and clicked the door open. So far, this had been easy, but that only meant something wasn't right. At least, that was how it happened in her mystery stories. But this was reality, not fiction, and she wasn't going to pass by an opportunity if it presented itself.

Her head spun as she held on to the wall, descending the stairs. She tried listening for any sounds in the house, but the pounding in her head overrode anything else. Regardless, she would keep pushing forward and take one minute at a time.

She reached the bottom and stopped, listening again. Her heart hammered faster. She mustn't allow this weakened emotion to take control. How could she escape if fright consumed her very being?

Taking a deep breath of courage, she turned the corner and headed toward the kitchen. Since Theresa considered herself a *lady*, Alexandria figured she wouldn't enter this particular room because it was beneath her to reside in a place where servants congregated.

Alexandria entered and blew out a relieved sigh. She had been correct. Her kidnapper wasn't here.

She aimed her focus on the back door. Freedom was within walking distance.

I can do it, she repeated in her mind as she moved toward the door. Three more steps…now two…one…

She gripped the doorknob and turned until it clicked. The grounds in the back of the cottage welcomed her, and she was grateful to see the outdoors at last. She had made it this far, which meant she would make it the rest of the way. She prayed Julian was already on his way to save her.

She stepped out of the house and onto the grass. Birds flew high in the sky, and at the nearby pond, toads croaked. Hopefully, she wouldn't disturb them and alert anyone that she was escaping.

Moving along the cottage wall, she kept an eye out for anything out of the ordinary. Concentrating was still difficult because of the fierce beating in her head, but she tried not to think of the pain. There were more important things that could occupy her mind right now.

Just as she reached the corner of the cottage, she heard the snort of a horse. The sound was much closer than she had expected. Silently, she prayed that someone had come to help her. She didn't know what she would do if it were Theresa.

CHAPTER TWENTY-NINE

"T HERE YOU ARE."

Fear weakened Alexandria's legs, and she collapsed against the brick wall. The chilling voice of Theresa was right behind her. How had she not heard the woman sneaking up on her?

Theresa gripped Alexandria's arm and yanked, making her fall to her knees. Tears filled Alexandria's eyes, blurring her vision, but really, she didn't have to see the terror unfolding before her. She didn't *want* to see the evil lurking in Theresa's glare.

"Where do you think you are going?" Theresa snapped.

"Away from you," Alexandria whispered.

"That is not going to happen."

Growling, Theresa pulled Alexandria back toward the cottage. She had no other choice but to stand and go along. The throbbing in her head grew worse, and all she wanted to do was close her eyes and pretend this was all a nightmare and that she would wake up soon and be in Julian's protecting arms.

Once they reached the front of the house, Theresa shoved Alexandria to the worn couch. Although the piece of furniture was rickety and dirty, she was grateful for the respite it offered her shaky limbs.

She rubbed her forehead, trying to alleviate some of the pain. "Tell me what you plan on doing with me now." Although she shouldn't have asked, she needed to know if her life would end right here and at this woman's selfish hands or not.

"I honestly don't know." Theresa raked her fingers through her hair as she paced the room. "I never thought I would do something like this myself. Too bad someone couldn't do it for me."

Obviously, she was confused in the head. "If you never thought to kidnap me, then why did you do it?"

"You don't understand." Theresa waved her hand. "I have *thought* of doing this, but I never believed it would actually happen."

Either Alexandria's head injury was getting worse and took away the ability to think straight, or this crazed woman wasn't saying the right words. "Would you make sense so I can understand you?"

Theresa stopped her pacing in front of the window. Leaning her shoulder against the frame, she peered out. "It's difficult to explain."

"Please try."

Theresa exhaled. "I have been so very upset with Julian for ruining my life, as you probably have suspected. He joined the military and built himself an exemplary reputation. He became a major, you know. I couldn't understand why Julian reaped the rewards of a good life, and I could not. After all, he was the one who ruined me."

Alexandria bit her tongue, not wanting to argue. They didn't need to get into that again. She remained quiet, waiting to hear what else the lying woman would say.

"Not long ago, I had an incredible idea for revenge that I shared with a few friends. They, of course, told me not to think about it ever again, because that kind of imagination would get me thrown in the gaol."

"What were you thinking?" Alexandria asked hesitantly.

"I wanted Julian dead." Theresa paused as her bottom lip trembled. "It wasn't fair that he lived a carefree life, and I couldn't. But I didn't want anyone to think I had killed him. I had actually created a way in my mind to kill him and have everyone believe it was an accident."

"How?" Alexandria asked, dreading the answer.

Theresa turned, leaned her back against the wall, and folded her arms. "I was going to find someone who had access to a cannon, and I would pay them to hit a mark nearby Julian and some of his men."

Alexandria's fears had been confirmed. She gasped before she could control her reaction.

"Yes, that was my idea," Theresa continued, tears coating her eyes, "but believe me when I say it wasn't my doing. I had only created the concept. After I told my friends, I realized how ludicrous the idea sounded, and they were right. I didn't want to end up in the gaol. Four days later, I heard that Julian died after a cannonball exploded near him and his men."

Alexandria couldn't believe what she was hearing. "You didn't do it?"

"No."

"Who did?"

"I wish I knew. At first, I thought it was the friends I had told, but they do not have the brains to carry out such a plot. And, of course, they didn't hate Julian as I did."

Alexandria remembered that one of the people involved would have a bullet wound in their arm. Yet it didn't appear as if Theresa had been injured recently, especially if she'd handled Alexandria by herself to get her to the cottage.

Theresa moved to the hearth. She knelt beside the low-burning fire, pushing the logs with the poker.

"The news shocked me," she continued, "for I had actually thought about it, and yet it really happened. Then reality struck me hard, and I mourned. I was sick for several days, thinking I was the one who'd killed him, even though I hadn't." A tear streaked down her cheek. "When I discovered he was still alive, I was relieved. I felt as if I had been given a second chance at winning him back." She swung her head toward Alexandria and glared. "Then *you* came into his life, and I couldn't allow you to wreck my plans."

"Is that why you tried to kill us in the coach accident?" Alexandria really hadn't believed Theresa was behind it, but it was definitely a possibility.

Theresa gave a small laugh. "Actually, no. Killing you in a coach accident was not something I conjured up, unfortunately."

"How had you thought of killing me?"

"You enjoy riding your horse. I had thought about doing something to loosen the saddle so you would fall off. Of course, in my plan, you would strike your head against a large rock and die instantly."

Alexandria bunched her hands into fists as anger rose inside her. "And that is why you were meddling with Buttercup's saddle when I caught you in the stable."

"Well, yes. Although I didn't want to do it, I thought I needed to help fate."

"Fate." She shook her head. "Is that what you call it?" This woman had lost her mind completely.

"Yes, of course."

"And what has *fate* got planned for me now?"

"I don't know that answer, which is why I'm so very confused. As mentioned, my plan was for you to die falling off your horse, but since that hasn't happened, it's left me confused. Whatever happens to you, I don't want to be blamed. If that happens, I won't have any chance of winning Julian's love."

Alexandria couldn't believe this woman. Theresa wouldn't stop until everything went her way, and that frightened Alexandria to death.

Stalling for time and hoping she would think of a way out, she glanced around the meager room. It was hard to believe that a place like this belonged to Lord Trenton, since he hadn't done anything to repair the cottage or even decorate it with newer furniture. Obviously, he didn't bring anyone here.

"Tell me something else before you take my life in cold blood." She looked back at Theresa. "How does Lord Trenton fit into your twisted scheme?"

Theresa's eyebrows arched. "What makes you assume Lord Trenton is involved?"

"Because this is his cottage."

Theresa gripped the handle of the poker tighter. "How do you know that?"

"My husband brought me here once."

Theresa's haughty expression grew darker, and she lifted her chin. "I suppose I should tell you, since I don't plan on your being alive much longer."

Crushing despair made Alexandria's heart heavy. No, there must be a way out of this nightmare. "Please tell me," she said in a choked voice, wishing she could control her fear better.

"Not too long ago, Lord Trenton decided to make me his mistress." Theresa shrugged. "After all, I am considered a fallen woman because of what Julian did, so no decent man will have me for his wife. Nevertheless, Lord Trenton made me an offer I couldn't refuse. And I have to say, we are quite happy now."

"Why didn't Lord Trenton want you for his wife, if you two are so happy together?" Perhaps Alexandria shouldn't rub salt in the wound, but she just couldn't help it.

Theresa's features hardened, and she slammed her hand against the wall. "Actually, it is the other way around. I didn't want *him* as a husband. He will only be an earl."

"Oh, so you are after someone with a higher title?"

"But of course."

Alexandria shook her head. "But when you fell in love with Julian, he was only the second son of a duke. Why would you want a man like that?"

Theresa huffed, placed the poker against the wall, and paced the floor. "Julian was closer to being a duke than Vincent. Besides that, Julian's family was wealthier."

"And you needed to find a husband who could keep you

living in the lap of luxury."

She grinned. "You understand now."

"Are you still Lord Trenton's mistress?"

Theresa's smile faded as she paused in front of Alexandria. "Well, I haven't kept in touch with him lately. He has been so busy."

"Does he know you are using his cottage?" Alexandria asked.

"No, and if I have it my way, he'll never know. However, the duke's dead wife will be found in this pitiful shack, and everyone will believe Vincent killed you." Theresa threw up her hands. "Thus, my plan for revenge against him and his friend will be complete."

"Well, Miss Dickson, it sounds like you have everything thought out. However, I think you overlook one important matter."

"And what, pray tell, is that?" She folded her arms and cocked her head.

"If I am dead, my husband will be distraught, and it might take some time to make him fall in love with you. Julian and I may have only been together a short time, but he truly loves me, just as I love him." Tears stung Alexandria's eyes as she recalled their last moments together, the last time he touched her, their last kiss, and his last words spoken. For a certainty, her husband loved her with all of his heart. "I imagine," she continued, trying not to cry, "that it will be difficult for him to find another woman who will be able to make him forget me."

Growling, Theresa turned away and marched to the window. Thankfully, she was quiet now. Of course, Alexandria didn't know how long that would last, and what worried her more was that the evil woman was plotting some way to kill her.

Alexandria's headache worsened, but that wasn't the reason her stomach churned. She didn't want to die. She wanted to live forever with her wonderful Julian. She wanted them to have children and grow old together. Yet right now, her defender was not here to protect her. She would have to be the one to free herself from this situation and return to the man she loved.

Her attention fell on the poker resting against the wall—the same wall that was very close to where she sat on the couch. She snapped her attention back to Theresa, who hadn't moved. This was the perfect chance to take control of everything and become as heroic as one of the characters in her stories. Alexandria was closer to the weapon than Theresa. If only her spinning head would stop so that she could stand and find the strength needed to grab the poker.

Silently she prayed everything would work in her favor. Strangely, she *felt* Julian's strength. In her mind, she heard him calling for her, begging for her to return. She must not let him down.

Taking a deep breath, she slowly scooted to the edge of the couch. Willing her limbs to work properly, she focused on her goal. Before she could talk herself out of it, she jumped from the couch and leapt for the poker. She grasped it tightly and turned to face her foe.

Theresa had spun around, and her eyes widened in panic. Color faded from her face.

"Wh—what are you doing, Miss Templeton?"

Alexandria really wished the insipid woman would get her name straight. "You don't know?" she asked, finally feeling in control and enjoying the power it gave her. "Can I assume you didn't *think* of what would happen if I somehow became fearless?" She tightened her fingers around the handle, raising the poker slightly.

Theresa shook her head. "You are too weak because of your head injury. I can still overpower you."

Energy climbed higher inside Alexandria, steadying her limbs and, remarkably enough, calming the pounding in her head. "Shall we test your theory?"

She didn't know if she was encouraging the madwoman or not. But right now, she wanted this over with. She wanted to be back in Julian's loving arms.

She studied Theresa's eyes, waiting for her next move. When color seeped back into her face and she narrowed her eyes, Alexandria realized the snake was about to strike.

Theresa lunged toward her, and Alexandria quickly jumped aside. Theresa smacked against the wall with a loud thud and crumpled to the floor. Alexandria raised the poker and brought it down soundly on Theresa's head.

The sound of bones cracking made her stomach roil, but it was the sight of blood that made Alexandria gag. Sobbing, she stepped away from Theresa, backing up toward the door. She kept her gaze on the unmoving body.

Never before had she killed a person, and she prayed that she hadn't killed one now. Yet she didn't know what would happen if Theresa was left alive to follow through with her threats. Neither she nor Julian would be safe.

Alexandria's legs wobbled slightly as she ran out the door and to the lone horse grazing in the yard. She didn't know how she got the strength to jump on its back, but she did. She kicked her heels into the horse's sides and held on to the reins, riding as fast as she could.

When her hand began to ache, she realized she was still holding the poker mixed with blood and some of Theresa's brown hair. A cry broke loose from her as she threw the weapon down as though it was on fire. Tears stung her eyes as she pushed the animal faster toward home. Nothing was going to stop her now. Her nightmare was finally over.

CHAPTER THIRTY

JULIAN WAS AT his wits' end and running out of ideas. He had sent the servants scampering around the estate, and some of them had even ridden into town to find Alexandria. It had been hours since he realized she was missing, and helplessness washed over him, growing stronger by the minute. If he didn't find her soon, he would go stark raving mad.

He couldn't stay still to heal his leg injury. Instead, he paced the floor in his bedroom, in his study, in the dining room, and the sitting room, but none of these rooms left him feeling at peace. He wouldn't feel calm until he was able to see his wife and know that she was all right.

He marched outside. His leg ached and was swollen, but he didn't care. For the sixth time since he'd discovered Lexie was missing, he hurried to the stable, hoping she would be there by some great chance.

The stable boy's head had been bandaged, and although John had a headache, he still completed his duties. Earlier, Julian had caught the boy crying because he felt it was his fault that Lexie had been taken. Julian tried to convince the lad differently, but John refused to be swayed from the notion that it was his fault for not stopping his attacker before Her Grace was taken.

If anyone was to blame, it was Julian. If he had stopped his cousin by now, Alexandria would be at home, where she belonged.

On the horizon, the sun had started its descent. If they hadn't found Alexandria by nightfall, he didn't know what he would do. Naturally, he would continue searching for her, but it would be harder in the dark.

He moved to Buttercup and stroked the mare's mane. Would he ever see the woman he loved more than life itself riding her favorite horse and enjoying life to the fullest? It was difficult not to think negatively, especially when so many horrific things had been happening in his life. He had lost his father and brother, and Julian knew that losing Alexandria would literally kill him.

The echo of horses' hoofs pounding from up the hill pulled him from his dismal thoughts. Hopeful that someone had heard something and was coming to inform him, he rushed out of the stable to see who was riding toward the manor. At first, he recognized Vincent's tall frame and gray stallion, but the horse and rider following behind didn't look familiar. Both men stopped their horses, and as the dust around them settled, Julian could clearly see the other rider.

He gritted his teeth. *Martin!* What was he doing here?

Julian broke into an odd mix of skipping and running while cursing his wounded leg for slowing him down. As he approached the two, he noticed his cousin's hands were tied in front of him and attached to the saddle horn. Martin aimed a burning scowl at Julian.

"What is the meaning of this outrage?" Martin snapped. "I was taken from my house against my will, shoved on this animal, and tied to the beast. And if that wasn't degrading enough, I was then forced on a jarring ride to a place I have had little desire to visit of late. I demand to know why I am being treated like a prisoner."

Vincent jumped off his horse and strode to Julian. "I heard about Alexandria's disappearance, and the first thing that came to mind was to bring your cousin here so you could talk to him."

"Talk?" Julian arched an eyebrow. "I would rather discuss this matter with my fists."

"You have got to be jesting," Martin said. "You actually believe I'm involved with the duchess's disappearance?"

Julian limped to the horse and looked up at his cousin. "Can you give me a good reason why I shouldn't think you're involved?" He growled and pointed to the ground. "Vincent, would you take my cousin off the horse and put him in front of me? My neck is getting a kink from looking up at him."

"Yes, Your Grace." Vincent didn't remove the rope from around Martin's wrists, but he untied him from the saddle horn and pulled him off to stand in front of Julian.

Martin's glower was hot enough to burn the sun. Julian matched his cousin's expression.

"Why do you think I'm trying to hurt your wife—my own sister-in-law, mind you?" Martin snapped.

"You were eager enough to be rid of her before I returned. Shall I remind you how you wanted to sell your sister-in-law to the highest bidder?" Julian shook his head. Martin's face paled. "Ah, so you recall that now, don't you?"

"Yes, I recall. I know you will not understand, but the truth is, I sought to marry Alexandria off not because I wanted to harm her, but to harm my wife."

Julian's eyes widened. "You make little sense, sir."

"Because the two sisters are so close, I knew by marrying Alexandria off, it would hurt my wife."

"Are you telling me you don't know where she is?"

Martin swallowed hard. "I will not take responsibility for your wife's disappearance. I had nothing to do with it. I swear on my father's grave."

Julian studied his cousin's fierce expression. Although he didn't know whether to trust Martin, he did recall his cousin having a very close relationship with his father. Julian remembered hearing that the old man's death nearly shattered Martin. Could he be telling the truth now? Julian didn't know what to believe. He just wanted to find his wife quickly.

"Tell me truthfully," Julian said, stepping closer to Martin, "did you have anything to do with my father and brother's deaths?"

Martin shook his head. "Absolutely not! I looked upon your father as my own, especially after my sire died. After you left to join the military, your father helped me out of many embarrassing scrapes, putting me on the path to a better life. I wouldn't even think of harming your father. He was my mentor."

Julian's mind wanted to doubt Martin, yet his heart actually believed the story. Julian's father would have been generous to one of his own family members. He would have tried to help Martin the best he could.

However, there was one more test to see if Martin was lying. Julian tightly grabbed his left arm. Instead of yelping because of an injury, Martin appeared confused.

Julian rubbed his forehead and closed his eyes. As much as he wanted someone to blame for all the horrid things that had been happening to him lately, his cousin was not the culprit. Not now. But if Martin wasn't responsible, then who was?

"It just made sense," Julian muttered, "that you would want the title, since you were next in line."

"Julian." Martin's voice softened. "I have never wanted the title. Even after it was given to me, I tried to find someone else to take it. The duke's responsibilities are too much for me to handle. If you don't believe me, ask my wife. She can attest to the fact that I struggled to accept the title."

Julian lifted his head and met his cousin's stare with renewed anger. "And what about your wife? Why did you want her dead?"

"Dead?" Martin paled. He shook his head, but Julian was having none of it.

"The carriage accident," Julian replied. "You paid two imbeciles not long ago to create an accident. Have you forgotten about that so soon?"

Martin exhaled and shuffled his feet in the dirt. "In hindsight, I never really wanted to do bodily harm to my wife, but I did not wish to be married any longer. I was at a low point in my life. I'd just been given a title I didn't want, and I realized I was married to a woman who wanted to run my life. I also realized she had never loved me. I don't know why she still agreed to be my wife, though." He shrugged. "But I wasn't thinking straight the night I paid Walter and Sam. I'd been drinking heavily and was desperate for a new life. I will always regret paying those two. In fact, after a few days of sobriety and when no accident occurred, I wondered if they had somehow cheated me out of my money. My wife had made me a very unhappy man, but I decided I didn't want her dead, only to make her suffer for her treatment of me." He boldly met Julian's stare. "That is why I wouldn't allow Alexandria to visit her sister and why I wanted my sister-in-law married off. I wanted to make my wife as unhappy as she had made me. Keeping her sister from her would make my wife miserable. I never meant to harm Alexandria. I should have tried harder to call off the accident, but as I said, I thought the men had simply taken my money and labeled me a fool."

Julian glanced at Vincent, whose expression relayed the same conclusion that Julian had come to. They both thought Martin was being honest.

"Can you tell me why you were at the inn with them yesterday?"

Martin nodded. "I always frequent that drinking establishment, and when I saw them, I asked for my money back. I was well into my cups, so when they explained they had spent my money, I didn't push them for it. I knew they would never return it, anyway."

"Did you know my driver was involved with Walter and Sam?" Julian bunched his fists, recalling the horrible events of the day. "Yesterday, my wife and I were in the coach when it tumbled down the hillside and into a ravine. Did you demand a return on your investment? After all, they failed to kill your wife, so they owe you now. Did you wish me dead, too? I was in the vehicle as well."

Martin shook his head. "Forgive me, cousin, but I never thought it would happen to you. Indeed, I had been a drunken fool the night I paid Walter and Sam. Can you find it in your heart to forgive me?" He stepped closer. "If you will untie me, I shall do everything in my power to help you find Alexandria."

Julian untied the ropes at Martin's wrists. "Currently, I need all the help I can get. I'm putting my trust in you. Do *not* let me down, or you will never get another chance to gain my grace again."

"I won't disappoint."

Julian turned to the butler who stood nearby. "Higley, show my cousin into the house and see that he is washed and fed quickly, but make haste. We need him as soon as possible to help find my wife."

"Yes, Your Grace." Higley led Martin into the manor.

Sighing heavily, Julian looked at Vincent. "Do you think I made the right decision to trust him?"

Vincent nodded. "After watching his expression, I felt he was telling the truth."

In the distance, another rider came toward the manor. Julian swung his attention toward the cloud of dust. All he could see was long, dark blonde hair flapping in the wind and a dark blue jacket and skirt.

His hopes rose as he ran toward the rider barreling down upon him. Was he seeing things that weren't there, or was this truly the woman he loved finally coming home? "Alexandria!"

"Julian," she cried out, waving her hand frantically.

When the horse drew near, he reached for the reins, pulled hard, and stopped the animal. He reached for her, and she fell into his arms, sobbing uncontrollably. Tears of happiness and relief streamed down his cheeks as he pulled her closer. He kissed her as much as he could.

"Oh, Julian." Her voice cracked. "I never thought I would see you again."

He braced his hands on each side of her head and looked into her watery eyes. Scratches marred her skin, but nothing that appeared to be too bad. Her hair was very dirty, making it look darker than its original color, and streaked with dried blood. Her riding habit was caked with dirt and mud, and the material was torn in several places. "Where have you been, my love?"

Vincent and other servants joined them, each wearing wide smiles.

"I was in his cottage," she said, looking to Vincent. "The same one you took me to the first time we met."

Confusion swept through Julian, and he looked at his friend. Vincent appeared as flummoxed as Julian felt.

"Why were you at the cottage?" Vincent asked.

"Well, you see"—she stared at Vincent—"Miss Dickson kidnapped me and took me there."

Vincent's jaw dropped. Shock was a mild word for what Julian felt right now. "Theresa?"

Lexie nodded, stroking her husband's arm. "She knocked me unconscious and took me there. She wanted to kill me. She thought I was standing in her way of becoming your wife." Her voice broke again.

Julian held her tight as she explained what had happened. She trembled, which made him hold her closer. Anger built inside of him. He wanted to throttle that woman and torture her for what she had done to his poor, defenseless wife. Yet pride filled him as his love for Alexandria grew in leaps. She was definitely an incredibly brave woman to fight her abductor and get away.

"I hit her in the head with a poker and escaped." She took deep breaths. "Julian, I...I...think I killed her."

"Theresa is dead?" Vincent asked.

Alexandria nodded. "I believe so, but I didn't stay around long enough to check."

Vincent turned to one of the stable hands. "Come with me, and we'll ride to my cottage and make certain."

The stable hand nodded. "I'll saddle a horse."

"No, take this one," Alexandria said, pointing to the brown

horse she had been riding. "This was Theresa's."

Vincent quickly mounted his gray steed just as the stable hand climbed on the other. Together they rode toward the cottage.

Never had Julian hated a woman as much as he did Theresa. And he prayed God forgave him for having such harsh feelings. But he truly hoped that when Vincent arrived, he found a dead woman.

CHAPTER THIRTY-ONE

M OANING, ALEXANDRIA RUBBED her head. Julian's heart twisted. He hated to see her in pain. But as her fingers moved against some dried blood matting her hair, Julian noticed the gaping wound on her scalp. His heart dropped. Not another head injury!

"Lexie, we need to get you to your room." He looked at John. "Are you up to locating my physician?"

The boy's shoulders straightened, and he smiled. "Yes, Your Grace."

"Tell him my wife has had a serious head injury."

John nodded, turned, and bolted toward the stable to fetch a horse.

Julian lifted his wife into his arms. She clung to his shirt as he gently carried her into the house, up the stairs, and to their room. Her maid, Johnson, rushed to them, eager to help.

"Draw a bath for Her Grace," he told the maid. "And help me get her ready for the physician."

"Of course, Your Grace." She curtsied before rushing to do her duties.

Julian sat on the settee with his wife on his lap. Her eyes were closed as she leaned her head against his chest. With great tenderness, he stroked the side of her face, happy to be doing this again and grateful that God had given him the opportunity to take care of her. Julian would always be eternally grateful that she had come back to him alive.

Yet all of what she had gone through was because of him. Emotion clogged his throat, and tears stung his eyes. "Can you ever forgive me?"

Her eyes fluttered open. She weakly lifted her hand and cupped his face. "For what, my love?"

"For not being able to save you from that evil woman. And for allowing this to happen to begin with."

"No, Julian." She gently kissed him on the lips. "Theresa told me she wasn't the one who killed your father and brother, and she wasn't the one who shot the cannonball at you, either. Although she admits it was her idea."

He scowled, wishing he had never met that woman. "And you believed her?"

"I had no reason not to. She seemed perplexed as to why she could *think* something, and it would suddenly happen." She shrugged. "Either that or she was insane."

"I believe it was the latter."

"Very true. I think she is insane. However, there was no wound on her left arm."

Irritation settled over him. If Martin or Theresa weren't responsible for the deaths of his father and brother and for Julian almost losing his life, then who was the person who wanted his family dead? He couldn't go another day without discovering the truth.

Johnson bustled in, carrying the water and preparing a bath for Alexandria. Julian wouldn't leave his wife's side and even insisted on helping her undress. Thankfully, she didn't appear bothered by it.

The bath went quickly, and soon Alexandria was out, dressed, and in bed. When the physician came, Julian again refused to leave the room. His wife assured the physician that Julian could remain.

As the older man examined Alexandria, Julian cradled her

hand in his and caressed her arm. He couldn't tear his gaze away from her enchanting sapphire eyes…eyes that had captured his attention from the day they met. In his mind, he repeated his thanks to the Lord for bringing her back home safe.

She watched the physician as he examined her, but quite often, her focus reverted to Julian, and when it did, she smiled. His heart leapt every time. He could tell in her eyes how much she loved him because it touched not only his heart but deep into his very soul.

"Thankfully, you don't need stitches," the physician said to Alexandria, "but the wound will take some time to heal, as all head injuries do, so continue to add this ointment several times a day." He handed her a bottle.

"I thank you," she said.

Julian didn't want to tear his eyes away from his wife just to look at the doctor, but he knew it would be rude not to. He stood and shook the older man's hand. "I appreciate you coming to examine her so quickly."

"She needs rest." The physician looked to Julian's leg. "And so do you. I'm certain that if I examine your leg, it will be swollen."

"You are correct," Julian admitted.

"Then I suggest you and your wife lock yourselves in this room for several days and not go anywhere."

Grinning, Julian looked at his wife. He winked, and her face bloomed red. "You can bet that is exactly what we will do."

Chuckling, the physician gathered his things and left the room. Julian sat back on the chair and took Alexandria's hand again. "Are you hungry, my love?"

She nodded. "A little, yes."

He looked at Johnson. "Will you have the cook prepare us dinner and bring it up here, please?"

"Yes, Your Grace."

Just as the maid was leaving, Higley met her at the doorway.

"Your Grace, Lord Trenton is downstairs and needs to talk to you."

Julian frowned. He didn't want to leave his wife. But he figured his friend would let him know what happened to Theresa.

"Higley, I know it's not proper, but tell Trenton to come up here. The physician has instructed my wife and me not to leave our room."

Higley smiled widely. "I shall bring him up directly, Your Grace."

Alexandria gasped. "Julian, Lord Trenton cannot come in here. I'm in my nightclothes."

"Well, he will have to, because I'm not about to leave you for one moment." He pulled the blankets up to her chin. "Just keep yourself covered. He'll understand."

She shook her head. "The servants will tittle-tattle, you know."

"When haven't they?" He laughed. "But I'll fire anyone who says an unkind thing about you."

Within minutes, Vincent came up the stairs, following Higley. When Vincent stepped to the door and peered inside, a blush stole across his expression. Julian wanted to laugh but refrained.

"Your Grace, are you certain—" Vincent began, but Julian waved his hand.

"Come in and sit with me on the settee. I assume you have come to report your findings at the cottage?"

"Indeed I have."

"Well," Lexie said. "Was Miss Dickson still there?"

Taking a deep breath, Vincent raked his fingers through his hair. "She was still at the cottage but wasn't dead."

Alexandria hitched a breath and put her fist to her mouth.

"What did you do with her?" Julian asked.

"When the stable hand and I arrived, she hid in the bushes by the front door. She jumped your stable hand and knocked him to the ground. She held a thick piece of wood and tried to beat him over the head with it. I noticed her own head was bleeding profusely, probably from when your wife hit her with the poker. I feared Theresa was half-crazed, so..." He cleared his throat. "Forgive my bluntness, but I had no recourse but to shoot her. She is dead now, God rest her poor soul." He looked at Alexandria. "Forgive me for being so descriptive, but—"

"Do not be sorry, Lord Trenton." Alexandria shook her head. "I feel terrible that she had to die in such a tragic way, but she was not well in the head. She was dangerous."

"I'm also grateful she is not around to bother you." Vincent offered a small smile.

"How is the stable hand?" Julian asked. "Is his head all right?" He wondered if he needed to summon the physician back to attend to another servant.

"He is fine," Vincent said. "Thankfully, he was able to block her with his arms."

Julian sighed heavily. "Well, I suppose we need to inform Theresa's brother."

"I shall do that at once." Vincent stood. "Take care, and I'm very happy you are back home and safe, Alexandria."

"I'm very happy as well." She relaxed against the pillows.

Julian shook his friend's hand, and Vincent left the room. Once the door was closed, he was relieved it was just him and his wife again. He crawled onto the bed next to her, wrapped his arms around her, and softly rubbed her back. Closing his eyes, he breathed in her feminine scent. Lilacs...always lilacs.

"I love you," she whispered into his shirt.

"I love you more than you'll ever know." He hugged her tighter and kissed her forehead.

"I think I do know," she answered softly. "Your feelings are in your eyes. I can see it when you look at me."

"Indeed?" He lifted her chin so she could meet his eyes. "I was thinking the same. I'm so very fortunate to have a woman who loves me the way you do."

"Oh, Julian. When will this turmoil finally come to an end?"

"I know not, my love. All this time, I thought my cousin had been the guilty person, but I talked with him earlier today, and he explained things that made me realize he couldn't possibly have been the one who killed my father and brother and tried to kill me."

She pulled back slightly and looked at him with wide eyes. "Are you certain you trust him?"

"Believe it or not, I am. Even Lord Trenton felt as I had. Martin was telling us the truth."

"If he didn't do all those dastardly things to your family, then who did?"

He shook his head. "I wish I knew. Could it be that this whole time what I thought was conspiracy to take over the dukedom was not? Could my father and brother really have died from a plague-like sickness? And could the cannon blast that nearly took my life have been mere happenstance?"

She frowned. "It doesn't seem possible. The incidents are too surreal."

"Indeed, they are, but what if they really are just accidents?"

"I don't dare hope."

"Me either." He released a despondent sigh.

She buried her face back in his chest, and he smiled. He would never tire of holding her and feeling her hot breath against his skin. He would always enjoy the touch of her hand and the sweetness of her lips.

"So, my wonderful husband, what have you planned that will keep us entertained while we recoup over the next few days?" Her voice held a touch of impish humor.

He grinned. "I'm certain we'll find something to keep us occupied. In fact"—he lifted her chin again until she met his eyes—"I have an idea right now." He stroked her bottom lip. "And we don't have to talk unless we really want to."

Her smile made her eyes sparkle. "Oh, please tell me all about it. I'm eager to start on whatever activities you have spinning around in your brilliant head."

As she wrapped her arms around his neck, he gently guided

her down, lying halfway on top of her on the bed. They joined their mouths immediately, hers just as fervent as his. Passionately kissing her like this took his mind off his worries, just as it had always done. It felt as though they lived in their own little world…a world he never wanted to leave.

Although he should not rush things, he couldn't convince himself to take things slow. Having her safe and with him once again made him want to show her how much he loved her in every way he could.

He trailed kisses across her cheek and down her neck. She arched her neck, giving him better access, and when he nibbled on her collarbone, she giggled. He grinned and lifted his head to look down at her.

"Ticklish, are we?"

"Just a little."

Moving his hand to her waist, he squeezed certain places on her body that had her writhing against him. She laughed louder.

"Julian, really! Do you have to do this now?"

"But of course, my dear. You forget, we have all the time in the world." He tickled her ribs again.

Laughing, she grasped his hand. "Enough." She took a deep breath. "This isn't fair. Why can I not tickle you?"

"Probably because I won't allow it, my love."

She tried to tickle him, but when she encountered a spot that made him jump, he took her hands and held them above her head.

"Now you are trapped."

She breathed heavily. "I suppose I am under your control from here on out."

He released a deep growl and captured her mouth with his. But through the stillness of the room, the floor creaked, alerting his defenses. Quickly, he sat up and spun toward the intruder.

A woman wearing the brown dress and white apron of one of the maids crept toward them, holding a pistol. Her blonde hair was pulled back with a tie away from her face. Her eyes were puffy and red, as though she had been crying for several hours. But the color of her face had him curious. Her skin was grayish, and the dark circles under her eyes made them look like they were sinking into her skull.

"Your Grace," Johnson snapped, pointing the pistol at Julian. "I think it best if you get out of bed now. This is not where I plan to kill you."

CHAPTER THIRTY-TWO

JULIAN DIDN'T DARE move. What was going on here? Insane women were popping up like flies in his life.

Alexandria shifted on the bed. He blocked her with his body to protect her.

"Johnson, I don't know what you're doing, but I can tell you now, it is a huge mistake."

"You, sir, are not the one in charge. I am." Johnson took another step toward him. "Now do as I say, and both of you get off the bed."

"Dawn," Alexandria said. "Why are you doing this? I thought you were someone we could trust."

The maid's eyes moved over Julian in an unhurried perusal. By her strange expression, he wondered if she was delusional. Hard to believe, but this woman had changed quite drastically since he hired her. Sad to think she was recommended to him by one of his associates.

"Johnson," he said gently, "I don't know why you are doing this, but if it is money you're after—"

"I don't want money."

"Then why?" Alexandria's voice broke.

"I'm after revenge." Johnson squared her shoulders, but her eyes filled with tears. "Because of you, a very good friend of mine is dead."

Alexandria shook her head. "Was your friend Miss Dickson?"

Johnson's expression turned darker. "I had been her maid for several years until Lord Greystone ruined her. I couldn't stand to see my friend go through the heartache that *he*"—she motioned her pistol toward Julian—"put her through. When I heard her talk about her plan to kill Julian's family, I decided to do it myself."

Anger filled him, and he wanted to strangle Johnson. He hadn't noticed that her left arm was injured, but then, he didn't dare look now. After all, she was the one with the weapon, not him.

He licked his dry lips and slowly stood from the bed. "You are the one responsible for my father and brother dying?"

She nodded. "They were visiting Lord Senwick one day, and I poisoned their drinks. I knew Miss Dickson was still hoping for you to return from the military and marry her. She wanted to become Duchess of Linden one day, so I decided to assist in any way I could."

Julian gritted his teeth. He had never harmed a woman, but he was ready to strangle the life out of this one. "Did you try to kill me by shooting a cannon at me?"

Johnson arched an eyebrow. "Of course, Your Grace. That was the only way I knew to get you back home so that you could fall in love with Miss Dickson again."

Behind him, Alexandria's breaths shook uncontrollably. He realized she had become close with the maid, and the shock would be devastating.

"Dawn," she said. "Please put the pistol down. We can talk this out."

"I'm sorry, Your Grace, but talking will not work. Because of you, my mistress is dead. I can never forgive you now." Johnson huffed. "I'm tired of waiting. Both of you come outside with me or I'll shoot one of you right here."

Worry tightened Julian's chest. Both he and Alexandria knew firsthand how impossible it was to compromise with people who had lost their minds. For the moment, it seemed as if Johnson wanted them to leave the house. He would do as she wished, only to give him a better chance of catching her unaware.

Taking calculated movements, he grabbed Alexandria's wrap from off the chair and handed it to her. Slowly, she climbed off the bed and put the garment on. He then took her hand and gave the maid a nod.

"We are ready to go now."

Gradually, Johnson lowered her arm and stepped toward the door, keeping her gaze on Julian. He prayed that once they left the house, he would know what to do to save his wife's life.

"Johnson, I don't know what you have to gain from killing us," Alexandria said.

"Revenge is what I seek. It is what Miss Dickson would have wanted. Your husband is an evil man for breaking her heart. If only you hadn't become his wife, then perhaps I would have let you live."

"But Dawn, Julian did not love Miss Dickson. He never did." She squeezed Julian's hand. "But I have fallen madly in love with him. Julian Stratford has been nothing but kind and thoughtful. He really is my protector in all ways."

Happiness grew in his chest again, and he wanted to take her in his arms and shower her with his love. Hopefully, they could get the pistol away from the maid so that he could hold his wife once more. "And I love you, my darling Lexie."

"Enough of this!" Johnson screeched. In a flash, she raised the pistol toward Alexandria.

Anger filled Julian again. "You are correct, Johnson. This is quite enough."

He stepped toward her, and she jerked back, bumping into a table. The quick movement made her stumble, and she knocked her left shoulder against the wall.

Crying out in pain, she quickly cradled her arm. A spot of blood gradually grew on the sleeve, spreading over the material as though it was in a race to color the material red. A pungent, almost decaying odor permeated the room. Her face turned ashen, and for a second, Julian thought she might empty her stomach on him. At least he now knew what the stench was. Her arm was terribly infected. He had seen this with a few of his soldiers.

Johnson released an unsteady laugh and shook her head. "Don't get any ideas, Your Grace. I'm still strong enough to kill you and your wife."

He inhaled a deep breath for courage as he pulled Alexandria against him. "We shall see. I love my wife dearly, and I'm her protector. I shall do everything in my power to stop you."

Johnson's eyes widened and a grin touched her mouth. "Challenge accepted."

⟫⟫⟫✦⟪⟪⟪

ALEXANDRIA'S HEART BURST with an overabundance of love for her husband, yet at the same time, it painfully broke into tiny pieces because of her maid's surprising mental condition. Dawn was deranged, and Alexandria feared that she would follow through with her threat of killing them.

"Oh, my dear, wonderful husband." Alexandria laid her head against his chest. "I love you so much—"

Dawn screamed, a sound so evil it sent chills up Alexandria's spine. Never had she heard that tone before. She never wanted to hear it again, either.

"Will both of you be quiet?" Johnson yelled. "I don't want to hear or see you two fawning over each other anymore. It makes me physically ill to watch."

Alexandria scowled. How dare Dawn try to take this moment away from her? If this was the last hour with her husband, she wanted it to be meaningful.

"Come on, the both of you," Dawn snapped, and motioned the pistol toward the door. "We are going outside."

Alexandria frowned. "Why?"

Dawn swayed but quickly righted herself. "Because I don't want to drag you outside to bury you."

"Listen here, Dawn—"

"Lexie," Julian said calmly. "We shall do exactly what the woman requests. If she wants us to leave, we shall leave without arguing."

A victorious smile claimed the maid's face, making Alexandria want to scream with frustration. She studied Julian's aloof expression. Why was he acting this way? She wished she knew what was going through his brilliant mind. He didn't appear frightened of the prospect that Dawn could shoot and possibly kill him. In fact, Alexandria received the distinct impression that he was trying to communicate with her through his eyes. Unfortunately, she didn't understand him at the moment.

Julian led the group, moving at a slow pace out of the room and heading down the hallway toward the back stairs used by the servants. The house grew quiet as they made their way down the winding staircase. Alexandria prayed one of the servants would see what was happening, especially since they'd told the butler that they would remain in their room for a few days.

She stayed close to Julian as they quietly moved toward the kitchen and to one of the many back doors to the grand house. As they walked outside, Julian took hold of Alexandria's hand and stopped, waiting for further instruction from Dawn.

The maid closed the door securely and faced them, holding the pistol toward Julian.

"Go to the stable. We need to get…those…tools." She slurred the last words.

"What are you talking about?" Alexandria asked.

"You know…those…picks."

Alexandria shook her head. "Dawn, you're not making any sense."

"Do you mean shovels?" Julian added.

Blinking, the maid nodded. "Yes, shovels. We need two shovels."

Alexandria wished she knew what was wrong with her. Although her words were slurred now, Dawn hadn't seemed like the type of woman who consumed a large amount of spirits. She even swayed a time or two, so perhaps she was slightly tipsy tonight.

"Whatever do we need shovels for?" Alexandria hesitantly asked.

"To dig your graves." Dawn belted out an evil laugh.

Alexandria's stomach twisted as bile rose to her throat. Julian didn't argue with Dawn and led the way toward the stable.

With each step, tears burned in Alexandria's eyes. How could they get out of this? How could they convince the maid she was wrong? Julian wouldn't hurt Dawn, because he wasn't like that. It would be up to Alexandria to cause some kind of commotion and distract Dawn so that Julian could snatch the weapon away.

Anxiety and fear pumped through Alexandria's body, making her tremble. Taking deep breaths, she tried to gain control. *Be a character in your book. They'll know what to do.* Yet, although the idea was clever, fear had immobilized her mind. She couldn't think of what needed to be done and felt like such a failure.

Julian didn't say a word as he casually walked into the stable and found a shovel hanging on the wall.

"Get two of them," Dawn snapped. "Your wife needs to assist."

"No." Julian shook his head. "I shall dig both graves. I don't wish to cause further pain to the woman I love. Besides, she was badly injured earlier today by your so-called friend, Miss Dickson."

Dawn rolled her eyes. "Your wife got what she deserved, and soon the both of you will meet your maker and answer for your sins."

Tears fell unhindered down Alexandria's face. She had finally found her prince and lost him just as quickly. She clutched her hands against her chest and slowly died inside.

CHAPTER THIRTY-THREE

JULIAN GRIPPED THE shovel handle tighter. Couldn't Johnson see what kind of agony she was putting Alexandria through? Then again, the woman's devotion to her dead former mistress overrode any connection she had made with his wife.

Perhaps if he swung the shovel fast enough, it would knock the pistol from her hand. What were the odds that he and Alexandria could just take off running into the shelter of the shadows and escape the insane maid? Yet he didn't want to do anything to endanger his loving wife. She had been through enough already. Julian didn't want to miscalculate and have Johnson fire the weapon and shoot one of them.

However…

He bit the inside of his cheek. Little did the maid realize that by giving him the shovel, he now had a weapon to defend himself. She wanted him to dig his own grave, but there was so much more he could do with a sturdy shovel and some dirt. It must have slipped her mind that he had been a decorated soldier in the war. His military skills were second nature to him. But he would play her game until it was time to change the rules.

Another thing in his favor was Johnson's sickness. True, she was mentally deranged, but she was physically ill as well. Being in the war, he had seen many wounded soldiers die from serious infections. And since Johnson had been battling her injury for several weeks, he figured she was near her deathbed. Not only could he see the effect it had on her, but he could smell it.

He couldn't help but notice how weak she was now. A few times she had stumbled but quickly regained her bearings. Her confusion was obvious as well. When she first entered his room, the moisture coating her pale face was obvious. These were signs that her wound was severely festering. If not treated immediately, she would surely die. But even if she was treated, the infection might be so acute it would take her life anyway.

For now, he would wait until she lost consciousness, which, with any luck, would be shortly. She blinked quite a bit, which told him she was fighting the darkness trying to consume her vision. He prayed she didn't try to shoot him before she fainted. If he moved slowly, with any luck, she would pass out soon so that he could take control.

"I'm not sure if you realize this," Alexandria said to the maid, "but one of the servants might have seen us leave that house."

The slow chuckle from Johnson soon accelerated into a full-blown evil laugh. "That's impossible, Your Grace. I know your husband dismissed the servants for the night."

"Then I'm certain my sister might wonder why I haven't checked on her tonight and come to find me."

Johnson shook her head, still grinning victoriously. "I wouldn't count on that, either. You see, before coming to your room this evening, I made sure that your sister won't be coughing anymore."

Julian didn't like the sound of that. "What did you do to Lady Hinsdale?"

The maid shrugged. "Let's just say that I cured her malady quickly, and now… Well, now she is in a more peaceful place."

Alexandria's body grew limp against him, so he quickly wrapped his arms around her. Tears filled her eyes as the realization of what Johnson had said finally hit. Seconds later, Alexandria released a heart-wrenching scream and fell against him.

"Johnson, you have gone too far this time," he growled. "I promise you that you'll not get away with this."

Johnson's laughter died down, and she shook her head. "There won't be anything you can do, since I'm killing you shortly." She motioned to the grove of trees nearest to the stable. "Now go…over there."

Julian took a glance in that direction. "Over there?"

"Yes. To the trees."

"Are you certain?" he said. "There is not much light when you enter the grove, and the moon isn't full tonight."

"Uh…" Johnson swayed again but then blinked and shook her head. "Alexandria, go back in the stable and fetch a…a…candle."

"Fetch it yourself," his wife snapped.

His heart broke for her misery. If only he could comfort her during this time of grief. "I'll fetch it, but I think you mean a lantern. Not a candle."

"Yes, of course that is what I meant," the maid snapped.

Julian released his wife long enough to hurry into the stable and grab the lantern. When he returned, he took Alexandria back into his arms and held her as they walked toward the trees. Her body shook with sobs. His throat was tight with emotion, but he must be strong for the woman he loved.

He wasn't sure just how far back Johnson was, but he knew she wasn't close enough to hear if he whispered something to his wife. He should ease Lexie's worries slightly. Then again, he didn't dare give her too much hope. There was still the chance the maid could shoot him.

"Lexie, my love," he said softly.

She looked up at him with those big, watery eyes. "We need to stop her, Julian," she whispered.

"We will. But from this point forward, don't make her upset."

"I'm so afraid. And I want to see my sister one last time."

"I understand, and I promise you will see her. But I have a plan."

Her eyes widened. "I trust you. I shall do my best to keep her calm."

He paused for a moment. "I really love you, you know, and I'm so happy that you are my wife."

She hiccupped on another sob. "I love you more with every breath I take. I feel like the luckiest woman alive to have you as my husband, yet…" She swallowed. "I'm so afraid I'll lose you, too."

"Don't think that way, my love. Trust in love. Trust in me."

A tear slid down her cheek. "How can I not? You have taught me well."

Love burst inside his chest, and it was all he could do not to take her into his arms and kiss her passionately. But this was certainly not the place to shower his love on his wife, and if he didn't want Johnson upset, he couldn't outwardly show Alexandria his affections. However, he had wanted his wife to know how he felt just in case his plans didn't work the way he hoped.

Stop thinking negatively, he silently scolded himself. He would make certain his plans worked. He had been through many battles in the military and only been injured a few times. He wasn't about to allow a disturbed woman to steal his life and destroy his happiness.

They reached the grove and waited for Johnson to join them. She wobbled like a newborn calf. He suspected she would lose consciousness very soon. But her stubbornness surprised him.

She pointed to the ground. "What are you waiting for? Start digging."

He met Alexandria's gaze again. Her lips trembled. He leaned down and kissed her briefly on the mouth before turning toward his task. Johnson wouldn't shoot him before he dug a hole large enough to bury him and Alexandria, only because she didn't want to dig it herself, so he must take his time with the task.

Nothing was spoken between the three of them as Julian pushed the shovel into the ground and threw back the dirt. Occasionally, he glanced at Johnson. A frown marred her face as she gently rubbed her injured arm. She flexed her fingers quite a bit, which told him her arm was growing numb. How much time he had before she lost consciousness, he didn't know.

"Dawn?" Alexandria said in a quiet voice.

"What?" the maid grumbled.

"What will you do after we are dead? Where will you go work?"

Johnson took a deep breath and released it slowly. "After I kill you both, I plan on...making Martin Hinsdale love me. He'll be the next duke, of course, and I've always dreamed of being a duchess." She was slurring again.

Julian watched Alexandria closely, and it appeared as though she was fighting with her emotions. She struggled to show her maid a pleasant smile as she bunched her hands into fists by her sides. He prayed she would keep her temper under control.

Alexandria took slow steps toward Johnson. "I think once you let Martin get to know you, he will fall in love with you. In fact, I would like it if you took over my title when I'm gone."

"You woo-od?" Johnson slurred, continuing to blink rapidly. "I dish—deserve this after all I've put up with."

"Indeed you do." Alexandria shrugged. "I have always thought you were a kind woman with a large heart."

Julian tried not to grin. *That's my girl.* Alexandria was actually the one with the large heart. It thrilled him to see his wife using her wits to ease the maid's anger.

Johnson swayed again but righted herself before she could topple over. She held the pistol on Julian as she stretched her infected arm. "What's...takin' so long?"

"You look as though your arm is hurting," Alexandria said. "Is there something I can do for you?"

"No, I shall be fine. I assure you." Johnson swung her attention to Julian and scowled. "Keep digging. You're too slow."

"Forgive me. I'm injured. But more than that, I'm tired," he lied, and moved the shovel slower. He pretended that he struggled to breathe. "I'm just so very...very...tired." He spoke sluggishly, hoping it would have an effect on Johnson and make her more tired as well. When she swayed, he nearly shouted with joy.

Alexandria looked up. He was certain she had not been able to see the sky very well, so he wondered what she could possibly be searching for. He peered upward as well.

"Oh my," Alexandria said softly. "Look at the white owl perched on that branch. I've never seen one so lovely."

He snapped his attention back to Johnson. Thankfully, she took the bait. Tilting her head back, she lifted her eyes heavenward. She swayed, and this time she closed her eyes and crumpled to the ground.

Alexandria gasped and knelt beside her. Julian dropped the shovel and hurried over to them, grabbing the pistol out of Johnson's cold, clammy, and weightless hand.

"Is she breathing?" he asked.

Alexandria leaned her face closer to Johnson's mouth. "I cannot tell." She placed her ear on Johnson's chest. "I don't detect a heartbeat."

Julian moved Alexandria's head so that he could listen. Holding his breath, he tried to hear her heartbeat, but he feared the maid's infection had finally claimed her life. When she looked up at the owl, blood had stopped flowing to her head, which was the reason she finally collapsed. Perhaps her body had decided to stop working at that exact moment, as well.

He placed his fingers on her neck, trying to feel for a pulse. Again, he didn't feel anything.

Exhaling a frustrated breath, he sat up and met Alexandria's teary eyes. "My love, we can relax now. She's dead."

Lexie shook with silent sobs as tears streamed down her face.

He moved closer and gathered her in his arms. "Don't fret, my love. You know I will take care of you and get your sister ready for her burial."

"I just wish"—she sniffed—"I wish my sister had lived long enough for me to talk to her one last time."

He kissed her forehead. "She will be your guardian angel

now, and I'm certain she knows you loved her dearly." He withdrew just enough to look into her eyes. "Keep your memories close to your heart. That will help you through the grieving process."

She nodded and pressed her face against his chest again. "We need to tell Martin. I know he didn't love Charlotte, but they are still married."

"I'll tell him tonight. We'll return to the manor and you can be with your sister while I tell him."

She nodded. "Thank you, Julian. You don't know how much this means to me."

"I think I do." He tightened his arms around her. "And for your happiness, I'll do anything."

For the next few minutes, she cried in his arms, and he comforted her. He also grieved with her now that the truth about his family's deaths had finally come to light. Perhaps now he could go on with his life with his beautiful wife by his side.

Four months later

ALEXANDRIA EXITED THE house and strolled onto the front lawn. She smiled. The early autumn sky was so lovely this morning, and she just couldn't stay inside the house one moment longer.

Ever since Dawn and Theresa's untimely deaths, Alexandria and Julian's life had gone smoothly. No more threats. No more accidents. Nothing but pure paradise and wedded bliss.

Sighing, she closed her eyes. Her peaceful grin stretched her face so wide it made her cheeks ache, but she didn't care. She was so very happy and wanted everyone to know it. Her life had changed for the better, even with all the heartaches she had gone through just to reach this point.

She was certain nobody wanted to be kidnapped, but the event was the very thing that had brought her out of her shell.

Being with Julian through all the ups and downs was the best thing that had ever happened to her. No more was she the shy wallflower, afraid to meet new people or talk to men. Julian had cured her. His love had made her blossom like a flower in sunshine.

Keeping her bundled pages against her chest, she carried the writing quill and ink, heading toward the wicker chairs Julian had purchased as a gift to her not long after Charlotte's burial. He told Alexandria he wanted her to have a safe haven where she could write to her heart's delight.

She sighed dreamily. God had blessed her by sending her a man who was as kind, giving, and loving as the heroes she wrote about in her stories. Julian was such a thoughtful husband. How had she become so fortunate?

She couldn't wait to write a letter to her cousin, which would be first on her agenda. Maxey would be shocked to hear what had transpired at Linden Hall since the letter Alexandria had sent four months ago, and, of course, she would be heartbroken about what happened to Charlotte.

The letter Maxey wrote to Alexandria had been short and sweet. Uncle Stephen still worked for Chief Magistrate Tingey, and Maxey was spending her time with the children down the road or assisting at the library. Maxey had given Alexandria advice about her woes during that time the letter had been written. Her cousin said to have faith and continue to be forgiving and sweet, and surely Julian Stratford could come around and see Alexandria for the woman she was.

Alexandria chuckled. Although she hadn't received the letter until after everything was said and done, that was exactly what she had done. She had always cherished her cousin's advice.

As Alexandria neared the outdoor furniture canopied by the large birch tree, she noticed Julian sitting in his favorite chair, reading a newspaper. He looked so relaxed, and she truly believed her husband was the most handsome man in the world.

"Good morning, my blossom," Julian said without looking up

from his newspaper.

She sat on the wicker chair and placed her paper, quill, and ink on the table. The large tree beside her gave the shade she needed, and the peaceful outdoor setting helped her creative juices considerably. It thrilled her that Julian was so supportive of her writing.

"Good morning, my love. Is there anything interesting in the paper today?" she asked.

"Nothing as interesting as the person with me now." He folded the paper and placed it on the table.

Her heart did silly little flips again. It always did when he stared at her with such adoring eyes.

"You flatter me too much," she said.

"Nonsense. I don't flatter you enough."

Closing her eyes, she tilted her head back and let the sun's autumn heat warm her face. She took in the enjoyment of feeling free. Free from an overprotective sister and demeaning brother-in-law, and especially free from jealous women who wanted to be duchess. Being married to Julian didn't make her feel sheltered at all. He allowed her to do anything she wanted…as long as he could enjoy it with her.

She opened her eyes to find Julian was still watching her. "So, tell me something." She leaned her arms on the table. "Have you talked to Martin lately? I wonder how he is faring as a widower."

"I spoke to him just last night, in fact. He informed me he has decided to join the military and make something of his life."

"How amazing. I'm very happy for him. I'm certain he felt like my sister was holding him back."

Julian nodded. "When I confronted Martin during the time Theresa had taken you, he shared with me something very personal as well. First, I want you to know he told me he was only mean to you to hurt Charlotte. Sad, but true. His marriage to your sister had made him a very unhappy man."

"That is good to know." She waved a hand to dismiss those bad memories. "And I shan't hold that against him any longer."

"Also, while it was true that Martin had set his sights on your sister before they married, even though she could have had any man she wanted, apparently, he never could understand why she picked him. Especially since Lord Trenton had always wanted to court her."

Shock hit her, and she gasped. "That is amazing. But of course, we should help Lord Trenton find a wife soon."

Julian chuckled and shook his head. "As long as he doesn't suspect we are trying to push him toward the altar. I fear he would hate me if he knew what I was doing."

"My lips are sealed."

"Oh, and speaking of Lord Trenton…" Julian reached across the table and patted her hand. "Vincent wants us to come for dinner soon at his cottage."

She grimaced. "His cottage? Are you jesting? He didn't have any dishes the last time we were there."

Julian chuckled. "That is what I thought when he first mentioned it. But as it turns out, he decided to fix the place up. He hired builders and decorators, and Vincent is quite impressed with the cottage now. That is why he has invited us."

"That would be lovely." She squeezed his fingers. "It will bring back memories."

"Only good ones, I trust."

She nodded. "Theresa is in the past. And while it is true that I was scared for the first few hours after you kidnapped me, my fears eased once you realized I was not my sister. I sensed you would be kind to me, and, of course, you were. I might not have started to fall in love with you at the cottage, but definitely during that next day."

He winked. "The same with me, my blossom."

From the corner of her eye, she saw Higley walking toward them carrying a silver tray. As he drew closer, she could see it was a letter. Dare she hope it was from Maxey with more news about her life in Wales?

"Your Grace, this came for you." He placed the tray in front of Alexandria.

"Me? Who could have sent me a letter?"

"Why don't you open it and see?" Julian grinned. "You'll never know unless you read it."

As she took the letter, a knowing glint shone in his eyes. Did he know about this? The corners of his mouth rose, but he appeared as though he were trying not to smile. Very peculiar indeed.

She opened the letter and skimmed it. Confusion filled her as she read.

"What is it, my blossom?" Julian asked with a touch of laughter in his voice.

"I'm not certain. It says they are making me an offer to…" Excitement rushed through her, shaking her hands.

"An offer for what?"

Goosebumps rose on her arms. This couldn't be real. "The letter is from a publishing company, and they are offering to publish one of my stories." Emotion choked her voice, and she cleared her throat.

"That is marvelous, my love."

She shook her head. "I don't understand. I have never sent my stories to anyone. I'm a woman and was told nobody would take me seriously."

Julian moved around the table and knelt beside her, resting his hand on her knee. "Vincent has connections with this particular publisher, and that is how he was able to get your story in front of an editor. Vincent told me the publisher wanted money up front, but he assures me that you shall be reimbursed in abundance when the book starts selling."

"Does this man know the writer is a woman?"

Julian nodded. "He does, and is *still* very interested in your stories."

Tears of happiness filled her eyes, and she threw her arms around her husband, giving him a bear hug. "You are truly amazing. I'm so blessed to have you in my life."

He captured her mouth in a heated kiss, moving his hands in circles over her back, warming her quickly in more ways than one. As he pulled back, a twinkle lit his eyes.

"I'm the one blessed. I ended up with a treasure when I kidnapped the wrong sister."

Sighing, she stroked his strong jaw. "You did more than steal the duchess—you stole my heart."

"Then I was repaid well, because you stole mine just as quickly."

Julian leaned in to kiss her once more, and she returned it passionately. She wanted to show him how much this letter meant to her, to actually have one of her books in print. But it was more than that. She wanted to tell him how important it was to have a husband who supported her. She also wanted to share with him her own surprise but didn't know how to bring up the subject.

He broke away and gave her a wink. "Are you thinking what I'm thinking?"

She arched an eyebrow. "And pray, what would that be, my love?"

"That you want to take a break from writing and join me in our bedchambers for the next two hours?"

She laughed and stroked his chin. "That, my dear, isn't quite what I was thinking."

His smile disappeared. "No? Then what was going through your mind just now?"

The disappointment on his face was quite comical, but she refrained from laughing. "I was actually thinking about finding a way to share some more good news with you."

The corners of his mouth rose. "Good news, you say? How good is it?"

She shrugged. "I'm not sure. It depends on you and how much you want to be a father."

The humor in his face vanished, and his eyes widened. "A...father? You are with child?"

"Either that or I'm thinking about purchasing a puppy," she joked.

He whooped with joy and lifted her from the chair. "I'm going to be a father," he shouted.

Giggling, she nodded. "Am I to understand you like this news?"

"Absolutely, my love. You will be the best mother in all of Britain."

"And you, my wonderful man, will make the best father in all of Britain."

He gathered her tighter in his arms and kissed her forehead. "Life with you will make me a wonderful father and husband. Only with you by my side can this be accomplished."

"And that is where I'll be. Forever and ever."

He sealed the promise with a kiss that she was certain would end back in their bedchamber. But it didn't matter. She was blissfully in love, and she would never hide it again.

The End

About the Author

Marie Higgins is a multi-award winning, bestselling author of sweet romance novels, from refined bad-boy heroes who make your heart melt to the feisty heroines who somehow manage to love them regardless of their faults. She has been with a Christian publisher since 2010. Between those and her others, she has published over a hundred heartwarming, on-the-edge-of-your-seat stories and broadened her readership by writing mystery/suspense, humor, time travel, and paranormal, along with her historical romances. Her readers have dubbed her "Queen of Tease" because of all her twists and turns and unexpected endings.

Website – www.authormariehiggins.com
Facebook – facebook.com/marie.higgins.7543
Instagram – instagram.com/author.mariehiggins
Bookbub – bookbub.com/authors/marie-higgins
Twitter – @mariehigginsxox